P9-CNG-798

THE TASHKENT CRISIS

BOOKS BY WILLIAM CRAIG

The Fall of Japan

The Tashkent Crisis

THE TASHKENT CRISIS

A NOVEL BY

William Craig

A RICHARD W. BARON BOOK

E. P. DUTTON & CO., INC.   NEW YORK   1971

Copyright © 1971 by William Craig
All rights reserved. Printed in the U.S.A.
First Edition

No part of this publication may be reproduced or transmitted
in any form or by any means, electronic or mechanical, including
photocopy, recording, or any information storage and retrieval
system now known or to be invented, without permission in writing
from the publisher, except by a reviewer who wishes to quote brief
passages in connection with a review written for inclusion in a
magazine, newspaper or broadcast.

Published simultaneously in Canada by Clarke, Irwin & Company Limited,
Toronto and Vancouver
Library of Congress Catalog Card Number: 74-125549
SBN 0-525-21435-6

To my wife,

Eleanor,

and to my children,

Ann, Richard, William, and *Ellen*

A NOTE TO THE READER

Because the events in this book span three continents, the reader should be aware of the precise differences in time zones.

Like the United States, the Soviet Union also has several time zones. Soviet Central Asia is three hours ahead of Moscow. Moscow is two hours ahead of Western European cities, such as London, Geneva, and Paris. Western Europe is six hours ahead of cities in the eastern time zone of the United States, such as Washington and New York.

For example, when it is 11:18 P.M. in Washington, it is 5:18 A.M. in Paris, 7:18 A.M. in Moscow, and 10:18 A.M. in Tashkent, Soviet Central Asia.

Prologue

I t was spring in Washington, D.C., and tourists thronged the esplanades around the Potomac basin, admiring the cherry trees in full bloom. Some wandered over to the memorials for Lincoln and Jefferson and recited the words the Presidents had left for future generations to ponder. Others went to the halls of Congress where their representatives were deliberating issues that affected their daily lives. They invaded the galleries of the Senate and House and saw the machinery of government running sluggishly in the chambers below. At the end of the dull sessions, the tourists dispersed through the stately corridors. A few brushed by a door in the Senate Building where a guard stood watching the visitors with bored detachment. None of the tourists stopped to ask the guard what he was defending. If they had, he would have said, "A closed session of the Appropriations Committee," and no one would have bothered to press the issue with him. The guard watched the last straggler pass by and shifted his tired feet while he waited for the senators to emerge and let him go home.

They had been inside for five hours, listening to Administration representatives stressing the urgency for increased funds. The senators were not hostile to these messengers from the White House. Horace Eubank, the white-maned chairman from Louisiana, had been a member of the Appropriations Committee for over thirty years. He was acknowledged to be a strong advocate of American military superiority over any potential enemies and

3

had even been nicknamed among certain elements in the country as Attila the Reb.

Eubank did not worry about his enemies. Elected six times to the Senate, he hoped to retire to his bank in Baton Rouge after this term and leave affairs of state to younger men. But he did worry constantly that his country was falling into ruin after years of protest and rioting in the streets. Vietnam and the entire Southeast Asian debacle had caused convulsions in almost every segment of American public opinion. Most people were simply tired of the constant warfare on the frontiers. Some had succumbed to the incessant blandishments from the new left and radical groups and decided that the first order of business was to correct the inequities so apparent among the country's more than 200 million inhabitants. Others had embarked on a campaign of repression against those who wanted to bring down the established order.

The result had been a new isolationism, a creeping withdrawal from foreign involvements and a gradual return to the concept of Fortress America, once only a slogan of the right.

Presidents were forced to tread carefully in the discharge of their duties. Often, against their better judgments, they retreated from decisions which only decades earlier would have been popular. In this atmosphere American influence lessened noticeably in sensitive areas of Europe and Asia.

For some Americans this was only good. For others it was a tragedy. Always before in world history, these people reasoned, the strongest had survived by staying strong. The weak were always present, anticipating the time when Goliath would let his guard down and fall to the jackals. It was national suicide, they believed, and yet they were nearly powerless to stop it.

Horace Eubank had tried. For several years he had managed to secret large sums of money in his budget for research and development of strategic weapons systems. He had aided the White House as much as he could by burying these grants under

4

innocuous classifications, and the White House had been properly grateful. But each year it had been more difficult to find the huge funds needed to keep the United States at least even with other countries in military hardware.

Horace Eubank could recall the long list of projects which had been regretfully shelved by the government till another day and another fresh wind of change blew down on Capitol Hill. He also had at hand intelligence reports describing Soviet research and knew that several systems, if perfected in time, could irrevocably alter the balance of power in the world. All of this was in Eubank's mind as he looked over his horn-rimmed glasses and smiled graciously at Gerald Weinroth, the President's scientific advisor.

"Professor, I think you know how kindly disposed this committee is toward your advisory board. We are always trying to help your little endeavors along to fruition, but," and he shrugged his shoulders sadly, "we can only do so much. We get whittled back each year and have a devil of a time scraping up what we do get for you. With the nation in the shape it's in now, I am not at all surprised at what's been happening. Why, pretty soon some of these people will be insisting we turn the ration's defenses over to the Black Panthers and the SDS."

The remark brought laughter, but Eubank was suddenly grim. "Seriously, Professor, this government is so paralyzed by the reluctance of the American people in general and the crackpot radicals in particular that I am getting scared to death at what will happen. We congressmen have to answer to the people at home and the word is out: 'Screw the military. They screwed us in Indochina and everywhere else.' So when you ask for money for items which I consider essential to the continued security of the country, I fear the worst. I am convinced we are in the midst of a retreat from reality. And some day we'll wake up dead."

Gerald Weinroth sat nodding his head vigorously in agreement. He waited to see whether Eubank had anything more to add, then hunched forward in his chair and addressed the five-man committee in a low, passionate voice:

"Mister Chairman, when I took over this job, I analyzed our position vis-à-vis the other side and concluded that we were at least even in most important areas. But it's also my job to predict the future and here I'm in terrible trouble. Because with the funds drying up, I can't even begin to fulfill the essential research work on systems we know the Russians already have off the drawing boards. And you all know that the real function of my group is to keep the other fellow from ever being able to get the drop on this country."

Weinroth smiled ruefully at his friends on the panel. "And I now have an ulcer to prove I have great trouble sleeping nights worrying over just such a calamity."

An oppressive silence followed. Finally, Horace Eubank looked at his watch. "Well, sir, we'll get you something for your pet projects but nothing like what you really need. Meanwhile, gentlemen, why don't we adjourn to my office and see if we can't calm the professor down with a shot of Jack Daniels."

The chairman rose, put a folder marked TOP SECRET under his arm, and marched out of the committee room. Gerald Weinroth popped a white pill into his mouth for his nerves and joined the safari to Eubank's whiskey oasis.

Monday,
September 9

WASHINGTON

MOSCOW

AT 6:30 A.M., the lobby of the Metropole Hotel was almost deserted. A middle-aged Russian woman sat behind the reception desk and watched John Brandon indifferently as he struggled with his heavy bags toward the door. Two porters sweeping the floor did not even look up as he passed.

Brandon was in a hurry. His plane was leaving at 8 A.M., and he had forgotten just how long it took to get to Moscow's international airport.

In front of the hotel, he put his bags down and looked for a taxi. Only one car was on the ramp, a private one, which now rolled suddenly toward the American. The door opened and a smiling man in a lumpy gray suit emerged.

"Mr. Brandon?"

"That's right."

"Jump in. I'm going your way."

The confused American got in with his luggage and the car moved away from the hotel. The driver was pleasant and gregarious.

"You've finished your research here?"

Brandon nodded.

"How did it go?" The man had no trace of an accent. His English was impeccable.

Though still puzzled by the stranger's familiarity, Brandon began to talk about his summer's stay in the Soviet Union, during which he had spent weeks in the Archives rummaging through records of the Napoleonic campaign against the Russian people in 1812. Brandon had been pleasantly surprised by the cooperation of the Soviet authorities in giving him access to materials no Western scholar had seen before. He knew that he had in his briefcase the ingredients of a book that would establish him in the academic world and guarantee commercial success as well. Brandon told all this to the stranger as the car left the center of Moscow and headed out into the country toward Sheremetyevo Airport.

A few trucks were on the highway, and a few people waited patiently at bus stops along the route. Otherwise, the summer landscape was almost deserted except for the two men conversing animatedly in the little car.

The stranger introduced himself. "I'm Grigor Rudenko, Mr. Brandon, and I work for Tass. I've known about your work here, and I though maybe some day we might get the opportunity to meet. Perhaps this is the best way." Rudenko smiled, almost to himself, as he said this. Brandon wondered suddenly if Rudenko had something more in mind.

Rudenko continued, "You know, I grew up in Philadelphia." He looked at Brandon for a reaction. John Brandon just stared back through the haze of his cigarette smoke. "My family came to America in the twenties and I went to high school there. But then the war came with Germany, and I guess the old loyalty to the motherland had never died because I decided to fight the Fascists myself. This was all before Pearl Harbor, and so I applied to the government for permission to join the Red Army, and it was granted. I spent the rest of the war in the cavalry and wound up picking my way through the streets of Berlin in 1945." Brandon was astounded but did not interrupt.

Rudenko lighted a short nonfilter cigarette and inhaled deeply.

"Then instead of going back to America, I stayed on with my adopted countrymen and renounced the evils of capitalism forever." At this remark, Rudenko laughed uproariously and winked at Brandon. "At the press agency, I have since contributed my talents to keeping the cold war cold." Rudenko waited for a response.

Brandon was extremely careful by now. All during his time in Russia, he had expected trouble. In talking to people who had studied in the Soviet Union or spent any length of time there on business, he had learned that, not infrequently, the Soviet Committee of State Security, the KGB, tried to compromise foreigners by involving them in unpleasant little intrigues, which ended in blackmail against the individual or international repercussions from a spy scandal. For the first time during his stay, he felt himself in the presence of such a situation. So he picked his words slowly.

"It's about time the cold war between our countries ended, don't you think? I must say, I've felt a great sadness while in this country at the thought that America and Russia might some day kill each other over one thing or another. It's a damn shame . . ."

Rudenko nodded vigorously and added, "I'm glad you feel that way because I, too, am discouraged at the prospects for survival." Rudenko's voice was suddenly tense, his manner subdued. He stubbed out his cigarette and watched a sign coming up which pointed the way into the airport. "Brandon, I want you to do me a favor."

Here it comes, Brandon thought. The overture is ended and the curtain is going up.

As the car slowed down, Rudenko steered it into the parking lot in front of the terminal building. He parked in an area where no cars were within fifty feet.

Turning to his passenger, he said, "When you get to New York, stay long enough to call a man named Karl Richter at the State Department in Washington. Tell him you were contacted by me and that you have something for him." Rudenko drew a bulky manila envelope from his inside suit pocket, Brandon stared at it in disbelief. He was being offered the bait that would land him in jail. "Make sure you deliver this into his hands within forty-eight hours of your arrival. That's all you have to do, believe me." He could see the turmoil in Brandon's face. "Don't worry, Brandon. You have nothing to fear. I'm not trying to trick you into something. What I'm giving you is vital to what we just talked about. Richter can act on it and prevent something far bigger than the Cuban missile crisis back in 1962."

Brandon suddenly said, "No, no, I won't do it. I'm not the type to get involved in these things."

"Brandon, don't talk nonsense. We're discussing something far more important than either of us. Why do you think I met you this morning? I know you're afraid that you'll be stopped by the customs men, but it won't happen. They know you and won't touch you. You're from Winnetka, Illinois. You're a bachelor. You have two brothers and a sister. Your parents are dead. You were in the U.S. Army during Korea . . . you were a sergeant in a rifle company. You later went to Purdue, and today you teach history at Lake Forest College. You're clean as far as the KGB is concerned. You have no ties to the U.S. intelligence community. Correct?"

Brandon nodded in wonder at this verbal dossier.

Rudenko looked at his watch. "You have about forty minutes to plane time. Take this envelope, please." His voice was urgent, almost pleading. Brandon reached for it and thought, Jesus, here I go into the bottomless pit. He took the package, put it into his jacket, and opened the door and started to get out. Rudenko leaned over and repeated, "Karl Richter at the State Department. He'll know what to do." Rudenko smiled and put out his hand. "Relax, Mr. Brandon, and thanks for trusting me." Brandon shook his hand perfunctorily. He wished the man had never come into his life.

He took his luggage on into the building. At the customs desk, he filled out a form declaring how much money he had spent in the Soviet Union. He also changed his few Russian rubles into dollars. Then he brought his baggage and the declaration to the desk. His luggage was weighed and put on a pile to be taken to the Pan American plane. It was not inspected.

In the waiting room, Brandon paced up and down, waiting for the call to board. When it came, he went down a long corridor to a final checkpoint, where Russian soldiers examined boarding passes and passports. The phone at the desk kept ringing constantly, and, each time, Brandon wondered if the listener would turn and beckon him into oblivion. The minutes passed. Then the gate was opened, and Brandon and a crowd of passengers were led down a ramp to a waiting bus. Out on the runway, he saw the familiar blue Pan Am emblem rising from the tail of a Boeing 747 in the September sunshine.

When he entered the plane, a smiling hostess, an American girl, welcomed him into the long tunnel of seats. Brandon realized how long it had been since he had actually talked to an American woman, all fresh and made-up and distinctly midwestern. He smiled back and went to a window on the right side where he sagged into a chair, putting his briefcase under it. He wanted to smoke badly but the No-Smoking sign prevented that. In a few minutes the motors started, and slowly the jet moved off down the runway to the takeoff position. Brandon looked around at his fellow passengers. The plane was only half-filled, and he found it difficult to type his companions. He tried to imagine who might be a secret policeman, but no one stood out in the group. Then Brandon caught himself and tried to analyze the situation. He had passed customs. No one was suspicious. If anyone had been, he would not have made it this far. And certainly, the Russians would not have put a secret policeman in a seat on an American plane just to follow him all over the world. They would get him while he was still in their camp. At this point in his analysis, John Brandon relaxed. The envelope in his pocket still intruded on his thinking, but

13

he knew that he had gotten through the final barrier. While he watched, the ground rushed by him and Pan Am Flight Number 101 was airborne to New York.

He waited impatiently for the No-Smoking sign to blink off and then he lit the most delicious cigarette in his entire life. Beneath the jet the lush countryside receded below the clouds.

A huge lunch was served as the plane passed west of Norway and headed over the North Atlantic. The menu included chilled turkey slices followed by a fileted steak. John Brandon devoured the entrée, left the apple strudel dessert, and drank two cups of coffee. When the movie began, he watched for a few moments, then dozed off with his headset tuned to Beethoven's Eroica Symphony. He slept for over an hour.

When he awoke, the North Atlantic was still beneath him. He got up from his seat and threaded his way to the bathroom at the rear. Inside, he combed his hair and washed the fatigue from his face. Then he thought again about Rudenko and the envelope. Pulling it from his inside jacket pocket, he held it in front of him and examined it in the harsh fluorescent light. In the upper left corner, there appeared to be some sort of address. Brandon read the smudged Cyrillic characters and made out the words. Soviet Society of Theoretical Physicists. Beneath that, in smudged ink, was an address, Number 10 Tolstoy Prospekt. That was all. The society itself was not familiar to him. But then he was a historian, not a scientist. He was terribly anxious to know what was inside the package but resisted the temptation to tear it open. It was enough to deliver it to Mr. Richter.

Brandon walked back to his seat and put his headset on. *The Afternoon of a Faun* lulled him back to sleep.

At 3:15 P.M., New York time, the plane landed at Kennedy Airport. Brandon went through customs quickly and looked for a pay phone. He called a hotel in Manhattan, then placed a second call to Washington and the State Department. When the operator there answered, he asked to speak to Karl Richter. In thirty seconds, a girl's voice with a cool Southern accent came on the line, and Brandon asked again for Richter. The voice said, "Who's calling, please?" Brandon gave his name. The voice excused herself for a moment, and then Richter came on the line. "Yes." He sounded remote, vaguely unfriendly.

"My name is John Brandon, and I have something for you from Grigor Rudenko in Moscow. He said it was urgent that you get it promptly." Richter's attitude changed. "When can I see you, Mr. Brandon?"

"Well, I just checked into the Chatham Hotel here in New York, and I'm really bushed from the flight. How about tomorrow morning?"

"Fine. Take the shuttle from LaGuardia at nine, and I'll have someone meet you at the gate. Make yourself known at the desk, and he'll take you from there. And, by the way, Mr. Brandon, how did you meet Rudenko?"

Brandon gave the whole story to Richter, about his own background as a historian, his summer of research in the Soviet Union, his curious trip to the airport on the final day. When Brandon finished, Richter told him he looked forward to seeing him in the morning, then hung up.

John Brandon undressed slowly in the welcome air-conditioning of his hotel room. He put the manila envelope on a night table and hung up his lightweight suit. Then he put on a bathrobe over his underwear and took his toothbrush and shaving equipment out of his luggage. Before going in to shower, he called room service and ordered a bacon, lettuce, and tomato sandwich and a pot of coffee. Refreshed by a cool shower, John Brandon stretched out on the bed to watch the evening news. He had missed television during his many weeks in Moscow.

A knock sounded at the door. Brandon tightened the sash

of his robe as he opened the door to let the waiter in. A man stood there, dressed in a fall topcoat. He was swarthy; his face had several ruts in it, and his beard was bluish. The man asked, "Mr. Brandon?"

Brandon replied, "That's me."

The man pulled a peculiar-looking instrument from his right-hand pocket and put it directly in front of Brandon's nose. He pulled the trigger, and although no sound came from the gun, John Brandon staggered backward, clutched at his face, and then sagged to the floor.

The man stepped over the body and walked about the room. He spotted the manila envelope lying on the table and went directly to it. Tearing it open, he looked swiftly at the collection of blueprints and memoranda within. The man shook his head in seeming amazement and then stuffed the material back inside the envelope. He put it into his inside jacket pocket.

Then he walked to the corpse on the rug, turned it over, and stared into the sightless eyes of John Brandon. The man put his hands under the corpse and, grunting, carried it the short distance to the bed. Pulling the blue covers down, the killer tucked Brandon beneath the blankets. He propped a pillow behind his head and folded his hands in front of him. Then the man stepped back and looked a last time about the room. Satisfied, he went to the door and picked the Do-Not-Disturb sign from a wall hook. In the corridor, he placed it on the outside door knob and then strolled casually fifty feet to the elevator. As he entered it, a waiter carried a sandwich and a pot of coffee past him down the corridor. The waiter stopped in front of John Brandon's room and stared in confusion at the sign on the door. He knocked very softly, hesitated, and then turned away with the food order.

Down in the lobby, the man in the fall topcoat mingled with crowds of strangers in summer clothing and disappeared through the glass entrance into the warm night.

16

Tuesday,
September 10

WASHINGTON

MOSCOW

AT 10:15 A.M., the next morning, Karl Richter was told by the man he had sent to the airport that no one named John Brandon had gotten off the plane from New York. In his air-conditioned sixth-floor office at the New State Department Building, Richter sipped a Dixie cup of black coffee and digested the news. Probably Brandon had just overslept and would catch the next shuttle flight due in at 11. He told the man to wait there and call him as soon as contact was made.

Ever since Brandon's call the previous afternoon, Richter had become increasingly alarmed at the strange circumstances surrounding his impending visit. At the root of the mystery was the worry over Grigor Rudenko's unorthodox manner of transmitting information. Grigor must have been in a desperate situation to have used an innocent man as messenger between Moscow and Washington. Always before, Rudenko had operated strictly according to the book as written by the CIA. Always before he had passed his information at the appropriate drops, whether they were embassy parties or clandestine "chance" meetings in playgrounds or at street corners. He had always been prompt, efficient, and the most productive operator working inside Russia. Rudenko must have sensed surveillance while possessing material too urgent to delay transmission.

Karl Richter felt particularly unhappy and frustrated because Rudenko was different from the others Richter dealt with in the espionage profession. Richter had known several men who were finally exposed and died in anonymity. It was the ultimate hazard of the business. But Rudenko was special. He and Karl Richter had been close friends since high school. They had met at lunch one day and discovered an instant rapport over things like the lowly state of the Philadelphia Athletics and the supreme joy of riding a horse in the sweet fragrance of an early morning mist. After the first day, they had slept at each other's homes, shared shirts and ties, and double-dated with girls in Karl's Studebaker convertible. Richter was particularly enchanted with the stories Grigor's parents told of Russia in the old days, when the Czar was ruler and the winter snows hid the landscape but not the misery of the peasants, who bore the feudal life with stoic passivity.

In June of 1941, the two boys had graduated from high school and both were to go to Haverford College in the fall. But Grigor's world changed forever on June 22nd, when Adolf Hitler invaded Russia.

His family had left Russia in 1928, not because they were totally disenchanted with communism, but to find a more immediate better life for themselves and for Grigor, then four years old. Sacha and Sonya Rudenko knew that Russia would improve under Stalin; anything would be better than life under the Romanovs. But they did not want to wait. The Civil War had ended; Lenin's Five-Year plans were struggling along to fruition. But Grigor was the Rudenko's only child, and they wanted a better world for him at once. Because relatives in Philadelphia had urged them to come to America, they packed their suitcases and left the steppe country around Rostov for the last time. For them it was heartbreaking; for Grigor it was an adventure.

In 1941, when the motherland was threatened and Stalin appealed to his countrymen to defend it, not communism, from the invader, the Rudenkos felt the tug of patriotism. Grigor went to fight in their place.

When the war was ended, he was nearly twenty-two and had

met a nurse named Tamara, whose entire family—except for an uncle, Andrei Parchuk, the world-renowned quantum physicist—had been killed in the massacre of Kharkov. Grigor married her in Moscow in 1946, and immediately went to work for the government press agency Tass. He wrote faithfully to Karl Richter, who had just returned from the Pacific where he had served on Admiral Bull Halsey's staff. Richter was finishing his education at Yale and planning a career in the Foreign Service. Rudenko's letters were marvelous accounts of life in Moscow, of the new society building in Russia, of his hopes that the two friends might meet again soon. He often wrote of the days before the war and the people they had known in school. In 1948, the letters stopped coming, and, when Richter visited Rudenko's parents to find out about Grigor, they admitted sadly that he did not write to them anymore, either.

Karl Richter joined the Foreign Service and was posted to a succession of assignments in South America, then on to Paris, and finally in 1956, to the embassy in Moscow. He had married the daughter of a prominent Main Line doctor in 1951, and she followed him around the world, hating every minute of it. They had no children, and the tedium of diplomatic life claimed her as a victim. She began to drink, at first socially, then to blot out her boredom. Richter watched her disintegrate but could do nothing to arrest her destruction. Just before they were to leave for Moscow, she went into the bathroom of their Paris apartment and swallowed thirty-five sleeping pills. She was dead when he found her.

Richter went to Moscow a broken man. He plunged into his work as cultural attaché and began the inevitable rounds of cocktail parties at various embassies. At the Swedish Embassy, he met Grigor Rudenko, now plump and jolly. The two friends did not embrace. Richter instinctively knew that he should not betray their long acquaintance. Grigor shook his hand warmly but otherwise held his own emotions in check. They talked briefly about their families, and Rudenko offered his condolences to Richter about his wife's death. Richter was positive then that Grigor was involved in Soviet secret police activities, for only the KGB would have a full dossier on him. At the end of the party, Grigor shook hands again with Karl, who felt a piece of paper stick to his palm. He casually put it in his pocket and went out to his car where he unfolded the tiny scrap and read, *"Karl, meet me at Dynamo Stadium, soccer game, 2 P.M., Saturday, Gate C."*

Richter checked with his superiors, who told him to proceed with the meeting. At 1:55, Richter met Grigor, who walked in front of him to the ticket-taker and handed over two tickets. Then the two men went into the stadium and sat down to watch the game. Grigor ignored him for a few moments. The crowd was in an uproar, cheering on the Dynamos against a team from Kiev.

"Great sport, Karl, isn't it?"

"Almost as good as watching the Athletics."

Grigor laughed deeply and put his hand on Karl's wrist. "We have a lot of catching up to do, don't we?"

He began to talk. He had stopped writing because of his new job with the KGB. Grigor wanted to know about his family, and Karl assured him they were fine, if a bit hurt that he did not correspond. Rudenko grimaced at this news, but did not comment.

"Karl, I made a bad mistake, staying here in Russia. I was so enchanted with the victory over Germany and the hopes for this country in the postwar world that I threw everything over for it. Now I'm in it up to my neck. I can never go back." Richter watched the game while his friend went on. "But I've been thinking there may be a way I can still be an American, in spirit at least." Rudenko leaned over and whispered, "Karl, I'm going to pass information to you. Only you. You have to be my contact at all times."

Richter nodded impassively and Rudenko sat back, seemingly purged of his burden.

At half time, the two men got up and wandered down the ramp under the stands. They separated there with smiles, and Rudenko walked to Gate D and through it. Richter went out through Gate C.

In the next two years, Grigor Rudenko kept his word. He and Karl met in restaurants, at receptions, and on long walks at night through side streets, where they fleshed in the missing years of their lives and talked about the cold war. Each time they met, Rudenko handed over microfilm, papers, and copies of orders, whose contents provided American intelligence with a staggering insight into Soviet plans. Richter was afraid for Rudenko and told him not to risk his life. Rudenko always laughed and said he was too highly placed to be followed, too important to be suspected. The meetings continued.

Rudenko never brought Richter to see his wife and two children. Once he did show him snapshots of his family, and Richter made appropriate comments on their appearances. Rudenko was pleased but did not speak about them further.

In September, 1959, Karl Richter had to leave Moscow. His tour of duty was up, and, if he had requested an extension, the Russians would have been suspicious. That would have endangered Grigor. The old friends met for the last time at the British Embassy, where Richter introduced Rudenko to Anthony Carter, who would be Rudenko's new contact. Carter would funnel all information to Richter in London. Rudenko seemed satisfied with the arrangement.

He stood before a buffet table and raised a Scotch and soda to Karl Richter, "Karl, let's drink to the old days." Richter looked at Grigor and wanted to cry. His double life was surely going to envelop and crush him someday, but the man was remarkably composed and almost fatalistic in his acceptance. Richter drank to the old days.

Richter went to London and then to Washington, where he became second in command at State Department Intelligence. Always he handled Rudenko's material, which by now centered on Soviet missile production and silos. The data helped American planning for defense all during the Kennedy, Johnson, and Nixon years. Anthony Carter and others delivered back to Rudenko letters from his parents in Philadelphia and notes from Richter, who used the code name Haverford in case the papers fell into the wrong hands. The contact man said that Rudenko appeared in the best of health. His spirits were always good. Only two weeks before, when Grigor had dropped a container of microfilm at a trade fair in Moscow, he had appeared jovial and unconcerned. And yet, he had now sought out a stranger, John Brandon, within the past twenty-four hours and entrusted him with something for Washington. Richter was deeply concerned for his friend.

At 11:10 A.M. on that Tuesday morning, Richter's messenger at the airport called once more to say that John Brandon had not emerged from the shuttle plane.

Richter went into action. He called the Chatham Hotel in New York and asked to be connected to John Brandon's room. The phone rang ten times. Richter told the operator to send someone up there quickly to find out if Brandon was ill.

The bell captain found John Brandon in bed, facing the television set showing a Charlie Chaplin comedy. The bell captain said, "I'm sorry to intrude, sir, but a friend of yours . . ." Then the bell captain stopped talking, for he had seen Brandon's eyes, fixed unwaveringly on the picture screen. They never blinked. The bell captain went to the phone and asked the operator to let him speak to Richter. He said, "I'm sorry to tell you this, sir, but Mr. Brandon seems to have passed away during his sleep."

24

Karl Richter was not terribly surprised. He ordered the hotel manager to hold the body for a police autopsy, then spoke to FBI headquarters in New York and told the bureau chief to search the room immediately for a manila envelope among Brandon's personal effects.

Karl Richter waited beside his phone. He drank another container of coffee. He contacted the traffic department in the basement of the building and asked them to cable the American Embassy in Moscow for information on the whereabouts of Grigor Rudenko. He cautioned the embassy to be extremely discreet in its inquiry since Rudenko might be under surveillance or worse. Richter told the clerk to use the Croesus code in relaying the message to Moscow. Later, after reading two urgent reports, he ate a sandwich at his desk.

Finally, the phone rang. The FBI reported that after a careful search, they had found no manila envelope in John Brandon's room. Richter was now certain that the messenger from Moscow had not died from a heart attack. He told the FBI to look for death by "unnatural means" and to stay with the coroner until something definite emerged from the autopsy.

Richter went to the elevator and down into the basement garage at the State Department. He drove his car up the ramp and into the early afternoon stream of traffic heading past the Lincoln Memorial and across the bridge into Virginia. Ahead lay the hill where John and Robert Kennedy lay at rest. The late summer foliage wrapped the hillside in lush warmth. Tourists formed a line around the memorial to the assassinated President. Richter watched the antlike column of mourners idly as he swung the car off the bridge and onto the road leading into the country and the headquarters of the Central Intelligence Agency fifteen miles away in Langley. He found himself thinking of those terrible days in the fall of 1962 when the Kennedy brothers had confronted the Russians over Cuba and won the "eyeball to eyeball" duel. Richter shuddered slightly as he remembered the unbelievable tension of those hours. It had been too close a thing to romanticize the affair even now. And still, the cold war went on. Richter thought of Grigor sadly as he drove along the highway toward the agency.

On the second floor of that sprawling main building which housed the men and apparatus that monitored enemy intentions, someone else was remembering the days of the missile crisis with the same feelings of subdued horror. In his walnut-paneled office, Director Samuel T. Riordan had wheeled his chair around to the window and tilted it back with his feet propped up against the pane. He drummed his fingers against the arm of the chair as he looked out at the rolling hills surrounding his domain. Riordan was uneasy. Years of training in the intelligence business had honed his instincts for danger to a high degree of sophistication. Riordan's instincts were now working overtime. Something was wrong in the world, and the director felt it strongly. In his lap lay pieces of the puzzle, reports from agents and data from eavesdropping devices which clearly indicated an extraordinary turn of events somewhere in the world. Riordan was nagged by the similarity of this situation to the Cuban crisis when the constant filtering of bits and pieces of data pointed to a highly irregular activity on the part of the enemy. Only at the last moment had the pieces fitted together and enabled the President of the United States to counter the threat.

Samuel Riordan was suffering the same dreadful reactions on this lovely September day. He turned wearily back to his desk and sorted out the information one more time.

Item:

From Commander-in-Chief Atlantic Fleet:
Flotilla of twenty-two Soviet naval warships including four Polaris-type missile carriers passing south of Newfoundland, bearing southwest at twenty-four knots. Complete radio silence being observed. Being shadowed by units of Allied fleet in area. Probable

destination unknown at this time. Present speed and course if maintained suggests rendezvous off Virginia coastline with large fleet of Soviet trawelrs presently in area.

MOORE, Admiral

Item:

CIA, HQ, Frankfort, Larsen:

Seven Soviet diplomats, including ambassadors to Belgium, France, West Germany, and Yugoslavia, have within past forty-eight hours, emplaned for Moscow. No explanation of departure. Also KGB activity in Western Europe appears in state of flux. Resident agent in Bonn has not been seen in his usual cover as press officer at embassy for ten days . . . supposed to have the flu . . . What do you have from your end on all this? . . .

Item:

MOSCOW, Sept. 5 (Reuters)—Premier Valerian Smirnov was reliably reported today to have gone into the hospital for tests to determine the cause of a persistent stomach disorder. Bulletins will be issued by the Soviet government at periodic stages of the medical diagnosis.

Item:

Norad to Langley, August 10, 3 P.M.

Soviet space base at Baikonur has fired six satellites into orbit within three-day period. Each satellite contained eight-in-one packages now distributed in a global arc seven hundred miles high. Chain of satellites grapefruit-sized. Assume navigational aids for Soviets but no confirmation.

Item:

To Riordan from Nichols, Director National Security Agency:

On August 14 and 22, Midas infrared detection satellites recorded intense heat emissions of fourteen to eighteen seconds duration emitted from a position in area north of Tashkent and also region fifty miles east of Vorkuta just north of Arctic Circle. No hydrogen tests possible since other detection apparatus failed to give corroborative signals.

Item:

HAVANA, Sept. 7 (AP)—
A delegation of Soviet generals and other officials landed today in Havana to pay a courtesy visit to Fidel Castro, leader of the Cuban people. They are expected to stay approximately ten days before journeying on to Algeria on the last leg of their goodwill trip to friendly nations.

Samuel Riordan knew something more about this news dispatch. An agent working in the Cuban Foreign Office had passed word along that the delegation was no ordinary group. The generals included a rocket expert, a long-range bomber man, and the deputy chief of Soviet land forces in Central Europe. The civilians in the gathering were an especially interesting collection of scientists: one, Zabin, had helped father the Soviet H-bomb; Zakharov was a pioneer in the development of the Fractional Orbital Bomb system, now in operation for several years; Bessanova was a theoretical physicist, out of circulation for the past eighteen months, and last reported somewhere in the Urals on a secret project.

Riordan kept coming back to this news from Havana and wondered why such an outstanding collection of brains and prestige was gathered together for Fidel Castro's benefit. It just did not make sense, unless something was going on again in that island off the Florida coast.

The director's musings were interrupted by the intercom:

"Charlie Tarrant would like to see you immediately."

"Send him right in, Margaret."

Charlie Tarrant, a slim, Brooks-Brothers-clothed deputy director, came into the room trailed by Karl Richter, who knew

Riordan from their many years together in intelligence work, Riordan was pleased to see him and welcomed him warmly. The three men sat in a corner of the room and coffee was brought in.

Riordan asked Charlie what the problem was. Tarrant said, "We seem to have another item for today's briefing. Karl has just told me we may have lost Rudenko. Karl, you may as well tell the story from the beginning."

Richter did so, and Riordan sucked on his pipe while the man from the State Department spoke about Brandon and the envelope. Then Riordan offered, "I'm really terribly sorry, Karl, because I know how close you were to Grigor." Richter nodded, and Riordan continued, "And this Brandon fellow, just an innocent victim. Isn't that awful! What about his family?"

Richter said he wanted to keep the government out of it and therefore, the New York City police had agreed to say that he had died of a heart attack in his sleep. His sister was on the way to claim the body.

Riordan went on: "I wish there was something we could do for his family, but it would only make the whole thing a bigger mess right now. They might even be bitter enough to go to the papers with it, and we don't need that kind of publicity. Maybe someday we can explain it to them and help them financially. Perhaps we can find some way to get an insurance policy payment to them. Something like that might work."

The other men agreed wholeheartedly. Richter said, "The manner in which Rudenko involved Brandon in his problems suggests to me that he must have believed that the end was near for him. Otherwise, he would have used the usual means of communication with the boys at the embassy, the drops in Gorki Park, the meetings with agents from the British Embassy. For him to collar Brandon at a hotel and then give him an envelope instead of microdotting the material can only mean he was a goner and knew it. And whatever was in that letter must have been worth dying for, I suspect."

29

Riordan's right hand tightened around the stem of his pipe as he knocked the ashes from it. For the first time, Richter noticed the large wart that disfigured the director's ring finger. It fascinated him.

Tarrant broke in, "What the hell could he have gotten that was so worth dying for?"

Samuel Riordan sucked on a fresh pipe while he pondered the question. "I don't know, Charlie, but maybe he had the answer to what's bothering me." Riordan glanced at his watch and started to rise. "I expect the situation will be bothering a few other people before the day is out."

A full-scale briefing was held that afternoon in the office of the Joint Chiefs of Staff at the Pentagon. As four o'clock neared, men entered Ring E of the massive building and showed their ID cards to guards at the desk in front of a barred door. The participants had come at the express request of the President of the United States, who had been alerted to the situation by Sam Riordan from CIA. Riordan had called the President shortly after noon and briefed him on the disquieting intelligence reports flooding in from around the world. The President had told Riordan to convene the special session and invite every intelligence-gathering unit in the government to send representatives. From the meeting, something should emerge, some pattern or clue to the intentions of the other side. The President expected Riordan, who arrived with Charlie Tarrant and Karl Richter, to make a personal report to him at 8 P.M.

At 4:10, General Stephen Austin Roarke, chairman of the Joint Chiefs, called the meeting to order. Fourteen men sat with Roarke around a huge oaken table, which he had moved into the conference room from his home in Texas. It had been his family's dining board for over one hundred years, since the time of the Alamo. Roarke was proud of his family, his state, and

30

his own rank as the leading American military personage next to the President of the United States.

"Gentlemen, we're all here to add whatever we can to a clearer picture of the enemy's capabilities and motives on this beautiful September day. While I have no doubt we have a true picture of him, the President feels we should pool our information and distill it for his personal evaluation. Therefore, let's begin with a general rundown or the world as seen from Langley. Mr. Riordan, would you take over."

Sam Riordan took the floor and told of his fears. He admitted that his agency had not been able to diagnose any unfriendly act in the making. He described the various bits of intelligence that bothered him, including the probable loss of a top Soviet informant. He added two items that had come in overnight. A man named Cherkovinin, from the Soviet Embassy in Paris, had been found shot dead and floating in the Seine. Karl Richter, sitting next to Charlie Tarrant, leaned over and whispered, "He's a friend of Rudenko. Worked for him once at Tass. He's a courier."

Richter's face was pained. "They must be making Grigor talk."

Riordan was still speaking. "The other piece of trivia is this. Russian troop units on the West German border just came off summer maneuvers three weeks ago. And yet they are now beginning new movements toward the frontier, nothing threatening to us but highly unusual, based on their past performances."

Charlie Tarrant passed Riordan a note about Rudenko's friend floating in the Seine and Riordan pursed his lips. But he sat down without making any reference to it in front of his colleagues.

The representative from the National Security Council followed with his own report. Eavesdropping radar and telephonic equipment had noticed a startling increase in Soviet radio conversations between army units, but it only indicated what

31

Riordan had already said. The Soviets were maneuvering again at a time when they should be dormant. By contrast, the Soviet Navy was quiet, especially the group moving toward the open Atlantic and possibly the United States east coast. The missile sites ranging across the spine of Russia were in their usual state of readiness; monitors detected no overt sign of aggressive intent. The man speaking wore spectacles and read from notes like a teacher charging a class with responsibility for knowing the reasons for the decline and fall of the Roman Empire. He was boring his listeners with his recital. Then he brought up the heat-sensing devices in the sky, which had alerted their masters to the pulsing emissions from the ground.

General Roarke broke in, "Have they been testing above-ground?"

"No, all evidence denies that. It could be something else, like a laser weapon. We've been working on the same thing, haven't we?"

Roarke and the others looked at Gerald Weinroth, head of the President's scientific board. The shaggy-haired, rumpled professor nodded vigorously and stood up.

"Project Jerusalem has been going forward for over three years. We hope to have a workable model in three to six months. It has been in many ways a more difficult task to organize this effort than the original atomic bomb back in 1945. But when we do get it, it will revolutionize warfare. We'll have come up with a death ray."

Roarke interrupted again, "Where are the Russians on this one?"

Riordan took the floor again, "We know they've been working on the same idea for some time. But like their missile program, it may be they've run into economic difficulties which have slowed down their progress. It's like the time they tried to beat us to the moon and fell so far behind, mostly because of finances and also a certain lack of sophistication in gadgetry. Look how long it was before they finally got to the Sea of Tranquillity. At any rate, the information we get back from agents on the ground is that they have gotten bogged down. Now as to those Midas readings, I'm not quite sure if that's a prototype that was fired. I can only hope they didn't break through on this. It might get sticky as hell . . ."

At 6:45, the meeting adjourned for a light supper, and the participants went to the next room for a meal of chicken salad and black-eyed peas, General Roarke's favorite delicacy. White-coated waiters passed among the officials and served impeccably from gold service, bearing the seal of the U.S. Army. The conversation was relaxed and warm. Most of these men were comrades from many crises during the cold war and often entertained one another at intimate parties in the suburbs of Washington. They spoke the same language professionally and faced the same problems in their tiny fiefdoms. In the dining room at the Pentagon, they were comfortable and confident over coffee and brandy.

Across the river, the White House basked in the brilliant sunshine. In the Oval Room, President William Mellon Stark sat with his Secretary of Labor, Bruce A. Hinton, and discussed a proposed bill to enlarge relief benefits to migratory workers scattered across the land. The secretary was telling the President how much the passage of the measure would ingratiate him with the liberal community, which would be convinced the President was finally moving on the human-rights issue. Stark was bored by the whole discussion and particularly by the secretary. Hinton had been forced on him by certain people who had contributed heavily to his campaign. Because of this, Stark put up with his constant ramblings about minorities and whatever else he preached about as the months went by.

Stark himself was more interested in a long-postponed vacation, due to start in two days. His wife was joining him at a retreat near Bar Harbor for two long weeks. Since the children had their own families and jobs to think about, that would leave him alone with Pamela for the first time in two years. Stark was tired of being President, tired of constantly watching over the fate of the nation. He had lost that drive which once ate at him, forcing him to grasp for the shiny gold ring. Once he got it, the challenge was met and the fires had been banked. The President of the most powerful country in the world just wanted to serve out his first term and then quit and go fishing with his wife of twenty-five years. He owed it to her and to himself.

So Stark listened to his Secretary of Labor and found him a bore. The secretary did not seem to notice and kept up his dreary monologue.

In the basement of the building, another man sat before a machine. Master Sergeant Arly Cooper watched indifferently as he read a poem before him on a teletype; it was in English but it was from *Eugen Onegin* by Pushkin:

> I write you; is my act not serving
>   As an arrival? Well I know
> The punishment I am deserving
>   That you despise me. Even so,
> perhaps for my sad fate preserving
>   A drop of pity you'll forbear
> To leave me here to my despair.

Fifty-one hundred miles away in Moscow, a Russian soldier was tapping out his favorite lines to his American counterpart in the Situation Room deep beneath the White House. The two men manned the hot line which traversed the Atlantic Ocean and then went through Scandinavia on into the heartland of

Russia. Every hour on the hour the Soviet technician cleared his machine to guarantee its dependability. Each hour on the half hour, Arly Cooper or his replacement did the same. Cooper, a black man, always used Lincoln's Gettysburg Address for his message. He would type out: "Four score and seven years ago, our fathers brought forth on this continent a new nation conceived in liberty and dedicated to the proposition that all men are created equal." Cooper did it with a certain relish, as though in the process he was educating the enemy to the real meaning of America. Cooper felt as though he personally was piercing the Iron Curtain with his own brand of propaganda. It was a game which helped him while away the monotonous eight hours a day he spent locked in this walnut-paneled nerve center of United States military communications. The hot line was manned on three shifts by both countries. Cooper's counterpart in Moscow was always the Pushkin lover. He often wondered what the man looked like, whether he too was a master sergeant, or if he too wished he could be somewhere else, doing something more interesting. Arly Cooper would never know, but he thought about it often.

The transmission ended at 7:05 P.M. and Cooper acknowledged. He then went to the coffee urn and poured himself a cup, black with no sugar. In twenty-five minutes it would be his turn to promote the cause of Abraham Lincoln behind the Iron Curtain.

At the Pentagon, the intelligence meeting had reconvened. The representative from the Defense Intelligence Agency, filling in for Secretary of Defense Clifford Erskine, who was in London, added his office's pieces to the world mosaic. He noted that a Soviet diplomat in Ankara, who had been friendly for years with Premier Smirnov, had been unusually garrulous at a reception for foreign ambassadors on the previous Tuesday. His garrulity seemed forced, and an informant reported he seemed extraordinarily nervous and agitated. No one had ever seen him act this way before.

Charlie Tarrant commented on this remark by saying that a pattern had been established in at least one area. The ranks of Soviet diplomats and secret police apparently were under some kind of internal stress. "Perhaps," offered Tarrant, "the Kremlin is undergoing a periodic reshuffle."

Claude Norton, from the U.S. Arms Control and Disarmament Agency, reinforced this argument by saying that the last meeting of the two great powers had been the most difficult in several months. The Soviet delegation was mute, completely intransigent. It was shocking to the Americans because Premier Smirnov himself had urged the Americans to stay at the conference so that an important breakthrough could be achieved in the near future. Smirnov was evidently pursuing the idea of disarmament despite increasing opposition at home from hawkish elements who feared he was giving away the security of the country. Yet, in the last meeting, Norton recalled, it had seemed just like the old days of Stalin.

General Roarke asked for any further comments bearing on the subject. Hearing none, Roarke continued, "Gentlemen, I think we can say that our immediate safety is not threatened by anything we've heard here today. Our missile strength is at least equal to the enemy. Our military posture is superb. There does seem to be some indication of a political upheaval over there, but it will take time to resolve the significance of it. Don't you agree? As to the mysterious Midas sensings, let's also suppose that the Russians are working on a project similar to ours, and are possibly proceeding at a faster rate than we thought. Still, Dr. Weinroth, what would that mean as far as capability if they are now testing a weapon?"

He turned to Weinroth again, and the scientist thought for a moment or two. Then he sighed and shrugged his hands in front of him. "I can't predict what they will do, but it would strike me they'd have to iron out the bugs for another year. By that time, we'll have an operational system ourselves and we'll be at parity just as in bombs and missiles." Roarke nodded happily and adjourned the group.

Sam Riordan went up to Roarke and told him he would brief the President personally on the meeting that night. Roarke put his hand on Riordan's shoulder and said, "Sam, tell him hello for me. I haven't seen the President for six months. And please give my best regards to Pamela."

Riordan said he would and went back through the barred doors into the corridor and on to his limousine which headed for the White House. The director was still a nervous man because the puzzle was not yet solved.

At 9:02 P.M., Washington time, a Midas satellite, moving 104 miles above the earth in its relentless orbit, monitored a twenty-two-second pulsing of heat estimated at an intensity of plus ten million degrees. Its on-board computer calculated the emission at a point north of the Caspian Sea in the area of Tashkent in Soviet Central Asia.

At almost the same moment, another Midas, circling the globe ninety-seven miles over the darkened jungles of Tanzania, recorded another emission in the area of the Negev Desert southwest of Jerusalem. It lasted for twenty-two seconds at an intensity of plus ten million degrees and was followed by heat ranging between one thousand and fifteen hundred degrees. The latter emission continued for some time as the Midas passed on over Bulgaria toward the Arctic Circle.

37

In the Mediterranean Sea, sailors of the United States Sixth Fleet on watch noticed nothing unusual.

In the ancient town of Beersheba on the edge of the Negev, guests at the Desert Inn, the only motel in the area, were wakened by a tremendous roll, like thunder, to the west. When several of them looked in that direction, they saw a cherry-red glow beyond the mountains. Someone remarked, "Al Fatah must have been caught in another ambush. Those bastards never give up, do they?"

On a hillside near Aqaba, the Jordanian port near Eilat, three men bent over instruments just inside the mouth of a cave. They watched sensitive needles recording wavy lines across paper and gauges which reflected a violent reaction somewhere within the range of the equipment. The three men conversed in low tones. They spoke Russian.

At a radar station in northern Turkey, an employee of the National Security Agency heard a voice coming from the radio. Beamed from near Tashkent to Moscow, it said simply, "Borodino." The NSA man noted that it was the first time Tashkent radio had spoken to anyone for over six months. He also noted that Borodino was the site of Russia's great victory over Napoleon.

In Washington, D.C., the lights had gone on in the White House. In an upstairs sitting room, Sam Riordan sat with his chief and explained the outcome of the Pentagon briefing. William Stark was not bored now. He had known Sam Riordan for too long not to detect in the man's attitude a note of urgency and, even more dismaying, a sense of frustration at not being able to pinpoint his fears.

Stark pressed Riordan several times on his own feelings, and finally the director of the CIA blurted out: "Mr. President, frankly I'm baffled. My instincts tell me that something bad is taking place in the world, but my intelligence cannot bring it to light. Maybe I'm getting too old for the job. Maybe I'm seeing things that aren't there. Perhaps I've been watching the Reds so long I've become paranoid."

Stark smiled at him and leaned over to pat him reassuringly. "Sam, you're still the best man the CIA ever had. Don't worry about yourself that way. What does concern me here is some item we all might have overlooked. Is there any area not probed yet by your people or the other agencies?"

Riordan searched his mind for a clue. "No, we've gone over the missile deployments, their outer-space platforms, the naval and army concentrations and even the internal condition of the Soviet Union. In several instances, the ones we discussed today, there are signs of trouble within the country, and there are unusual movements of ships and even diplomats. But by themselves they don't add up to any dangerous situation. Again, I go back to my own gut reactions, which are not good."

Stark ordered drinks from the kitchen, and the two old comrades sat under a portrait of Thomas Jefferson and sipped bourbon and branch water. The grandfather clock in the corner chimed ten as they continued to discuss the perplexing problem.

At Point Mugu, ninety miles north of Los Angeles, a Univac 5000 computer poured forth a torrent of words received from Midas 14 passing overhead. Midas 14 had analyzed the data collected in its pass over the Middle East and was now disgorging it to its masters on the ground. Midas 8 had earlier alerted Mugu to its detection of a single heat-emission from within the Soviet Union.

The Univac recorded its interpretation of the information while the Midas silently stole southward off Baja California. A man dressed in a white smock looked casually at the lined paper as Univac began its report. He suddenly snatched at it and ran to a telephone. He called NORAD—the North American Defense Command—and the operator pressed a switch. The line cleared immediately, and a man deep within the rock of Cheyenne Mountain in southern Colorado answered.

"Mugu here with a condition yellow from Midas. Only one sighting but suspicious outside Soviet border . . . but initiated within."

"Uh, roger . . . confirm condition yellow."

The officer at Cheyenne picked up another phone and in the Situation Room at the White House, Colonel Howard J. Landry answered. His face blanched as he heard the news and he immediately called upstairs to the President's sitting room. Stark and Riordan had just finished talking, and the CIA director had reached the door leading to the hall elevator. Stark listened without comment until the Situation Room officer finished. Then Stark said, "Keep condition yellow until further word comes in." He put down the phone and stared at Riordan. "Sam, your bones may be right. We've just had another Midas tracking, and this time it's somewhere in Israel."

Riordan put his coat down on a chair.

Two flights below, Sergeant Arly Cooper was still working. His reliefman had gone with his wife to the hospital to deliver a premature baby, and Cooper had volunteered to stay on until he returned. At 11 P.M., he had watched the teletype as a new Russian operator had printed out the first five lines from *War and Peace.* Cooper grunted with renewed interest as he read something other than Pushkin. At 11:05 P.M., the Russian signed off, and Cooper acknowledged the transmission. He stretched his legs for a moment, then went to the bathroom to revive by washing his face and dabbing cold water on his wrists and neck. Cooper walked back into the main room and poured himself another cup of black coffee. He had lost count of the number he had drunk that day. As he sipped, the teletype chattered suddenly. It was 11:18 P.M.

Cooper sat in front of the console and began to read the message:

TO THE PRESIDENT OF THE UNITED STATES OF AMERICA
FROM THE SECRETARY OF THE PRESIDIUM, UNION
OF THE SOVIET SOCIALIST REPUBLICS:
WE HEREBY INFORM YOU THAT WE DEMAND THE
UNCONDITIONAL SURRENDER OF YOUR COUNTRY
EFFECTIVE SEVENTY-TWO HOURS FROM THIS TRANS-
MISSION. RESISTANCE TO THIS ULTIMATUM WOULD
BE FOOLHARDY SINCE WE POSSESS A WEAPON OF
UNUSUALLY DESTRUCTIVE FORCE WHICH CANNOT BE
CHALLENGED. FOR PROOF EXAMINE THE REMAINS OF
THE ISRAELI ATOMIC RESEARCH CENTER WEST OF
BEERSHEBA. ARRANGE WITHIN TWELVE HOURS BY
THIS CHANNEL FOR INTERMEDIARIES TO MEET WITH
OUR REPRESENTATIVES IN GENEVA TO DISCUSS
DETAILS OF TRANSFER OF POWER. WE URGENTLY
REQUEST THAT YOUR ARMED FORCES MAKE NO
OVERT MOVES AGAINST OUR COUNTRY SINCE THAT
WOULD RESULT IN THE NEEDLESS DEATHS OF
MILLIONS OF YOUR PEOPLE. THE ALTERNATIVE WE
OFFER IS PEACEFUL OCCUPATION.
SIGNIFY RECEPTION OF THIS MESSAGE.

V. KRYLOV

Sergeant Arly Cooper was unable to move. His eyes were fixed on the words before him. He could feel his heart jumping in his shirt. The teletype asked again: REPEAT: SIGNIFY RECEPTION OF THIS MESSAGE.

Cooper roused himself and automatically acknowledged. Then he leaped from his chair and ran twenty-five feet to the desk of Colonel Howard J. Landry, night duty officer. "Sir, come quick." Cooper was stunned by what he had witnessed. Landry followed him to the piece of white paper and read the fateful words . . . "WE DEMAND THE UNCONDITIONAL SURRENDER OF YOUR COUNTRY . . ." Landry punched the button on the phone and called President Stark, "Sir, the hot line has just brought us a message from the Soviet Union. Could you come down here immediately?" Landry was trying to control his voice, but Stark could hear the wavering. He rushed out to the elevator with Riordan and descended two levels to the basement. At the door to the big room, he stopped and stared at Arly Cooper, mopping his face with a handkerchief. Landry was talking on the phone with someone. Stark said, "Let me see it." Cooper went to the machine, ripped off the transmission, and handed it to Stark, who read it silently and passed it to Riordan. Sam Riordan's world fell around him as he scanned the ultimatum. Because his intelligence network had failed, his country was about to pay the penalty. He looked up at Stark, whose face was ashen. Stark went to a chair and sat down for a moment, then got up and strode restlessly up and down the green carpeting. He suddenly whirled on Riordan and asked, "Have they got the drop on us or not, Sam?" His tone was demanding. Riordan's thoughts raced each other around in his mind.

"Honest to God, I don't know. They must be talking about that laser beam. That would explain the Midas sightings the past month and tonight."

The President stood still, trying to absorb the words. "Goddamnit! How could we let this happen? How could we?"

Riordan wished he could die.

Stark paced again, slamming his fist into his palm. He went over to Landry, who was standing quietly next to the teletype. "Colonel, advance alert level to orange."

"I've already done so, sir."

Stark seemed surprised but nodded. "Good. Call Roarke and the other chiefs and have them come to the White House immediately. Oh, and have them enter by the west door so the press won't get wind of this yet."

Landry hurried to the phone.

Stark and Riordan went back upstairs. Behind them they left Arly Cooper sitting tensely in front of the teletype that now linked him with a mortal enemy.

Stark had regained control over his momentary self-pity. He began issuing rapid-fire orders to Riordan: assemble the cabinet, the science advisory board, anyone who could counsel him on the matter of survival of the nation. He asked for an immediate report on the status of Soviet armed forces. Were they moving or waiting for Stark to give a final answer? While the President was speaking to Riordan, Pamela Stark came into the room in her dressing gown. "Bill, what's keeping you up so late? Hello, Sam, are you the cause of my husband missing his sleep?"

Riordan smiled painfully while her husband put his arm around her shoulder and led her to the door. "Pam, go to bed and don't worry. I'll fill you in on all of this in the morning."

The gray-haired woman knew she had intruded on forbidden territory and did not press the issue.

She smiled up at the stern face and said, "Don't forget our second honeymoon next week."

He did not answer and turned back into the sitting room. Bewildered and vaguely hurt by his coolness, she wandered down the hall to her bedroom.

Secretary of State Martin F. Manson was gulping down a glass of milk in his kitchen when word came to report to the

White House. When he ran upstairs to get his shoes and brief-case, he left a note for his sleeping wife on the night table by her bed.

In London, Secretary of Defense Clifford Erskine was sleeping at the American Embassy on Grosvenor Square when a Signal Corps man entered his room and told him the President was calling. Drugged with fatigue, Erskine barely registered recognition until Stark brought him to full awareness with word about the hot line. Erskine said he would catch a plane immediately, but Stark said not to move from London. He told Erskine he might have to send him to Geneva to talk with the Russians the next day. The stunned Erskine hung up and sat on the edge of his bed as dawn broke over the British capital.

Robert Randall, Stark's advisor on matters of national security and foreign policy, was also in bed. His arm cradled the blond head of his secretary, Mary Devereaux, who murmured sleepily as the phone rang. Randall slipped noiselessly away from her and picked up the receiver. Stark said simply, "Come quickly, west entrance." Randall began to dress in the dark.

All over Washington and in the suburbs, men walked out to waiting limousines, which drove through emptied streets toward an anxious rendezvous. In the Pentagon, all five floors were suddenly ablaze with light. Passing motorists questioned the squandering of taxpayers' money on so much electricity.

In the radio room of the building, orders were flashing to stations around the planet. In Montana, missile crews ran to silos to reinforce skeleton forces manning the Minuteman III weapons. West of Guam and north of Scotland, Polaris submarine commanders tore open sealed orders, designating primary and secondary targets within the borders of the Soviet Union. The klaxon horn dinned out Condition Orange; if it moved to Red, the Poseidon warheads would leave their sixteen tubes instantly.

In the forests of southern Germany, near the Czechoslovak border and East Germany, tank crews raced to their vehicles as the sun broke through the darkness of early morning. They gunned their motors and waited for further word from Washington.

Wednesday, September 11

WASHINGTON

GENEVA

MOSCOW

In the blackness of post-midnight, limousines glided quietly through the White House gate and up to the west entrance. Men emerged and blended swiftly into the shadows at the doorway. They were taken to the Cabinet Room, where President Stark greeted them with a brief handshake and told them to make themselves comfortable around the polished mahogany table. When the last person arrived at 1:10, the door was closed and William Stark went to his chair at one side. He sat down heavily and asked that all present listen closely while he read them a communication.

Outside the room, the low murmur of his voice reached the ears of a man waiting impassively. In his right hand he carried a black satchel. In the satchel were the codes to be used by the President of the United States to unleash a nuclear war. The bagman shifted his feet uncomfortably as he kept up his ceaseless vigil.

The President had finished reading the ultimatum. He put the paper down, and smoothed his hair absently as he watched for reactions.

Robert Randall was the first to recover from the shock. "Mr. President, the question is, are they bluffing?"

Stark answered, "I thought of that, and we'll have a report shortly from Israel. Sam Riordan has sent a man down from Tel Aviv by chopper to investigate. But it seems to me that the stakes are so big here that they would be risking far too much to be joking. No, I think they mean it, and it's up to us to figure an alternative."

General Stephen Austin Roarke spoke for the Joint Chiefs. "Mr. President, assuming they have managed to beat us to the draw, we still have our nuclear capability. They can't thumb their noses at that, can they? If they blast us with that laser, we can blast right back at them with H-bombs and they'll lose everything they've got in one day. Why don't we just bluff them back?

William Stark turned to Roarke and said, "General, if I understand you correctly, I have no intention of initiating a nuclear exchange. For the last thirty years, the leaders of this country have gone out of their way to avoid just such a calamity. President Johnson once told me that he spent many a night worrying that the Vietnam War would end in a confrontation between the big powers and he would be forced to let the missiles out of their silos. The thought of being responsible for the deaths of several hundred million people haunted him. And may I add, it haunts me, and I cannot accept the choice you offer."

General Roarke flushed. He kept his jaw down on his tunic while he tapped a pencil on a scratch pad in front of him.

Stark went on, "Short of going to war, what alternatives do we have? The Russians say they have us cold. What do you say, Weinroth?"

Gerald Weinroth's ulcer was making its presence known. When he had gotten the summons to the White House, the diminutive professor had been reading in his study. Unable to sleep well for days, he had been taking pills to ease the constant cramping in his stomach. Months of overwork on his job as the President's scientific advisor, directing military research and development, had sapped his physical and intellectual strength. He regretted deeply having left his chair at Cornell to join the Administration in the exacting role of arbiter between military and civilian teams engaged in top secret projects. Wein-

50

roth was sick of the bickering and infighting that marked the daily routine of his job. He had become a pacifier, a father confessor to slighted parties. Now he was being asked to explain the existence of the one thing his organization was supposed to thwart: a deadly peril to the country.

Weinroth adjusted his horn-rimmed bifocals. "Mr. President, if the Soviets have perfected a laser weapon, we have absolutely no way to stop it." He paused to let the point sink in. "They have one of the world's best men in quantum physics and optics in Andrei Parchuk. They must have solved the problem of directing the beam up into the ionosphere and then down to a targeted point with sufficient accuracy to obliterate the designated area. The laser was never the biggest obstacle for us. We worked out the theory months ago. Our dilemma has been getting the funds to change theory into reality. As you know, Congress has been extremely reluctant to funnel unlimited cash into the military. This situation goes back to the sixties when all that trouble was made over research contracts during Vietnam. Since that time we've been living hand to mouth. Perhaps the enemy has not had to answer to its population and gone way ahead in their research. That being the case, they could well have the weapon they claim. If so, they have the ultimate terror gun: a laser capable of total annihilation. It could, for instance, eliminate Washington."

The remark paralyzed everyone in the room. Stark stared at a portrait of John Adams hanging over Martin Manson's head and cursed silently.

Sam Riordan was sitting five chairs away to his left. He spoke now. "Mr. President, something we have so far overlooked should be discussed at this time."

"Go ahead, Sam."

"The ultimatum was signed by Krylov, not Smirnov. That must mean that he is the top dog there now and would also explain this whole nightmare. Krylov has been the leader of the opposition to Smirnov for years now. He was slapped down at the time of the Arab-Israeli Six Day War in 1967 for his part in fomenting the disaster. But he has kept his hand in and stayed around the fringes of power. He has that knack for survival. Krylov has always hated the West and preached the hard line with a vengeance. It's entirely possible that he's been waiting for some chance to throw Smirnov out, and the successful firing of the laser may have been just what he needed. Our reports indicate he's a reckless gambler, foolhardy and unpredictable. A few other points about him. He has a wife who suffers from diabetes, which necessitated the amputation of her right leg two years ago; he drinks great quantities of vodka but is not a drunkard as far as we know; he does use hashish, however, which is bought for him by a contact working with suppliers in Iran; Krylov has been 'turned on' several times at our embassy receptions."

Riordan handed a sheet of paper up to Stark, containing further biographical data on Krylov. Stark read it over and passed it along to Martin Manson.

Five hundred feet over the harsh terrain of the Negev Desert, a CIA agent named Michael Murphy looked down through the early-morning sunlight at what was left of the Israeli atomic center. He called to the helicopter's pilot, "Take it down as low as you can." The pilot shouted above the racket of the motor, "Murph, I don't dare go much lower. The updraft from the fires might catch us."

Murphy nodded and took notes on what he was witnessing. After ten more minutes, he tapped the pilot on the right shoulder and jerked his thumb to say, "Let's get out of here."

In eighteen minutes the helicopter landed on a runway at Lod Airport, south of Tel Aviv. Murphy jumped out while the dust was still whirling and ran to a small building at the edge of the main terminal. At the desk, an operator nodded to him, and Murphy went into a telephone booth and picked up the phone. He said, "Hello," and someone said, "Just a moment, please."

Then President Stark said, "Go ahead."

Michael Murphy glanced at his notes as he spoke to the anxious and wakeful leader of a sleeping nation half a world away. "Mr. President, the Israeli atomic facility is completely gone. Large fires over an area of two square miles. Of seven buildings, only one wall remains upright. The entire region has been cordoned off by the military, and initial indications estimate no survivors from a work force of one thousand two hundred. Also, the Defense Ministry has told me that fourteen atomic bombs warehoused in a concrete bunker were all detonated, at least the high explosives in them, and the fissionable material has burned up." Murphy nervously waited for a reaction from Stark. There was none. He read again from his notes. "The Israeli cabinet is now meeting in the Knesset. It seems totally unaware of the source of this attack. No one can believe the Egyptians could have anything so sophisticated." Murphy was finished with his report. Stark thanked him and told him to keep Riordan informed about the Israeli cabinet's actions.

Stark hung up and said, "The Russians are not bluffing. The Israelis have lost their atomic bombs."

Martin Manson covered his head with his hands. General Roarke scrawled on his work pad furiously. He kept writing the word "Shit" over and over.

Stark leaned on his elbows and continued, "We have to come up with alternatives. First of all, we can surrender in less than seventy hours—the deadline is Friday night at eleven eighteen. At this point, I cannot even contemplate that. Secondly, we

53

can fight them with our missiles, and, as I mentioned earlier, I cannot endorse that, either. Third, we can do nothing and wait for them to make the first move against the country. But that would be gambling with the lives of our people. Perhaps Krylov might shy away from mass killings. Maybe someone there will prevail on him to lessen his demands on us. That's a very faint hope, though."

Martin Manson, the white-haired Secretary of State, had been following the conversation carefully. His legal mind was seeking a loophole, a straw to grasp. In thirty-seven years of practice, he had acquired a reputation for exacting attention to detail which helped him become the foremost corporation lawyer in the nation. His reputation rested on his ability to sift available evidence and seize on a point and exploit it. "Since the Russians want us to meet with them in Geneva, why don't we just wait until we can size up their position face to face?"

At 2:45 A.M., the meeting broke up. Stark told the participants to be back at 8 A.M. to consider a final approach. The officials left by the same door through which they had come in, and the black limousines carried them off into the blackness. On the other side of the White House, two reporters from wire services dozed in a corner of the deserted press room. They were obvious to the coming catastrophe.

In the Situation Room, Arly Cooper had been relieved. The new man typed out a message to the Kremlin:

TO THE PREMIER OF THE PRESDIUM OF THE UNION OF SOVIET SOCIALIST REPUBLICS:
FROM THE PRESIDENT OF THE UNITED STATES OF AMERICA:

SECRETARY OF DEFENSE CLIFFORD ERSKINE WILL
ARRIVE GENEVA WITHIN THREE HOURS. SPECIFY
SUITABLE MEETING PLACE AND TIME FOR DISCUSSION
OF PERTINENT QUESTIONS.

STARK

ACKNOWLEDGE RECEIPT

Eleven minutes later, the teletype came to life:

FROM THE PREMIER OF THE PRESIDIUM, UNION OF
SOVIET SOCIALIST REPUBLICS:
TO THE PRESIDENT OF THE UNITED STATES OF
AMERICA:

MEETING PLACE RUSSIAN EMBASSY. REPRESENTA-
TIVES WILL RECEIVE ERSKINE AT 1300 HOURS SWISS
TIME.

KRYLOV

ACKNOWLEDGE

Stark read this over the shoulder of the operator. He thought,
Those bastards are already trying to call the tune. Imagine them
ordering us to see them at their embassy. Aloud, he said to
Manson, "What the hell can we do except go to them and find
out what they really want. But it's a bitch eating crow, isn't
it?"

Martin Manson shook his head in disgust.

Stark went up to bed. Though he was exhausted by the night's
events, he could not sleep. Dressed in a silk bathrobe, he drank
a cup of coffee slowly and tried to look ahead to the morning.
Not yet completely discouraged, he refused to think of the finality
implicit in the enemy ultimatum. At a quarter to four, William
Stark slipped into his side of the double bed. Beside him, Pamela
Stark did not stir. Stark felt her warmth and closed his eyes
in momentary respite.

It was seven hours since the White House had received the Soviet ultimatum, sixty-five hours until the possible annihilation of all mankind. The plane carrying Clifford Erskine circled over the beautiful lake bordering Geneva, the original home of the League of Nations. For many years the city had been host to a succession of conferences dealing with peaceful solutions to potential calamities in the world. It had become a symbol of good intentions among nations, an oasis where sanity ruled men's minds.

The military transport leveled off and touched down on the runway. A car flying the American flag on its right fender moved to the foot of the gangway at the rear door. Erskine emerged and walked down swiftly. At the bottom, he shook hands with a man and then entered the limousine, which drove away at high speed.

Noontime pedestrians in downtown Geneva, long used to diplomats, did not even pause to stare at the official vehicle. Inside, Erskine sat in air-conditioned comfort as he talked animatedly with Philip Bordine, ambassador to France, who had arrived just an hour before from Paris. Bordine had once been ambassador to Moscow, and Stark had requested his presence to help in any negotiations with the Russians.

At 12:50, Geneva time, the limousine entered the Soviet Embassy grounds. The embassy, a stately seventeenth-century mansion, renovated by the Russians in 1952, was the heart of Soviet diplomatic and clandestine activities in Europe. Today it served as the contact point for the greatest powers on earth.

The car stopped at the front door, and a courteous aide shook Erskine's hand as he got out. He led the Americans into the lobby, where four men lounged about, eyeing the strangers closely. Their carriage and looks revealed them instantly as secret police bodyguards. Erskine noticed something else almost immediately. A strong aroma of cabbage permeated the room. He murmured to Bordine, "Don't they ever go out to eat here?"

Bordine smiled and answered, "It's the same everywhere. They bring their kitchens with them from home. A touch of Mother Russia, I guess."

The aide led them up carpeted stairs and down a hallway to a conference room, where two men sat stiffly at a table. Erskine and Bordine were ushered to two chairs at the far end. Fully thirty feet away the two Russians watched them settle comfortably. One of them was a broad-shouldered, bemedaled general, who simply glowered at them. To his right was a balding civilian, dressed in a dark blue suit. He smiled benignly across the vast expanse of the room.

"Good afternoon, sir," he said to Erskine, "and hello, old friend Bordine."

He nodded grandly to the American ambassador, who returned the greeting.

"Mikhail, how good to see you again. How long has it been, five years?"

Mikhail shrugged. "No matter, but you're looking well and maybe even younger."

Bordine smiled his thanks until the Russian general spoke sharply to Mikhail, who suddenly became very serious and turned his attention to Clifford Erskine.

"Mr. Erskine, we assume you come empowered by your President to discuss terms of surrender?"

Clifford Erskine was astounded. His hands began to tremble, and he felt his mouth going dry.

"Mr. Erskine, I repeat my question. Are you here to discuss surrender seriously?" Mikhail was smiling through a cloud of cigarette smoke.

Erskine sputtered, "Mr., ah . . ."

Mikhail offered, "Darubin."

"I am sure you realize, Mr. Darubin, my instructions from Washington involve no thought of surrender. I am a devoted American, here at the request of President Stark and his advisors merely to learn your country's intentions regarding the diabolical plan we were informed of over the hot line last night. That is the extent of my mission."

Darubin nodded while an interpreter translated Erskine's remarks to the general. The general nodded grimly and spoke quickly to Darubin. Holding his cigarette daintily between two fingers, Darubin stood up and went to the floor-length window. Gazing out at the grounds, he asked, "Mr. Erskine, your CIA must have told you by now what has happened to the Israeli atomic arsenal?" He turned abruptly and shouted, "Have they not?"

Erskine did not reply. Bordine answered, "But, surely, Mikhail, your government cannot be serious about conquering the United States. For the past few years, the cold war has nearly melted away. Smirnov was anxious to reach a *modus vivendi* with us. Both countries have honestly grappled with the disarmament problem and avoided confrontations in the Middle East and Asia. Now this insanity . . ."

"Bordine, my old friend, it is not insanity. Smirnov went too far in accommodating the West. He was a fool to trust you. But he is gone now, and we can correct all his errors like that." He snapped his fingers.

The two Americans watched him as he went back to the table and pressed a button underneath. A motion-picture screen dropped from the ceiling in back of him, and the drapes at the windows closed automatically.

In the darkness, Darubin's cigarette waved about as he said, "Watch carefully."

A projector went on in the wall behind Erskine and Bordine.

In the white floodlight, they saw the general pulling his chair around to face the screen. Darubin remained standing.

An announcer spoke over the movie in Russian. Bordine understood him as he described the opening scene. It showed a vast forest flowing under the wing of a plane. The announcer said it was situated north of Irkutsk in Siberia. The next closeup was of a village made up of wooden houses. Nobody walked in the streets. It reminded Erskine of a western town in American films. The announcer did not name the village. The lens merely panned up and down the deserted streets. Then a high-altitude camera, possibly from a satellite, took over the visual presentation, and the annoucer, his voice rising with excitement, intoned the magical countdown, eight, seven, six . . . three, two, one. At one, the forest and village were still visible. At zero, they exploded in a sheet of light which brightened even the darkened room in Geneva. Erskine and Bordine leaned forward, their surprise reflected in their gasps of amazement. For possibly six square miles the forest burned fiercely. The village had disappeared in the inferno. The camera zoomed down and seemed to hover over the flames which filled the screen. It held that scene for two minutes. Then the announcer came back to the watchers and said, "A week later . . ." and the camera brought Erskine and Bordine into the village streets again. But the village was gone; a black smudge marked its grave. Then the long-range camera came back on and revealed the magnitude of the disaster. The forest had been scythed as though a giant meteor had hit and rolled along for miles. Bordine tried to estimate the extent of the ugly scar which had cut a swath through the woods. He could only think, It's the size of New York City. The picture faded away, and Darubin's cigarette glowed brightly in the void.

Then the window drapes parted, and Erskine squinted against the harshness of the afternoon sun.

Darubin and the general were back facing the Americans

in their chairs. Darubin was almost unbearable now. "You have your proof. That was not a hydrogen bomb. It was, as our message to you indicated, a weapon of unusual destructive force. And, may I reiterate, there is no defense against it."

Mikhail Darubin was enjoying himself immensely. He offered the Americans coffee or something stronger. They declined. He offered them cigarettes. They refused.

Darubin shuffled some papers and went on, "You are empowered, you say, to find out what we want from you. Mr. Erskine, we want your country. To that end, you have precious little time to effect an orderly transfer of power. We have men in Cuba who are waiting to be received in Washington. From there, you will take them to the missile centers, atomic plants, and storage areas. In approximately sixty hours, our warships will be off New York City and will expect the fullest cooperation from the U.S. Navy in disarming Polaris submarines at sea and in port. Army occupation units will arrive after the strategic weapons have been rendered harmless. Finally, your President will fly to Moscow at the end of the time period specified on the teletype. There he will enter into conferences with Comrade Krylov as to future relations between our two nations."

Clifford Erskine felt a sharp pain under his breastbone. His body was bathed in sweat. He wanted to vomit.

Darubin did not seem to notice his victim's discomfort. "In case anyone decides to ignore the obvious and fight, I give a final warning. If surrender is not indicated within five minutes of the expiration of the deadline, the city of Washington will be burned to the ground."

Erskine rose from his chair and screamed, "Darubin, you're a maniac! If you force us to the wall, we will surely fight against the Soviet Union, but it will mean the deaths of millions of innocent people. I have come to Geneva to warn you of my country's reaction. You can be sure that President Stark is a man who could not live with the thought that he had not tried to prevent the subversion of his country. As a sane man, he is sickened at the thought of using atomic weapons, but if you persist, you leave him no other reasonable alternative than to plan to destroy your cities and missile sites."

The Russian was unruffled. He came up to Erskine, who stood, fists clenched, rigid against the table.

"Mr. Erskine, if you fight, the decision to kill millions will be yours and yours alone."

He glanced at his watch and said, "You have only hours left to make your plans." Walking to the double doors, he held one open and said pleasantly, "Good day gentlemen."

Erskine and Bordine went past him and down the stairs to their car. In the conference room, Darubin and the general touched tumblers of vodka and drained them in a salute.

In Lafayette Park, pedestrians sat under trees to escape the heat, enervating even so early in the day. Across the street in the East Room of the White House, an early-bird tour group stood around a guide as she explained the history of the State reception room. The guide was telling them that the body of President Kennedy had lain in state there on November 23, 1963. The tourists stood hushed in the presence of history.

In another room in the same building, a preoccupied President William Mellon Stark talked with his closest advisors about the ultimatum from the Russians. The President had just heard from Clifford Erskine in Geneva that the enemy was adamant and Darubin wanted nothing short of total surrender by the United States. Erskine had given details of the movie and had closed with the Russian threat to obliterate Washington if their demands were not met immediately.

Stark was becoming increasingly despondent. His normally bright blue eyes were rimmed with fatigue. He had not been able to eat his usual breakfast of bacon and eggs. He just nibbled at a piece of toast and absently sipped a glass of orange juice. The President was increasingly aware that the Soviet Union was presenting him with an impossible situation. Erskine's report made it obvious the other side was convinced he was in a trap from which he could not escape. The Russians seemed to be counting on Stark's abhorrence of nuclear war.

The men with Stark were weary from lack of sleep. The impact of the ultimatum had struck them most forcibly after they had gone home and reflected on it behind suburban doors.

Martin Manson was outwardly calm as he listened to Erskine's report, but his stomach was churning.

Robert Randall, the sharp-nosed, wiry-haired foreign policy advisor felt strangely like the quarterback of a football team before the big game. His nerves were on edge and he was slightly nauseated, but his senses were unusually alert. Adrenaline was flowing swiftly through his body. To Randall, the problem before them was acute but a distinct challenge to his intellect. He was ready to compete for the highest stakes in the world.

General Stephen Austin Roarke was edgy. Still smarting from the rebuff handed him the previous evening by President Stark, Roarke had gone back to his quarters at Fort Myer, Virginia, and drunk three stiff bourbons. The tall, rawboned Texan, a widower, had paced the living room for some time until he finally fell into bed as dawn broke. Steve Roarke was a stubborn man, and as he rode to the White House a few hours later, he determined that he would continue to press his case with the Commander-in-Chief. It was his duty.

CIA Director Sam Riordan had come to the conference loaded down with information. Still feeling that he had let Stark down, Riordan had gone right back to his office in the early morning and napped for two hours on a couch. At 5:30 A.M., Riordan had assembled his experts and compiled a mass of data for the President. Along with it, he brought Charlie Tarrant, his deputy, to the conference.

Stark had weeded out unnecessary personnel for the morning briefing. Only Manson was there from the cabinet. Vice-President Richard Terhune, on a ten-day trip to Asia, had not been ordered back, to avoid arousing the suspicions of the press. Terhune was not even told of the peril.

Professor Gerald Weinroth sat at the huge table nursing his ulcer. Weinroth's cramps were no longer spasmodic; they now cut across his stomach like a knife. His face contorted, the owlish academician struggled to be attentive as Stark asked Riordan for further information.

The CIA man went to an easel set up in a corner. Tarrant followed.

"Here is the source of our trouble." Riordan motioned to Tarrant, who placed a huge blowup of a building complex on the easel. "This is the latest Samos photograph of the Soviet research center north of Tashkent. It was taken at an altitude of eighty-seven miles on the morning of August twenty-sixth. As you can seen, fourteen cars and trucks are parked near the main building, but otherwise there is no outward sign of life." Stark and the others looked intently at the place that threatened their lives. "We've watched it grow from the foundation up over the past four years. Traffic in and out has been very sparse. At no time has there been any radio communications until . . ." and Riordan paused, "until yesterday when a single word was beamed out of there to Moscow, 'Borodino,' which we can only assume was a code for Victory. It was logged approximately two hours after the strike on the Israelis."

Riordan pointed to another photo, and Tarrant put it over the first. "Another research center near Sverdlovsk. Same general characteristics as Tashkent, same *modus operandi* over the past years, no radio messages at all. Also no heat emissions from this general vicinity."

A third photo was put up. "Lastly, a relatively new location, as yet undetermined facility. This one is twenty-six miles east of Moscow and has been operating only a year. Smirnov himself was seen going in and out of there by one of our men—Rudenko, I believe. Rudenko went with Smirnov to inspect the latest Soviet contribution to world stability. But Rudenko never gave us anything out of this trip as far as hard intelligence is concerned. Now he's been exposed, and we have no idea what he knew about the Soviet laser program."

Sam Riordan continued: "So far the only emissions are from Tashkent. That doesn't mean they don't have the other sites in readiness. Still, the whole thing is insane because they can't have gotten that far ahead of us."

Stark interrupted his monologue: "Sam, it might be insane, but they nevertheless have at least one gun that works only too well. Murphy has reported in again from Tel Aviv. The atomic center there is still burning."

The President was irritable; he kept trying to blink the cobwebs away from his eyes. Nevertheless he was instantly sorry for being sharp with Riordan, knowing how Sam felt about the situation. Stark changed the tenor of the conversation.

"Philip Bordine was with Erskine at Geneva, and he knew the Russian Darubin from years before at the embassy in Moscow. Bordine says Darubin was the one who talked Khrushchev into taking the chance with the missiles in Cuba. Do you remember him, Sam?"

Riordan said, "Of course. He fell when Khrushchev did. We last heard of him working in Siberia as head of an electric power plant. If Krylov has him back in good graces, it would explain a lot. Darubin was the mastermind behind the attempt to achieve parity with us on missiles by installing them under our noses.

64

He sold Khrushchev the deal and very nearly pulled it off. He would appeal to Krylov because he thinks the same, staking everything on one roll of the dice."

Riordan was silent for a moment, as though weighing the emergence of a new approach. "It's entirely possible that the two of them cooked up this idea of facing us down with just one laser instead of waiting until they had twenty or thirty." Riordan slammed his hand against the table. "Of course, it adds up. They tested the weapon twice and then Krylov and Darubin moved in on Smirnov. They undoubtedly got the army to back them up by convincing them that they had a golden opportunity to tip the scales once and for all. Like us in 1945, when we went after the Japanese without first stockpiling a number of bombs. One test in New Mexico and the next one in Japan. Darubin's thought processes would work the same way today as they did in 1962. He'd still go for broke, especially after being stymied the first time."

Sam Riordan seemed pleased with his analysis and looked to the others for confirmation. Stark nodded: "That may be the key, Sam. He's bluffing us down but with a helluva hole card, an ace!" Stark shook his head in bewilderment.

Gerald Weinroth broke in: "Which complex do you think is the production facility for the weapons?"

Riordan said, "The one near Moscow must be the one. Bigger buildings, nearer to railway lines, larger workers' settlements. But it's only a year old, and we haven't seen anything come out of it yet."

Weinroth looked satisfied as he added: "From our knowledge, production on a finished weapon has to be six months minimum. Thus, the test firings could only lead to operational equipment by January at the earliest. They must have just one or perhaps two lasers at Tashkent and Sverdlovsk."

Weinroth forgot his ulcer for the moment. "Unfortunately it doesn't matter. One or two lasers can still destroy us." His voice was mournful. "They can reach Washington in less than thirty seconds and then swivel around to hit something else in minutes. In one hour, that damned machine could wipe out half our cities."

"Jesus H. Christ," General Roarke exploded. "Mr. President, I've been sitting here listening to talk about what the other side can do to us but no one asks what we can do to them. In the same amount of time we can put that country out of business. Moscow would go up within eight minutes. The Polaris is already waiting to hit more than five hundred silos and cities. We act as though we're helpless, hapless, and castrated."

William Stark stared at Martin Manson's mane of white hair. He was trying to control himself enough not to offend the speaker. Stark said icily: "Professor Weinroth, would you please give some statistics to this body on the results of a thermonuclear exchange."

Weinroth was only too happy to comply. He plunged into the results of such a nightmare. "In the first twenty minutes, one hundred and seven million Russians would be incinerated. Roughly, the same number of Americans would succumb, give or take ten million. I am leaving out those who would die of radiation fallout around the world in the next four weeks. That figure would approximate three hundred million. The net result of this exchange would be the deaths of more than five hundred million human beings, give or take, as I say, thirty millions."

Gerald Weinroth was enjoying Roarke's discomfort. "All of this excludes the possibility of bombs falling on Europe and Asia by mistake or plan of either of the main protagonists. In that case, the death rate would exceed one billion."

Weinroth sat down.

Roarke was not dismissed so lightly. The general lunged to his feet and snarled, "Professor, your figures are both impressive and correct. But you are ignoring one fact. We believe that it's possible to deal the enemy the first blow and cripple his

66

retaliatory strength within the first fifteen minutes. We've always planned for such a situation and are absolutely convinced that the Russians could only get off twenty-five percent of their missiles. Since some of those will be defective anyway, we're really discussing the detonation of perhaps one hundred and fifty incoming warheads. And of those coming in, our Vanguard anti-missiles will knock out seventy-five to a hundred. So actual impact will occur in only fifty or so areas with a death rate in the range of twenty million, tops." Roarke paused to look at the President, who was gazing at a new crack in the ceiling.

"Now, Weinroth, those casualties are acceptable in order to eliminate the menace we have before us. And it sure beats the hell out of giving up this great country to those bastards."

Steve Roarke could not think of anything to add to his argument. He was perspiring from the emotions he had unlocked within himself. The general took out a handkerchief from his trousers and wiped his forehead and neck. No one said a word. Weinroth looked disgusted. Manson was stunned, unable to take in the magnitude of twenty million bodies piled one on top of another. Robert Randall thought: You dumb son of a bitch . . . I'll bet you play home movies of the blast at Nagasaki for your friends.

Steve Roarke thought of something else: "To guarantee success, we have to lull the Russians to sleep on this one. Let's let them think we're going to quit so that they'll take their hand off the trigger. Then at the last minute, we can let the missiles go and get the few minutes lead time we need to hit the missiles in the silos. We always know where their subs are and we can use large-megaton warheads on them to cover the sea sector they're in."

President Stark had had enough. "General Roarke, it's your kind of thinking that has caused too many Americans to belittle the military over the past ten years. Goddamnit, when will your people get over the idea that you can solve the world's problems by blowing it up every now and then? Vietnam proved that a military solution is not necessarily the answer. The Pentagon is still trying to recover from that fiasco. You cheerfully enunciate that only twenty million Americans will die in a nuclear war and that's acceptable to you!"

Roarke was furious. His eyes were slits burning into the Chief Executive's.

Stark pointed his finger at him, "Well, it's not acceptable to me."

Stark was remembering his own past. "I was once a company commander in Korea. Headquarters ordered my regiment to go up Heartbreak Hill one more time. Everyone in the unit knew it was a crazy thing to do because the Chinese had not been bombed out of their holes and had gotten reinforcements while we bled on the slopes. But we went anyway, and it was the worst day of my life. I personally counted the casualties for over an hour. I saw my friends lying there without heads and with their stomachs scooped out. I counted a hundred and six bodies of men I had sent on a fool's errand. Next day Headquarters sent in planes to soften the enemy up, and we took the hill in a matter of minutes. So when we talk about body counts I cannot be impervious to the sight of blood and the smell of putrefaction. I must have another answer to the problem we have here today."

An uneasy silence followed. Roarke's stubborn chin mirrored tenacious belief in his plan. But the general was now content to let others pursue the solution. His seeds had been planted.

Martin Manson tried to breach the gap. The Secretary of State felt that all possibilities in the Roarke proposal had not been fully aired. "Short of an all-out nuclear war, we do have another option, I believe. The laser is the difference between us. That threat is the one thing that alters the balance of power. If we can find some means to surgically excise that, it would neutralize Krylov's ultimatum and make them back away for

68

good." Manson peered over his horn-rimmed glasses at General Roarke and asked: "In that case, General, what can you suggest to us?"

Roarke answered quickly, "We could send in an SR-71 reconnaissance plane fitted with a couple of megaton bombs, and, even with a near miss, that place near Tashkent will be leveled. The SR-71 flies over two thousand miles an hour at one hundred thousand feet and could be in and out of Russia before they knew it. As far as we know, they have nothing that can even come close to it."

Stark continued: "But such a maneuver would probably lead to instant retaliation by the other side. When they record an overt trespass into their heartland, we have to figure they'll think the United States has decided to fight. And God knows, when one or two hydrogen warheads detonate on their country, it would take a very cool head in Moscow to keep the beasts at bay."

Roarke flushed badly at this remark, and Stark hastened to cover the affront.

"You couldn't blame them for acting that way. By putting two and two together, they would have to believe the facts; an intruder plane had violated their airspace and within minutes dropped bombs on their country. The aggression would be too flagrant to confuse them, and their reactions would be, I would think, about what I would do if a Russian plane came down over Canada, was picked up on radar, and shortly thereafter blew up Chicago. I would mark it as a declaration of war."

The President smiled wanly at Roarke and added: "It certainly would solve the problem of the laser, General, but we'd be right back to the discussion of a body count in the hundreds of millions."

Robert Randall finally joined the dialogue. His incisive mind had picked something out of the confusion of ideas being sifted around the table.

"Mr. President, I think we have found the germ of a strategy. Roarke's theory is fraught with danger only because it is blatant. What we need to do is take out the laser by a subtle approach, a clandestine operation. Sam here could tell us if that's feasible."

Riordan said: "You mean a ground operation?" When Randall nodded enthusiastically, Riordan said, "But how the hell can we get in there? I don't have anyone inside Russia capable of doing it, and if I did, I couldn't get to them in time. Nor could I supply them with anything to make it work."

Randall was excited. The boyish-looking advisor exclaimed, "We have the men right here in America down at Fort Bragg. The Green Berets have been practicing this kind of thing for years. It's their meat."

For the first time that morning, William Stark felt a surge of hope. Randall's idea, though sketchy, offered some positive conditions lacking in Roarke's strategy. He urged Randall on.

"A small group of men might be able to penetrate the Soviet border and make its way to the area of Tashkent," Randall improvised, "There it would have to work out the best possible manner of destroying the laser. I can't pretend to know the best way now, but if they succeed, we have eliminated the danger, and the Russians will be hard pressed to start a war since none of our planes and missiles will be coming at them. In fact, we can order all our strategic weapons to stand down from alert."

Stark weighed the plusses and minuses. Roarke's mouth was drawn into a grimace of distaste. Weinroth's ulcer refused to quiet though its victim, like Stark, tried to analyze the chances of a coup by infiltrators. Sam Riordan was highly skeptical because he knew more than the others the odds against such a mission. Charlie Tarrant, at his right, fingered his Dacron summer suit and thought of the long list of men the CIA had sent into the Soviet Union who had never even performed one task before being discovered and killed.

Martin Manson had no opinion either way. He was only interested in exploring the issue to the fullest. "Mr. President, we ought to weigh the balance sheet on this one. As Bob has said, this strike would avoid directly confronting the Soviets and spare us the horror of precipitating a war, and I think if it was effective it would spare any Russian leader the decision to launch an attack on this country. It would pretty well immobilize them unless, and here we can't be sure, they've gone crazy. However, what are the real percentages in favor of this mission succeeding?"

Sam Riordan had an answer. The director stood up and solemnly shook his head: "Gentlemen, I cannot imagine leaving the destiny of this nation to a band of men sent on a suicidal venture. Randall is not wrong to suggest it, for God knows, we have very little going for us. But they would be doomed from the start. The nearest point of penetration would be on the southern rim of Russia, and they would have to evade detection for hundreds of miles, then get access to what must be the most closely guarded region in the country. And they have to get there and accomplish the task within—what is it now?—about sixty-two hours. I can't recommend it. To risk all on it would be madness on our part."

President Stark had lost his initial enthusiasm. The enormous difficulties in the plan were sobering.

General Steve Roarke interrupted the President's gloominess. "In Vietnam, our LURP teams went into North Vietnam regularly. Their mission was long-range reconnaissance of Charlie's intentions. These teams went in by chopper and raised hell along the Ho Chi Minh Trail. They were very successful on the whole, but that was because they worked in their surroundings so well. The jungle became their ally, and, of course, they were able to use native forces who looked like the enemy and knew the countryside like the back of their hands. In this case, we would have men going in with no natural cover and unable to blend into the local population. Unless you fellows," pointing to Riordan, "have a bunch of Russians holed up somewhere in Tashkent who love us more than Lenin." Roarke shrugged his shoulders. "It's just impossible to mount such an effort."

Stark was tempted to agree and move on to something more promising. But Sam Riordan was suddenly alert. "General, you just reminded me. In Germany we do have a group of men who love us more than Lenin. They're members of the NTS, an expatriate outfit which spends its time fighting the system back in Russia. We've been working these people through the Curtain for years."

Riordan waited for some reaction. Stark's was immediate. "How many of them would be able to do such a job as we have in mind?"

"I don't know. But I'll find out within an hour or two."

"Then see what you have and we'll break for some coffee in the meantime."

The Extraordinary Committee rose from the brightly polished table in the Cabinet Room. Riordan went to a phone.

At 10 A.M., President Stark walked into the press room that had been built over Franklin Roosevelt's old swimming pool during the Nixon Administration. He nodded to three reporters sitting there. He recognized Morris Farber of *The New York Times* and called to him, "Slow day, eh, Morris?" The reporter laughed and asked when the President was going to forget the cares and woes of office and leave for the Maine White House in Bar Harbor. Stark grinned back, "My wife knows all the details. You'd better ask her." Then he waved and turned back into the Executive Wing. Farber and the others resumed their gin rummy game.

At Langley, Virginia, an IBM sorting machine whirred busily as thirty-seven cards were fed into it. Six fell into a slot beneath, and an attendant took them upstairs to a file-lined office. There he extracted six bulging folders from a cabinet and walked briskly to a waiting car in the parking lot.

Gerald Weinroth led the group back into the Cabinet Room. He had not been able to eat because of his ulcer. The professor sipped a glass of milk while he read *The Washington Post* account of plans for a mass demonstration against birth control scheduled for the capital the next day, Thursday. Weinroth smiled ruefully as he folded the newspaper and went back to discussing the possible end of the world.

Sam Riordan had six folders in front of him. He and Charlie Tarrant had quickly absorbed their contents and placed two of them slightly apart from the others. Manson, Randall, and Roarke took their seats and waited for Stark to arrive. He came in huffing and apologized: "I had to say hello to a Boy Scout delegation from Iowa. I didn't want anyone to think it wasn't business as usual today. How does it look?"

"Out of six probables, Charlie and I think these two could do the job best. I'll read you a little about them. Peter Kirov, thirty-two, former lieutenant in a Soviet tank division, fluent in German, French, English, and, of course, Russian. He can even speak in the dialect of the Tashkent region. Three trips into Eastern Europe, including one parachute drop by night near Kiev, to set up cells of resistance. He's never failed yet."

Riordan picked up the other folder. "Interestingly enough, this one is a woman, Luba Spitkovsky, a Russian Jew, three members of her family in Siberia for 'intellectual provocations' against the government. Luba is a born killer. Twice she has gone in to assassinate agents in East Germany and performed beautifully. Her home for the first twenty of her twenty-eight years was the town of Chirchiz, about twenty miles northeast of Tashkent. Luba's home was no more than ten miles from our laser."

Robert Randall whistled appreciatively. Riordan seemed pleased with his choices.

"Both of these people could go on a moment's notice. But they will need more help, I'm afraid. Perhaps General Roarke can take care of that." Roarke asked for a telephone and called the Pentagon. He spoke briefly with the Office of Counterinsurgency, explaining what he wanted. The party on the other end promised to call back within fifteen minutes.

Stark said, "What about the details of their mission? Sam, you and the Pentagon better sit down on this in a hurry. Why don't you get going now? And Steve, you should get back to your office on this, too. When you have a plan and the team made up, let me have everything on it. Gerald, get your group together and give us all possible information on their laser and how it compares with ours. Let's have a final meeting at, say 2:30 P.M., in my sitting room. Say nothing to reporters, nothing to your wives, and above all nothing to your secretaries."

Robert Randall laughed sickly at the reference. Stark walked brisky out of the room and went down a corridor past the beautiful Rose Garden. His footsteps echoed loudly as he turned a corner and disappeared.

Martin Manson got up slowly and reached absently for his briefcase on the chair beside him. Randall said to no one in particular, "Do you think we can pull it off?"

Weinroth answered brusquely, "God help us if we don't."

In late summer, heat wraps the North Carolina countryside in a moist blanket of humidity. By noon, clothes are wrinkled and stained by the cloying dampness, which robs the body of vitality. On the outskirts of Fort Bragg, a column of ten men ignored these conditions and ran at double time toward their barracks. They were singing at the top of their voices. The men wore jungle camouflage fatigues and carried a variety of weapons over their shoulders. All had black smudge on their faces. In the midst of a quadrangle, the lead man shouted an order, and the column stopped. He issued another command, and they broke and disappeared at a trot into a long white barracks. The leader strode briskly away toward a line of houses in the distance. He was an impressive figure at six feet three and one hundred eighty pounds of taut muscle. His hair was closely cropped and blond. His eyes were a cold blue through the lampblack on his face. His chin was strong, thrust out jauntily.

By 1 P.M., the officer had entered one of the homes on Officers Row and gone upstairs immediately to the bathroom. He took off his sweaty clothes and stepped into a cold shower. He began to sing "Home on the Range" in a loud baritone.

In the hallway outside, a woman laughed softly at the noise and went on into the master bedroom at the end of the corridor.

In a few moments, the singing stopped, and the shower was turned off. The man emerged from the bathroom with a towel around his middle. He walked into the bedroom and saw his wife looking out the window into a play yard. She turned as he entered and said, "Joe, Tommy is really having a great time out there with the Jackson kids. He's running around like nothing ever happened to him." Joe Safcek stepped up behind his wife and put his arms around her. He looked past her to where his ten-year-old son was throwing a baseball with a neighbor's child. Joe felt a surge of paternal pride.

"Martha, the doctor said to let him do all these things. As far as he could determine, the skull fracture has healed perfectly, and he's as normal as any kid in town."

Martha turned into his arms, and he kissed her softly. He

felt her arms tighten around his neck. "Aren't we lucky," she said. "He could have died in that accident."

Joe hugged her closer. Outside, the shouts of Tommy and his friends echoed through the screen.

At 2:15 P.M., the phone rang in the Safcek home. Martha answered in the kitchen. She came running upstairs and shook her sleeping husband gently. "Joe, Joe, it's Washington calling."

He roused himself slowly and reached for the receiver. "Yes."

"Colonel, this is Dave Thompson at the Pentagon. We need you here for a special assignment right away. A plane is ready to fly you to Andrews within a half hour."

"Should I pack any special gear?"

"Everything will be provided for."

"Is this a repeat of the last time?"

"Negative, Joe. That's all I can tell you. See you shortly."

Joe Safcek sat for a moment, then shouted, "Martha, get some things together. I have to go away on a trip."

She stood against the sink, absorbing this news, and her lips began to tremble. "God, not again!" The dark night of loneliness, the nameless dread she always had that he would never come back from these trips. Martha began to pack his clothes.

Twenty minutes later an army car pulled up outside the house, and Joe went to his wife and Tommy to say good-bye. He reached down and tousled the boy's hair, then impulsively kissed him on the cheek. "Take care of Mother, Tiger, while I'm away, understand?"

"Yes, Dad, don't worry."

Joe was having trouble with his voice.

He kissed Martha once, then again hard. "I love you very much," he said, and went out the door to the automobile. Martha waved to him and called: "We'll be waiting."

He turned at the end of the walk and looked at his family for a moment, then grinned and saluted his son. Tommy's right hand went to his forehead as his father drove away.

The ultimatum was fifteen hours old, with fifty-seven hours left before the deadline. The wheels of the United States Government were meshing. Stark had given his subordinates orders which were being carried out with great speed and diligence. Specialists in guerrilla warfare had gathered at the Pentagon to plan an attack against the Soviet laser. They sat in an underground room and distilled years of experience in the art of clandestine warfare. In three hours they had arrived at a considered approach. At 3 P.M., the results lay on a White House desk.

President William Stark had napped for two hours. His fifty-seven-year-old body was rebelling against the fatigue and tension of the past hours, and Stark, helpless for the moment to alter events, had succumbed to sleep. Pamela Stark had not intruded on him. She had sensed all day that something grave had occurred in the world and did not attempt to bother her husband with any more questions about Bar Harbor. In his own good time, she knew, he would tell her what was troubling him.

Stark was in the Cabinet Room when the rest of the special committee entered. He greeted them curtly and asked Riordan if he had the details of the projected strike worked out. Riordan handed him a manila envelope, and Stark pulled out one typewritten page. He read aloud:

OPERATION SCRATCH

A thrust at the Soviet laser works twelve miles north of Tashkent.

Personnel: four-man team led by Colonel Joseph Safcek, U.S. Army, Green Berets.

Team will be transported by helicopter from Peshawar, Pakistan, across mountains of Afhganistan by night into Soviet territory east of Tashkent. Helicopter will fly through mountain passes at three hundred feet altitude to avoid detection by radar; at lower altitude over the desert. Personnel will be dressed in Red Army clothing.

Team will carry complement of handguns and automatic rifles;

also demolition charges (plastique) for use if they gain access to actual site. Otherwise, team will be provided with one atomic bomb, yield in ten-kiloton range for use in case access to immediate area of laser denied. Bomb is sophisticated to point where single agent can carry and trigger.

Helicopter pickup of personnel arranged for twenty-four hours after drop at same site.

Signed:
Bowles, Chief, Office of
Counterinsurgency

"Jesus," exclaimed William Stark, "we'd be sending those people to their deaths, no question about it. How can that helicopter possibly get through their radar?"

"We have two things going for us," Sam Riordan replied. "We've taped all their radar installations in the area. We know when they operate and have mapped the route to evade them. Secondly, the Hindu Kush Mountains are the most formidable natural barrier in the world—next to the Himalayas—and create the best possible interference to radar reception. That, with the chopper hugging the valley floors, will make it very difficult for anybody to pick them up. In the long run, we just have to hope that no one would think of looking for intruders coming through the Hindu Kush."

"Okay, and what about this bomb?" Stark asked. "Can they actually walk it in and still get away safely?"

"No problem there, Mr. President. We've sophisticated these weapons to the point where we could slip one into the American embassy in Moscow disguised as a can of tomato soup, set a timer on it, and get out long before the end."

Martin Manson shook his head. "Do they know the risks yet?"

Riordan answered, "The Russian agents won't be briefed until they arrive in Peshawar. Safcek is being told at the Pentagon. He'll go. The man has an amazing record in this field. He went into China two years ago to work with anti-Mao forces, and then another time he spent a week in Hanoi right under Ho's police trying to sabotage a waterworks that the bombers had trouble knocking out. He blew the plant sky high. Safcek is of Czech background with definite Slavic features. He speaks a passable Russian, enough to get by any ordinary situation. Safcek can work well with the group we have going in with him. They'll follow him because he makes people believe in him. The fourth man, from the CIA, is Boris Gorlov, who defected from the KGB three years ago and helped us clean up a whole network of Red spies in Western Europe. Gorlov has had plastic surgery, so no one will spot him in Russia. We doubt they'd be looking for him there anyway. They'd be more apt to expect to see him in a Mayflower Coffee Shop right here in Washington."

Stark bit his lower lip thoughtfully, then asked: "Has anyone come up with a fresh idea?"

General Stephen Roarke tried one last time to stress the efficiency of a single bomber strike. "These people won't make it, I tell you. The bomber will."

Sam Riordan interrupted: "General, our Samos camera satellites show the Soviets have, in the past ten hours, moved sixteen mobile SAM antimissile and bomber batteries around the laser works. The Samos has spotted them being deployed. So perhaps your bomber would never make it anyway. And if it did, we'd have the same problem of a possible all-out nuclear war staring us right in the face."

William Stark was tired of the constant reference to a third world war. Roarke's one-track mind annoyed him, and he was tempted to tell the general to go to hell. The President tapped his fingers impatiently. "Enough of this argument. If the team succeeds, the Russians will probably be so stunned that they'll forget all their big ideas. The bomber riding through their skies would most likely bring a counter-strike at us. So let's go with the less obvious and hope for a simple explosion on the ground which might take them weeks to figure out. By then, they'll have lost their hold on us."

Robert Randall said, "Great! It's the best thing to do."

Sam Riodan nodded through his pipe smoke.

Roarke stared straight ahead.

Stark asked one last question: "Sam, when would Safcek leave for Pakistan?"

"At 6 P.M., out of Andrews."

"Would you please ask him to drop by here on the way to the airport? I'd like to wish him luck."

Stark thanked the committee members for their help and dismissed them. Robert Randall went up to him and put out his hand. "Mr. President, it'll be all right. I'm sure it will."

Stark took his aide's hand and smiled sadly, "Bob, you once told me this is where the action is. But tonight I wish I was back in good old Pittsburgh, P.A., doing a crossword puzzle. Maybe I'm getting paid back for being too eager for power."

Randall did not reply.

Joe Safcek wanted desperately to call his wife. When he had heard the briefing officer at the Pentagon outline Operation Scratch, Joe was appalled. Always before he had been given tasks with acceptable risks but not this time. And no one at the Pentagon offered him any false hope. The men sending him into the Soviet Union were too professional in their field to attempt to deceive another professional about the odds on coming back. Safcek never thought of backing out. He could have. When Dave Thompson finished his instructions, he looked into Safcek's eyes and said, "You don't have to go, Joe, it's purely voluntary."

Safcek tried to grin but could not. "Dave, I'm your man. Have a brigadier's star waiting for me when I get back."

Thompson was glum as the two shook hands. "The President

wants to see you on your way to Andrews. The chopper will take you to the White House first."

Safcek was stunned and asked why.

Thomson shrugged, "Maybe you're getting the star tonight."

Safcek gathered his orders and went out to meet the Commander-in-Chief.

Stark met him at the door to the Oval Room. He shook the colonel's hand warmly and showed him to a seat in front of the massive desk. The President went to his chair and was framed against the famous window looking out on the South Lawn, where Safcek's helicopter now waited.

President Stark did not know quite what to say. He asked, "Well, Colonel, I suppose you've had all your questions answered across the river?"

Safcek assured him that he had. The President asked where he was from and Safcek told him McKeesport, Pennsylvania.

"Well now, that makes us neighbors. I'm from Pittsburgh."

Safcek said he knew that and that he had voted for Stark when he ran for governor of Pennsylvania. The President smiled and said, "Then I guess I can blame you a little for putting me in this chair tonight."

In turn, Joe Safcek did not know quite what to say. He was overwhelmed by the man who controlled the destiny of the world. The accumulated centuries of tradition in which the office was steeped left the colonel speechless.

President Stark wished at that moment that he had never invited Safcek to his office. It was an ordeal to look at this soldier, whom he was sending to a questionable fate. Stark hated to think of him with a wife named Martha and a son named Tommy. He would have preferred Safcek faceless, anonymous, just a name.

Joe Safcek noticed the deep furrows on the President's forehead and the baggy black pouches under his eyes. He felt a great sorrow for him and wanted to console the man behind the desk.

Stark roused himself from his depression. "Colonel, I know you have to get going. I just wanted to meet you and shake your hand. This country will owe very much to you shortly."

Stark had come around from his chair to stand in front of the Green Beret officer. He added, "God be with you" and stopped suddenly. Safcek mumbled, "Thank you, sir." They shook hands.

The President noticed that Safcek's grip was very strong, as he expected it would be. The colonel left the Oval Room while the President wandered back to the window and stared out at the Washington Monument. Stark saw a young officer counting the bodies of his friends on a hillside in Korea. Each corpse had Joe Safcek's face.

In a small waiting room at Andrews Air Force Base, northeast of Washington, Colonel Safcek met Boris Gorlov, the CIA man accompanying him. Gorlov, a squat, heavy-browed agent with a distinct Russian accent, smiled easily when Safcek said hello. The colonel observed how catlike Gorlov was in his movements. He had come out of the secret police jungle not long before and still retained the animal-like instincts that helped him to stay alive there. As a trained agent for the KGB, he had worked in Western Europe, infiltrating foreign espionage networks and exposing operatives marked for assassination. Gorlov had one day walked into the American Embassy in Bonn and offered his knowledge to the American government. He said he was tired of the Communist system, its corruption and narrow-minded insistence on world domination. His suspicious interrogators were astounded when he casually named one hundred and seventeen Soviet agents working with covers in Allied governments. His information was startlingly correct and led to the dissolution of clandestine Soviet activities in Europe for nearly a year. For that, his former employers had marked him for death. Plastic surgery had given him a new identity, but he lived always in great fear that somehow, somewhere, the Soviet government would reach out for him and snuff out his life. He often thought of Leon Trotsky whom Stalin never forgot and finally crushed, a pickaxe through the skull. Gorlov fought against his fears and the sickly debilitation that frequently invaded the minds of defectors. These people had rejected their heritage, their friends, their customs. For them life in America was a difficult adjustment. After the initial impact of leaving their homeland and the past, the defectors tried to settle down in obscure suburbs. Their names changed, their careers altered, their original lives erased by a master hand, which carved for them a fictitious birthright, they foundered in loneliness. Though protected from retribution, they had to live twenty-four hours a day in a limbo of artificial serenity, still pretending, as they had in their former clandestine lives, to be something other than they really were. It got to most of them. Gorlov was no exception. When the CIA was approached by the Pentagon for Operation Scratch, Sam Riordan had brought Gorlov forth for two reasons: he knew the man could be an invaluable guide and expert on Russia; secondly, he believed that the summons to duty would make him feel wanted. As therapy, it would be the best possible treatment for a man Sam Riordan knew was vegetating behind his false facade of security.

Safcek liked him immediately. They talked for a brief moment or two before an Air Force lieutenant came into the room and announced departure time. As the two men left the waiting room, Joe Safcek glanced one last time at a pay telephone in the corner. At the other end could be his wife, Martha, whose voice would be warm and reassuring. Safcek looked at the phone for a long moment, then said: "Let's go, Boris." They went by jeep along a runway, past administration buildings. Safcek saw a huge jet transport looming up at the far end of the field. When the jeep stopped, Safcek and Gorlov jumped out and ascended a ramp.

As they entered the aircraft, a voice called, "Welcome to the Pakistan Express." Out of the shadows stepped Karl Richter. As soon as they were all settled in their seats, the engines cut in, and the aircraft moved off into the late-afternoon light. At 6:04 P.M., the C-135 lifted off the ground, and Operation Scratch was under way.

In the inner sanctum of the New York Times Building just west of Times Square, the managing editor, Duane Brewster, sat in his book-lined office, his hand resting on the phone he had just hung up. On the other end of the line had been Daniel F. Michaels, the newspaper's bureau chief in Tel Aviv, where it was now well past midnight. Michaels had just returned from a highly privileged visit to the Israeli atomic test center, and he had an unbelievable story. Something had obliterated the complex, and the Israelis were at a total loss to pinpoint the source. The cabinet had been in almost continuous session for eighteen hours, and orders had been given to all army, naval, and air units to be on full alert. But strangely enough, Israel's natural enemies, the Arab states, were not even in a limited war condition. Michaels intimated that the Israelis were seeking advice and counsel from friendly powers. He thought the story was hot and wanted to know if the paper would keep a hole open on page one for him for the first edition. If so, he would file 1,500 words right away.

84

On a newspaper where the monthly telephone bill is $50,000, Duane Brewster could afford the luxury of telling Michaels that he wanted to do a little checking in Washington and then would call him right back.

Brewster dialed Robert Randall's private number and found him there. Randall was vague with the *Times* man. He professed ignorance of the disaster. When Brewster pursued the point, citing Dan Michaels's reputation for accuracy, Randall changed his approach.

"Duane, I'm asking you as a personal favor to kill the story."

Brewster refused.

Randall continued: "Then I ask you as a matter of national security not to print it. If you do, the President will be put in a terrible position, and believe me the man is up against it right now."

Brewster was struck by the urgency in Randall's voice. "Bob, is it that bad?"

Randall was quiet for a few seconds, then said: "Duane, please believe me, it's even worse than Cuba. I'm sorry I can't tell you any more right now."

"OK, don't worry. We'll keep this one on ice as long as we can, but if the wire services break it, we'll have to go ahead."

"Thanks, Duane. The President will really appreciate that."

Duane Brewster called Tel Aviv, and then sat for an hour longer in his office that night. While the clamor that accompanies the preparation of the morning edition continued outside his office in the third-floor newsroom, he could not forget Robert Randall's pleading voice. It radiated the fear which pervaded both the White House and the Pentagon.

At 9 P.M. in Washington, Robert Randall was telling William Stark about the call from Duane Brewster. Stark was grateful, and made a note to thank Brewster personally.

85

Randall had another worry. The Israelis had now asked the CIA to help investigate the attack that had destroyed their atomic arsenal. Stark moaned aloud: "Jesus Christ, we can't tell them we know. And I hate to do this to those people. They're our only real friends in that part of the world, and they must be going crazy trying to figure this one out. Worse, they'll know we know what caused it."

The thoroughly agitated President paced the floor of the Oval Room. Randall had never seen him look so worn. Though Stark was stylishly dressed in a dark blue pinstripe suit, his face betrayed his turmoil. His eyes were rheumy, veiled by fatigue and worry. He had even cut himself shaving. His skin was blotchy and marred by deep creases.

Stark whirled on Randall: "That brings us to our other allies. What the hell can we do with them? They have a right to know that the world is falling down all around them. But I can't tip my hand to them about Safcek. It'll get back to Moscow in hours some way. Every time we tell NATO something, it seems a report lands in the Kremlin the next day." The President shook his head. "No, I'll just have to let them hang until we know about Operation Scratch. It won't make any difference if it fails."

The next visitor to the Oval Room was Secretary of Defense Clifford Erskine, just back from Geneva. If Robert Randall was dismayed by the physical appearance of Stark, he was stunned by Erskine. The tall, slim secretary looked as though he had been visited by a ghost. The President himself was so moved that he immediately asked: "Are you all right, Cliff?"

The secretary, easing himself into a chair, said: "I've got the grippe or something. I've never felt so bad in my life. But if we get through the next few days, I'll go off on a vacation and relax for a while."

Stark wanted to know about the movie in Geneva. Erskine told it again, scene by scene, to the very end. He mentioned that Bordine thought he recognized the Soviet general in the

86

room. He said it might have been Marshal Moskanko, who put down the uprising in Budapest in 1956 and later faded from the scene with Darubin after the Six Day War. When Erskine ended by telling about Darubin's final threat to Washington and the country, his voice broke in anger. He apologized to Stark and then lapsed into moody quiet. Stark spent the next few minutes briefing Erskine on the arguments presented the previous day by the Executive Committee. When he mentioned Roarke's espousal of a nuclear strike, Erskine roused himself to grunt: "That damn fool! He's like a bull in a china shop. Did the other members of the Joint Chiefs go along with him?"

Randall said: "The Marines and Navy were against it, I beleive. But Air Force was all for it and so was Army."

Erskine got up to leave. "I'll speak to them later today to make sure no one goes off half-cocked. When does Safcek arrive at Peshawar?"

"Before midnight tomorrow, their time. That'll be about noon here. We're eleven hours behind him from here on in."

Erskine looked at Stark, who added, "And completely in his hands."

The Secretary of Defense went to the door and opened it. Pausing, he asked the man behind the big desk, "What kind of men would ever try what those damn Russians are pulling on us? They must have nerves of steel to match their ambitions."

When the door closed behind Erskine, Stark murmured, "And no feeling for anyone."

The room was simply furnished. A light-colored bookcase lined the right wall. A nondescript rug covered the floor almost entirely. Three functional chairs were drawn up near a table.

On the wall was a portrait of Lenin, his chest adorned with medals. Around the edges of the covered windows seeped the first light of day. A tall lamp still lighted from the previous evening shone down on a sallow-faced man sleeping on a couch tucked in a corner. His thick black hair fell onto his forehead. His cheeks and general facial contours suggested he came from Oriental stock.

He snored intermittently. His body moved several times as he lay on the couch. He seemed to be having a troubled sleep.

A door opened, and a man walked over to him. He tugged gently on the sleeping man's jacket and said: "Comrade Krylov, Comrade Krylov." Vladimir Nikolaievich Krylov struggled up from his bed.

"What is it, Alexei?"

"I am sorry to wake you so early, but Marshal Moskanko is outside waiting to see you."

"Send him in, Alexei. No, wait a minute until I wash up."

When the general entered, Krylov was sitting in one of the wooden chairs. His hair was combed, and his face was fresh and untroubled. "Dear friend," he asked, "how was your trip to Geneva?"

Marshal Moskanko, defense minister of the Soviet Union, was a bull-necked giant of a man who now nodded grimly. "Excellent, Vladimir Nikolaievich. The Americans were properly impressed. I thought Erskine would have a heart attack right in the room. But Darubin has probably already cabled you about the important facts."

"Yes, Mikhail Ivanovich was ecstatic. He particularly emphasized the importance of keeping up the pressure about destroying Washington. Like you, he referred to the impact that message had on the two guests. But then, General, I'd rather hear it from you because it was Darubin who convinced me that Nasser could handle the Jews with one hand tied behind his back." Krylov laughed loudly. "I lost my job because of that."

Moskanko did not laugh. "Mikhail Ivanovich told the truth about the Americans. They were terrified."

While Krylov poured coffee from a silver samovar left by Alexei, Marshal Moskanko stood before the portrait of Lenin. He gazed at the face of the man who had led the original revolution years ago. "Vladimir Nikolaievich, we can make all his dreams come true. In less than a week, the world will be communist, and he"—gesturing at the painting—"will be proven a prophet."

When Krylov did not respond, the defense minister turned. The premier was hunched over the table, stirring his coffee. "Don't you agree, comrade?"

The premier raised his eyes and smiled: "Of course, of course. But what if the Americans do not surrender. What then? We will have to kill all those people just to prove a point. And what if the Americans decide to die fighting. We will have millions of dead in our streets, too. Lenin would not have wanted that, I am sure."

Moskanko waved the premier into silence. "Let us worry about the American reaction. You just be calm and tend to your affairs. Remember, Vladimir Nikolaievich, we are directing this."

The defense minister finished his demitasse and strode out of the office.

Krylov put his face into his hands. The past few weeks had strained his nerves. A kaleidoscope of memories flashed through his mind; the call from Marshal Moskanko at midnight on the fifteenth of August; the visit to the defense minister's office the next day; the offer to back him as premier if Krylov would support the army against Smirnov; the initial flush of victory as he agreed to join forces against his old enemy, who had forced his ouster after the Israeli victory in the Sinai. Krylov's first days in office were filled with heady moments as he dismissed old rivals, men who had once been happy to see him banished from office. Krylov was vengeful as he checked off names of those who had balked him in his original quest for power.

Then came the fateful conference with Moskanko and the other three marshals of the Soviet Union. Krylov had watched the movie of the laser destroying the village and forest and was filled with awe at its colossal power. After the screening, Moskanko had told him the laser was the prototype of many more but that a production line could not manufacture a quantity for several months. Moskanko said the Americans were developing the same weapon and would probably have a working model within that time. He said it was imperative for the Soviet Union to use the time granted to correct the world situation. The marshals were convinced that the laser must be used immediately.

Krylov was aghast and refused to sanction such a proposal. The military men listened to his plea for a more rational approach, and then Moskanko said: "Vladimir Nikolaievich, if you refuse to concur with us, you will be replaced within the hour."

Premier Krylov, remembering the years of frustration and humiliation after 1967, sold his soul to the men who had given power back to him. The ultimatum to the United States followed, and Krylov retreated to his spartan office and brooded.

Now he rose from his chair and went to the window overlooking Red Square. Huge red stars shone from the pinnacles of the Kremlin. He looked beyond to the Moskva River, and the university behind it. It was the heart of his Russia, which had spawned him and molded him. He was the leader of a nation that had withstood the Hitler armies and given one of every nine people in death to deny the invader the soil of the motherland. And now, he, Vladimir Nikolaievich Krylov, son of a schoolteacher and a Hero of the Soviet Union, was endangering the lives of more than 200 million kinsmen because he was too weak to smash away the chalice of success and power. At the window, Premier Krylov wept softly.

At 9:45 P.M., Bob Randall had left the President. He went into the Situation Room to make one last check of the world fronts and found them deceptively tranquil. Though American forces were on condition yellow, the enemy was somnolent. The ultimatum was nearly twenty-two hours old. William Stark now had some fifty hours to answer the challenge. The Soviet task force in the Atlantic was still heading straight for the American coastline, but no hostile act was reported by shadowing ships. Randall almost wondered if he had imagined the ultimatum in a bad dream.

Randall went from the White House to Chez Camille, a favorite restaurant, where his secretary, Mary Devereaux, now waited for him. He kissed her lightly on the cheek, fleetingly brushing his fingers against her blond hair. Apologizing for his lateness, he settled into the booth.

"Bob, you look dead."

"I'm getting old, my dear. It happens to all of us."

The waiter took orders for a gin and tonic and a Cutty Sark on the rocks.

"What's going on at the big white house?" Mary asked.

"Nothing special, really. Why?"

"Bob, I've been around long enough to know when it's trouble." She stirred her drink and stabbed the lime slice with her swizzle stick. "The President looks as if he's had a nervous breakdown."

Randall eyed her closely. He enjoyed Mary immensely. In the first days after the bitter estrangement from his wife, she had filled the void. In his most candid moments with himself, Randall knew she was neither his equal intellectually nor as sensitive a human being as he would want for a partner. But she was a good companion in his loneliness, and she asked little of him.

91

He tried a smile at the worried girl and answered: "He's just tired from meeting all the ladies' groups and the Boy Scouts, I guess. What he needs is that vacation he's been planning for months."

Randall tried to change the subject but she persisted: "Then what about all those meetings you've been having with him at odd hours, like last night and this morning? That's not routine, and you know it."

Randall was annoyed. Mary was pushing him into a corner when she knew she shouldn't pry. He repeated that it was nothing. She gulped at the gin and tonic and examined him carefully: "No, Robert, you're treating me like a baby . . ."

He was suddenly tired of the game. "Goddamnit, Mary, drop it. You know I can't talk to you about these things."

Tears welled in her eyes, and she reached for her purse. "I'll be right back. I have to go to the ladies room." He let her go without a reply.

The waiter came and bent over Randall. "Sir, you're wanted at the White House immediately."

Robert Randall rose quickly, scribbled a note to Mary, and left it with the waiter. Then he ran outside and hailed a cab.

Mary Devereaux came back in five minutes, her face freshly made up and a pouting smile on her lips. She saw the empty booth and the note on her plate, which read: *"Have to go. I'll call you."*

She burst into tears and slumped into the seat.

A tall, elegantly dressed man noticed her distress and came to her side. "Miss Devereaux, may I help?" She stared up into the handsome face of Alexander Barnett, Washington correspondent for the CBA Television Network.

"Oh, hello, Alex," she sniffled through her handkerchief. "I'm all right, really. I guess I've had a long day and got a little strung out."

Barnett sat across from her and ordered drinks for both of

them. When he got his bourbon and soda, he leaned toward her and whispered: "Looked to me like a lover's spat. I saw Bob Randall run out of here and figured you had told him off but good."

When she failed to answer, he continued, "I didn't know you two were such good friends."

Mary Devereaux was confused. She wanted very much to tell someone that she was proud to be Randall's mistress, that he slept with her nearly every night, that she hoped to marry him someday. But she realized she could not confide in Barnett because Bob had told her the newsman was unethical. She waggled a finger at Barnett and smiled sweetly: "We're just here talking over business, Alex. He had to go back to the White House in a hurry, that's all."

"What's up?"

"That's what I'd like to know," she replied ruefully.

Barnett excused himself shortly and went to a phone. He left Mary Devereaux looking sadly into her third gin and tonic.

In the shadows of the big trees, Alexander Barnett waited with his photographer. When the door to the west entrance opened briefly, the photographer pointed the infrared camera and zoomed across five hundred yards to focus on the emerging men. He clicked the shutter three times and then pulled the camera down from his face. "That's all there are, I guess." The two men went up the street to their car and drove to a processing lab of CBA.

In thirty-five minutes, the photographer and Barnett were staring excitedly at the pictures laid out on a white cloth. Barnett picked up each one in turn and purred happily: "Old Sam Riordan himself, paying a social call on Bill Stark. Now what the hell would he be doing in the White House at midnight?

Sam hasn't been up past ten o'clock for twenty years, I bet."
Barnett tapped Riordan's picture against his teeth and said:
"There's a very rotten smell here. Let's see if we can smoke
it out of them." He went to a wall phone and put through a
call to New York and the director of CBA News.

Joe Safcek slept for hours in the uncomfortable cabin of the
C-135. When he awoke, the neat farmland acres of Germany
were underneath. Then the huge airfield at Frankfurt-on-Main
appeared, and the jet landed and taxied past the beautiful terminal complex on the right side, where commercial planes were
lined up at different gates. The C-135 pulled to the left and
cut its engines before an old hangar. When Safcek and Gorlov
emerged with Richter, four military policemen formed a body-
guard around them and escorted them into a lounge.

Safcek was amused by the special convoy and said to Richter,
"I feel like a VIP."

Richter answered: "You are. Their orders are to keep everyone away from you." He left unsaid what further orders they
had if anyone did approach the team.

The three men sat down at a table and looked at a menu.
The MPs got them what they ordered, and they ate in silence,
surrounded by curious busboys and the four MPs, who watched
stolidly while their charges finished their snacks. Karl Richter
had constant refills on his coffee. Joe Safcek drank coffee and
smoked two cigarettes. Gorlov asked for a tumbler of vodka and
swallowed it at a gulp. Then the MPs took them back to the
refueled plane. The doors closed, the engines roared, and the
C-135 went back into the air. It headed southeast toward the
Mediterranean.

Thursday,
September 12

WASHINGTON

MOSCOW

TASHKENT

MARSHAL MOSKANKO and his three deputies, Marshals Bakunin, Omskuschin, and Fedoseyev, were forty miles northwest of the Soviet capital, holding a morning situation conference. They had entered a bungalow at the top of a hill and descended an elevator five hundred feet into the bowels of the earth, where the defense command for all Soviet military forces maintained headquarters. A labyrinth radiated from a central control room lined with electric maps listing all American offensive and defensive weapons systems in position. Moskanko and his deputies went immediately to a huge television screen, which covered a fourteen-by-twenty-foot section of a side wall. They stared at the image, and the defense minister said, "They're still on a war footing. Look at those bombers taking off." The picture showed a long line of B-52 aircraft taxiing to the end of runways and sweeping down the long path into the sky. A Cosmos satellite hanging motionless over Torreon Airbase in Spain was relaying these indications of enemy readiness.

"Torreon normally handles only twelve planes on a daily basis, but now we can see at least twenty-four on the line," the ascetic-looking Marshal Bakunin, master of the rocket forces, said in his precise manner. "Not only that but each SAC station is similarly beefed up. The missile sites are also on at least condition yellow, so they are ready to go within twelve minutes."

Moskanko nodded acknowledgment to Bakunin, who was not only a fellow marshal but his brother-in-law as well. The defense minister left the television screen to go into a white-walled office. He greeted a man in civilian clothes who deferred to him by standing until he was seated. Moskanko was brusque with his visitor. "What about Rudenko?"

"He's still alive at Lubianka. We've had Fedor working with him for three days, and the pig is stubborn. He has admitted nothing of real importance, though he did testify that he knew some people at the American Embassy. Rudenko says it was merely in the line of duty. When we confronted him with the microfilming equipment from his apartment, he said it had been planted there."

The man speaking was Vassili Baranov, deputy director of the Soviet state security police. The hawk-nosed director continued apologetically: "We don't want to lose Rudenko before he tells us what we want to know. Fedor has had to be extremely careful with him."

Moskanko interrupted. "We must break him. Someone in our laser program gave him blueprints to pass on to the Americans. He could not just walk into the research center like a ghost. If you cannot do anything with your fists, use something else."

Vassili Baranov suggested sodium pentothal. The defense minister told him to arrange for it immediately, and the state security officer left by helicopter to execute this latest directive.

Marshal Moskanko rejoined his deputies. They were in the map room, standing over a table cluttered with charts of the frontier in Europe. The stocky peasant Omskuschin was explaining the disposition of NATO forces in West Germany.

"The Americans are in a terribly weakened condition. Their forces there are down fifty-five percent from their peak in 1965, and, of course, their allies have not made up the loss over the years. I have two tank armies poised along the Elbe which can reach the English Channel in fourteen days. The West German army is the shield. Once we have pierced it, there is very little to hold us."

Moskanko interrupted. "You will not even have to fight your way through, comrade. When the American President realizes the position he is in, he will not resist. You will be able to walk to the Channel and pick flowers all the way." The expansive Moskanko eased himself into a chair and smiled at his fellow marshals.

"Omskuschin," the defense minister continued, "I know how eager you are to test out your armored-warfare ideas on those flat plains, but you must prepare to be disappointed. Stark will fold up like an accordian, and your vehicles will continue to collect rust in their motor pools. It will not be like 1945 when you took your Stalin tanks into Berlin."

Omskuschin made a face at the defense minister, who laughed loudly and slammed the top of the table with his fist. "No, comrades, it will all fall into our laps without a man lost."

Marshall Bakunin did not smile at the remark. The bespectacled deputy stared moodily at the maps in front of him until Moskanko noticed his gloom.

"A problem?"

Bakunin stirred from his silence and turned his somber face to Moskanko. "Yes, a problem. I have been thinking of the one thing that could upset all our plans. What if the American Stark reacts differently from our expectations? What if his advisors convince him to fight? All indications show he would rather appease than face us. All indications show that the American people have lost their spirit, that they are divided among themselves and want to forget their commitments around the world. But, my dear friend, this is an entirely different situation. America is about to fall, and Stark may somehow find the strength to stand up to us. A rat scurries away until he is cornered, but then he fights to save himself from extinction. And we have not given Stark any alternative to total surrender. He is up against a wall and might just attempt to bring it down on us along with himself."

Moskanko was angry. "What is wrong with you, Pavel Andreievich? Are you losing your nerve?"

Bakunin flushed, but ignored his commander's remark. "I only know what power I have at my fingertips. I have seen the bombs go off at the test centers. I was there the day we misjudged the force of one hydrogen weapon and it killed more than fifty officials who were too close. Knowing that, I still went along with you because I believed that Stark would capitulate without a struggle. But I will be frank to admit I have had trouble sleeping nights, wondering whether he just might not surrender, that he might come to believe that it is better to die like a man than to consign his people to our domination. Man is the most complex of all primates, and his predictability is always open to question."

The defense minister had gotten up, and he came around the table and put his arm around Bakunin's shoulder.

"I am sorry for what I said to you, Pavel Andreievich. Please forgive me. Such arguments are out of place in a friendship as long as ours, which goes all the way back to Frunze Academy." Bakunin nodded grimly as Moskanko hastened to smooth over his insult.

"You were called 'the professor' even there, Pavel Andreievich. Spending all your time reading instead of chasing the women. My sister was the only one who could bring your nose out of those damned books. When you married, I was certain you would spend the honeymoon in some library." Moskanko laughed and Bakunin forced a smile.

The defense minister went back to his chair and waited for his friend to continue, but Bakunin had lapsed into another moody silence.

"You will see, Pavel Andreievich, it will turn out as I predicted. The Americans will not retaliate, and your rockets, like Omskuschin's tanks, will collect rust where they lie."

"I hope you are right, Viktor Semyonovich," Bakunin replied

to his brother-in-law. "I have seen the power of my rockets, and knew that someday I might have to use them. But this is different. We are the aggressors in this situation. If the world goes up . . ."

"It will not go up, I tell you. We will make it impossible for Stark to move in the next hours. We have a few more surprises that will render him absolutely harmless before the ultimatum expires."

The bespectacled Bakunin showed no interest in Moskanko's remark as he got up and went out to monitor the state of the enemy's defenses. Omskuschin and Fedoseyev watched him go and turned to Moskanko for a reaction. The defense minister shrugged.

"He is too intelligent for his own good. He might just lose the debate he is having with his conscience. And that would not be good for us."

Thirty-five minutes after having left the defense center, Vassili Baranov arrived at the infamous Lubianka Prison. Lubianka rivaled the Bridge of Sighs in Venice as a place where men's last hopes for life flickered and were extinguished. Baranov went to the second floor and nodded to a blue-uniformed guard who opened the gate to a cellblock. Baranov marched down the stone corridor and stopped before Cell 212. He looked in at the bed, where Grigor Rudenko lay inert. When the guard let Baranov in, he walked to the edge of the cot. Rudenko sensed his presence and rose up on an elbow. The secret police officer blanched when he saw the results of Fedor's careful handling.

"Rudenko, why don't you cooperate?" pleaded the state security man, looking at his battered prisoner. "Then you can rest."

Grigor's head rolled slightly before he summoned the will to answer. "Comrade, I have told your people everything I know." He smiled crookedly at Baranov, who then saw the blood dribbling down his chin in tiny rivulets. Baranov looked closer in the bad light and saw Rudenko's mouth. His teeth were broken and jagged, where Fedor's fists had smashed into them time and again and left the victim with a shattered face.

Baranov wasted no further time. He went to the door and muttered instructions to the guard. Shortly, two attendants brought a stretcher and lifted Rudenko onto it. As he lay with his face trailing over the edge of the cot, the prisoner spat blood onto the floor.

They took him down the hall to a room that smelled of ether. A Tchaikovsky ballet was playing somewhere, and Rudenko tried to follow it through the waves of pain that engulfed him. He sank into a real bed with fresh sheets and gazed through his good eye at a pink ceiling. It reminded him strongly of home, where Tamara's room had this feminine atmosphere. For a moment he mentally held her in his arms and kissed her cheek. Then a white form hovered over him and Baranov's voice cut through the fog: "Give him the maximum, Senski." The white form was pulling at his left sleeve, and then Rudenko felt something metallic burrowing into his arm.

The white form spoke to him; "Now, Grigor, please count backward from ten with me. Ten, nine." At the last second, Grigor sensed what they were doing and lashed out feebly with his arms. *But then he was on a meadow with the morning dew still on the grass. A horse was cantering toward him, and he shouted to it, "Archer!" The horse slowed and stopped before him. Grigor jumped on its bare back and rode through the sunlight, his hair blowing wildly into his eyes.*

Beside him, another horse and rider appeared, and Karl Richter shouted: "For a date with Sheila," and spurred ahead of Grigor who laughed excitedly and gave chase. The two boys went bounding over stone walls toward a red barn in the distance. At the gate to the stables, a girl with golden hair waited for them. She was jumping up and down and urging them toward her, and Grigor could see her teeth gleaming in the ruby mouth. He pulled Archer up before her and jumped off. Sheila came toward him and Grigor reached out to touch her hand . . .

"Grigor, who gave you the blueprints?"

". . . *Sheila, I just won a date with* . . ."

"Grigor, please tell us."

"You." And he held her hands and looked into her beautiful eyes.

"Who, Grigor?"

"Professor Parchuk, my wife's uncle. He gave them to me on September seventh."

"Why did he do it, Grigor?" and he kissed her on her ruby lips and felt her slim body cling to his. Karl Richter stood by, laughing, and said: "I'm going to shoot this old nag I've got. You and Sheila owe it all to him . . ."

"Parchuk found out what the laser was going to be used for."

"Who else helped him?"

"No one! No one helped him. He only came to me because he was desperate, and he trusted me completely."

"Where did you meet him?"

Sheila put her arm around him, and they walked with Karl to the main house, where Sheila's mother had a breakfast of pancakes and bacon ready for them. Sheila's eyes were twinkling with excitement and she tousled Grigor's hair; Karl Richter was hugging Sheila's mother who giggled and said, "Karl, I'm going to tell your father you're going around bothering old ladies." And they all laughed and Grigor sat beside Sheila.

"Where, Grigor?"

"At the GUM Department Store."

Another voice joined that of the white-coated man: "Enough . . . get me Tashkent on the special phone."

Grigor was walking again with Sheila, and the dew was soaking through their sneakers, and he was telling her he loved her, and Sheila was looking into his eyes happily.

103

William Stark had taken a sleeping pill at 1 A.M., but it had not brought him sleep. He tossed about in the bed until Pamela woke up and laid her hand on his shoulder.

Stark had been almost indifferent to her in the past two days. He had lied about the reason for delaying the trip to Bar Harbor, and she had been hurt when he explained that it was because of the pending passage of a conservation bill. Then she realized that the haunted look in his eyes hid a far more serious matter and she stopped pressing. Now in their bed, she asked again if she could help. President Stark lay against the pillow and poured out his turmoil to his wife of twenty-nine years. When he finished, she continued rubbing his back softly and tried to stop the fluttering in her own breast. Pamela was terrified not for herself but for the man beside her, who was faced with an intolerable choice—destroy the world or surrender more than 200 million people. Worse, she knew she could not help him except by her presence, by her devotion to him. And he needed more than that. Pamela Stark pulled her husband closer, and he fell asleep in her arms.

At 6:45 A.M., Leonard Thompson, the President's valet, knocked on the door and came in with breakfast. The couple sat up in bed. The night's conversation was an unmentioned presence between them. As a husband, Stark was relieved that he had confided in his wife. As the leader of the nation, he felt no let-up in his anxiety. And the malevolent influence of the laser continued to intrude into the Presidential bedroom. Almost thirty-two hours were gone; less than forty remained.

The valet switched on the television for the morning news, and Stark listened halfheartedly to the supposed state of the world as seen from New York. The announcer was saying something about an important meeting in Washington, and then Stark saw a picture of Sam Riordan fill the screen. The announcer spoke of rumors circulating through the capital that some unforeseen situation must have prompted the director of the Central Intelligence Agency to spend an evening at the White House with the most important advisor in the government. The broadcast switched to Washington and the suave Alexander Barnett, who told viewers that he had personally witnessed the rendezvous the night before and had also seen Mr. Randall called away hurriedly from a restaurant to attend the conference. Barnett took off his glasses, looked into the camera, and asked: "Why has the President postponed his trip to Bar Harbor and why the hush-hush meetings at the White House late at night? The American people would like to know, I'm sure."

Bill Stark turned to his wife. "Any advice for a rainy day, dear?" She leaned over and kissed him on the stubble. He rose to meet the deluge.

It was a special day in Washington for other reasons. The concerned members of the organization called Save Our Unborn Legions, popularly known as SOUL, were about to march through the city.

From all sections of the country, left, right, and center, they had come to voice their opposition to a bill before Congress that they felt was immoral and unconscionable. The measure had been proposed by Senator George T. Stratton of Colorado in the Senate and by Congressman Amos Seligsohn of Cincinnati in the House.

The Stratton-Seligsohn bill responded to a decade's alarmed attention to ecology, the study of man's environment. Scientists, viewing the deterioration of the planet's resources, had been making more and more dire predictions about the future of man. Some foresaw extinction within thirty-five years. Others wondered openly whether he would rot in our own garbage. Governments on both sides of the Iron Curtain had been laboring to cope with the universal menace. Billions were appropriated to eradicate smog and reduce water pollution, but efforts were too diffuse to combat the insidious by-products of man's technological development.

Two years before, a World Congress on Environmental Problems had been held in Vienna. Interested parties from seventy-four countries had presented their proposals. Birth control, the absolute limiting of procreation, was the antidote recommended by seventy-one delegations.

Just one year back, the Soviet Union, the United States, France, and Poland had asked for and received an audience with the Pope. Specialists from each country produced graphs and charts to illustrate the tragedy facing man. They expressed their conviction to the Pontiff that the best solution to the destruction of our resources was a limitation of the number of people on the earth.

The four nations wanted the Pope to make a pronouncement to the Catholic masses endorsing the concept of birth control by artificial means. The Pope promised an answer within one year.

On March 14 that year, he published an encyclical known as *De populis mundi,* from its opening words. In it, the Pope reiterated his belief that birth control by artificial means was contrary to God's law and therefore forbidden to billions of Catholics throughout the world.

In the United States, the disaffected and disenchanted condemned the Church for its blind obedience to what it termed "antiquated and irrelevant dogma." More and more enlightened priests broke with Rome over the position of the Pope.

When William Stark took office, certain forces in the nation were determined to override interference from outside interests. A campaign was mounted in all fifty states to educate voters to the calamity awaiting them if something was not done immediately to stabilize the country's population.

Television time was bought to explain the peril. One advertisement brought the viewer to a flat plain in Kansas. At first only a small group stood on it. Then hundreds and finally thousands arrived, pushing and shoving each other to maintain footing. At the end, children and old people were being trampled in a desperate attempt to salvage a piece of soil for themselves. A somber voice asked: "Is this the future for your unborn?"

Senator George Stratton was convinced his bill was the only reasonable solution. A religious man, himself, Stratton was immediately denounced by church groups and other factions, which characterized him as an insensitive monster, a *gauleiter* not unlike Adolf Hitler.

Stratton endured the villification stolidly. His biggest problem was encouraging other legislators to support the controversial bill. His colleagues had a terrible choice. Though most of them were convinced of the need to act, they had to face a divided constituency at home. When they read the significant passages in the proposed legislation, they quailed at two items. The first endorsed a fifty percent additional income tax on couples who insisted on having more than two children. The second asked that repeated violators of the limitation clause be forced to submit to sterilization at government expense.

Lawmakers in Washington knew that these provisions, if passed, could mean the end of their careers. Voters had not yet signaled a majority sentiment to the Congress, and the men on Capitol Hill could only sift the evidence at hand and relate it to their own precincts.

In large urban areas, where the black vote had to be cultivated, militant leaders told the people that the Stratton-Seligsohn bill was a thinly camouflaged scheme for black genocide by the white racist society—and many young radicals agreed. Moderate elements from coast to coast saw the Stratton measure as perhaps unfortunate but necessary. Though they deplored its possible infringement of personal liberty, they could see no alternative. In some conservative strongholds, rightists castigated Stratton as a tool of the left, who was trying to cripple the country while the Communists burgeoned on all sides.

In Washington, the members of Congress read these omens with growing apprehension. As the date for voting on the Stratton-Seligsohn bill neared, Capitol Hill was a wary camp of troubled politicians, wrestling with their consciences and their ambitions for continued power.

Into this uneasy situation marched thousands of people who saw the bill as an attempt by the government to practice Big Brotherism on them. Many of them had come to Washington before to protest the war in Vietnam and the oppression of black people and to advocate disarmament by the great powers.

Sharon McCandless had never demonstrated for or against anything in her life. But SOUL had brought her forth from Indiana to make her plea for sanity. A nineteen-year-old sophomore from Butler University, the hazel-eyed brunette had come by bus from Indianapolis with her boy friend, Tom Samuels. The overnight ride to Washington had been carefree and filled with gaiety. As the vehicle ghosted through sleeping towns in southern Pennsylvania, riders had drifted off to cramped naps. At 6 A.M. Tom shook Sharon awake at the base of the Lincoln Memorial where the bus had parked in a long line of vehicles. They tried to eat the peanut butter and jelly sandwiches they had brought in a knapsack, but it did not feel like breakfast, and the couple walked down past the Smithsonian Institution buildings on the Mall to a cafeteria on a side street. Inside were several cops munching doughnuts and coffee. When the proprietor saw the students approaching the door, he ran to it and pulled down the curtain. A sign waved from it: "Sorry, Closed for the Day." Sharon and Tom went elsewhere in pursuit of breakfast.

108

Henry Fuller was too busy to eat. As a group leader in the demonstration, he was responsible for the orderly procession of his five hundred people to the White House. The marchers were beginning to mass at the south bank of the Reflecting Pool, once the site of Resurrection City.

Henry worked at the Pentagon. A lawyer, he handled contracts with private industry for the peaceful development of atomic energy. He believed in this aspect of the government's program, but through his work he knew that in sixteen centers around the world, the United States had concentrated the equivalent of one trillion tons of TNT. Fuller could not live with this thought. As a man with a wife and six-month-old child, he refused to believe that these weapons would not be used someday. He wanted them dismantled by a worldwide agreement.

As to SOUL, he felt that denial of life by government regulation was as wicked as extinction by a bomb. Thus, he marched to protest this latest abomination. Fuller knew that if he was recognized during the parade by government agents, his top-security clearance would be lifted and his job would be jeopardized. But it was worth the risk to him to attempt to force the President of the United States to take a position. The youthful group leader passed among his charges for the day and issued further instructions. At precisely 10:30 A.M., he gave the order to move from the Reflecting Pool toward the Washington Monument, from there to the Capitol Building, and, finally, back by way of Pennsylvania Avenue to the White House.

Forty feet away from him, a man in a double-breasted brown suit watched him carefully. The man was swarthy. His shoes were distinctive, pointed, and of European cut. He held a large package in his hand, and he too looked at his watch when Fuller did. At precisely 10:31, he ripped a manila cover off the package and pulled forth a huge sheaf of handbills, which he began circulating to the crowd of marchers, happily leaving on their crusade for future generations.

William Stark had no time to worry about a demonstration in front of the White House. His mind was bedeviled by the pressing problems before him. He had just talked by scrambler phone to Karl Richter on the plane. Richter told him that he had briefed Safcek and Gorlov for the mission. Jump-off would be sometime after midnight, Peshawar time, near 2 P.M. in Washington. Richter was elated with his men. Safcek was the coolest man he could imagine in such circumstances. Gorlov was relatively calm, uncommunicative, but obviously efficient and ready. Stark told Richter he wanted to be in constant touch with the operation after they landed and would be available at any hour for consultation. Richter promised to keep an open line to the White House.

Stark had also met with Sam Riordan and Gerald Weinroth. Riordan told him Russian strategic weapons were no longer on alert. Samos detectors had come to the startling conclusion that the Soviets appeared to have declared a holiday for their personnel. No activity was apparent at missile sites. The Soviet naval task force in the Atlantic was still moving inexorably toward the East Coast and at present was three hundred miles northeast of Montauk.

Weinroth had consulted his own scientists and concluded that the laser, if operating efficiently, could be fired at Washington and then New York within ninety seconds' time. Stark pursed his lips in distaste, and Weinroth apologized for giving such awful news.

At 11 A.M., the White House press office was jammed with newsmen clamoring to ferret out the truth behind the meeting the night before. Edwin Rast, press secretary at the White House, told them the President would refuse to discuss such speculations at this time.

Alex Barnett said acidly: "I suppose the armed forces are on alert to defend the country against the marchers going by here soon." Rast refused to get involved with the acerbic representative of CBA Broadcasting and walked out of the room to a chorus of catcalls.

On the line of march, Sharon McCandless read a pamphlet someone had thrust at her. While attempting to maintain her footing in the crush of demonstrators, she managed to digest its contents. Clutching at Tom's arm, she screamed, "My God, did you see this?" He took the paper and read:

THE WHITE HOUSE

AS PER INSTRUCTIONS INITIATE CONDITION RED ON SEPTEMBER 16 AT 0900 HOURS.

ASSIGNED TARGETS IN THE SOVIET UNION AND ITS SATELLITES WILL BE RENDERED USELESS BY APPROPRIATE NUCLEAR CONFIGURATIONS. FINAL CODED SIGNAL FOR ATTACK WILL BE ISSUED BY MY ORDER AT 0800 HOURS SAME DAY. REPEAT MY ORDER ALONE.

STARK
COMMANDER-IN-CHIEF

Tom read it twice. "Where did you get this?" Sharon said a marcher had handed it to her as they were approaching the Washington Monument.

Tom was incredulous. "It's just a joke. Some underground group must have made it up to put a little spice into the protest. Forget it, honey. Let's enjoy the scene."

She was not so sure and felt a distinct wave of fear. "Do you really think it's just a hoax, Tom?"

"Of course. The United States would never do such a thing, and why should they? Everyone has been sitting down lately to talk about disarmament." The couple joined hands and walked on.

Others in the march were not so calm about the pamphlet. A tall, muscular man of about forty raised the paper into the air and shouted: "Look at what those bastards over in the White House are plotting now! Stark has gone crazy!" His voice was heavily accented, and his jacket bulged over the left breast. He shoved the pamphlet and others he had with him at curious paraders, who read them with growing indignation.

Henry Fuller had been pleased at the way his group of demonstrators were behaving. At first, the procession was slightly disorganized as thousands of citizens struggled to form into a reasonable facsimile of a parade. They wanted television cameras to record the truth, that this march was not an excuse for excess by a few against the Establishment. The past years had seen the bulk of the American people increasingly repelled by those who spoke disparagingly of an oppressive government and yet resorted to disruptive tactics to bring their own message to the people. Fuller and his followers marched with a sense of urgency but not in direct rebellion against their own governing process.

Fuller's glasses had begun to cloud over in the humidity of the late Washington summer. As he marched along wiping them carefully, he heard a discordant chorus behind him and turned to check. Two men were haranguing the increasingly agitated crowd. Fuller fought his way back through the press of onlookers to the edge of the disturbance. He could hear someone screaming: "It's true. This signature is Stark's. Somebody told me that a person in the Pentagon leaked it to us to expose the Administration's plans for a third world war."

Henry Fuller grabbed a pamphlet and read the fateful words. He could not believe them and shouted: "Who the hell are you?" toward the speaker. But the man was gone, swallowed up in the throng. Harsh voices beat at Fuller's ears, and he felt a sudden surge of anger. His demonstration was turning into a mob scene before his eyes.

A priest exhorted those around him to seek the truth immediately. He shouted, "Let's go to the White House! That man in there knows what's going on. Let's ask him directly."

A middle-aged woman in an expensive silk suit shrilled: "Father is right! We have a duty to find out whether this paper was signed by Stark. My God, imagine if it's true. We'll all be dead in a matter of days."

Fear had possessed the members of SOUL. Fear and a sense of righteous wrath had twisted the idealistic sentiments of thousands and was creating a mob.

In the growing frenzy, sane voices were drowned out. Henry Fuller was helpless. He tried to cajole, then to demand loyalty to the original reason for the march. He pulled at strangers and cursed the agitators who had transformed them. A fist rose from the crowd and smashed into his mouth. Fuller fell to the pavement, his blood staining the asphalt. A marcher kicked him in the ribs, and Fuller feebly attempted to raise himself to a sitting position. He heard people screaming in rage and anger and saw hundreds of shoes running by him as the line of march rushed past his body toward the citadel of power. Henry Fuller beat his fist into the ground in frustration and sorrow for his fellow man.

SOUL split into two groups, one of which doubled back to swing across the Potomac. Twenty-five minutes later, in front of the Pentagon, military policemen watched warily as the first of the protestors descended upon them. The angry shouts reached the ears of Colonel James Shelton, standing at the entrance to the massive building. He was appalled. Days of negotiations with demonstration leaders had convinced Pentagon generals that there would be no need to fear an invasion by dissident factions intent on humiliating the government of the United States. SOUL was sincere, sensible, and scrupulously correct.

113

It had refused to allow extremist groups to join the march. General Stephen Austin Roarke himself had signed the order permitting the demonstration in downtown Washington, and lesser Pentagon officials had not even thought to post soldiers from surrounding bases.

Colonel Shelton saw the hands waving hundreds of white slips of paper. He did not know the extent of the trouble that awaited him. In the mass of protesters who poured off the bridge and down the road leading to the stucco fortress, Sharon McCandless and Tom Samuels had been engulfed by the rising indignation at the "Stark" order. They had lost their objectivity along with thousands of others who heard the chorus of fear and frustration around them and denied their own instincts for order. Sharon was both exhilarated and frightened. She wanted direct action yet feared its consequences. Tom was feeling a great sense of guilt because he did not really believe the contents of the directive by Stark. Yet he had allowed himself to be swept along in the fury that suddenly veered from the announced line of march and swept into Virginia.

Hurriedly called MPs lined up across the entrance and stared over the heads of the mob descending on them. Colonel Shelton walked out in front and waited for the confrontation.

A native of Alabama, he had spent fifteen years in the United States Army, including two years in Vietnam as an advisor to South Vietnamese rangers. Shelton had lived with fear during that entire time and had acquitted himself ably. Yet today, basking in the warmth of a relentless sun, he felt a strange mixture of panic and helplessness. These people had ostensibly come in peace. But the front ranks of protesters were not filled with calm men. They were the enemy.

The marchers stopped twenty feet in front of him. Behind them hundreds of people bumped into one another like the cars of a freight train. The crowd reassembled, spreading out like a fan around the tiny line of soldiers.

Colonel Shelton breathed deeply. "May I ask who your leaders are?"

A delegation of five stepped toward him. Each held a white slip of paper in his hands. One old man wearing a seersucker suit was the spokesman. His face was wizened, and his white hair lay in wisps on his sweating head. The old man thrust his paper at Shelton and spoke in a thin, tired voice: "As you know, we came to Washington in peace. Our hearts break at the thought of our children and grandchildren living under the threat of a dictatorship which could force them to control their progeny." The old man paused to wipe his perspiring forehead. He glanced at the colonel, who was smiling pleasantly at him. "We, these people," and his hand waved behind him at the assemblage, "bear no ill will. And yet in the past hour, these people have been shattered by that paper you have in your hand now."

The old man stared directly into the colonel's eyes: "We must have an explanation from the government about this order. My friends out here demand a satisfactory answer."

He was not threatening Shelton. His voice was almost plaintive, filled with remorse for even an overtone of menace in his request. The old man was suddenly quiet. Shelton looked at the paper carefully. While he read, flags over the Pentagon snapped lazily in a welcome breeze whose coolness fanned the faces of the inflamed citizens. Shelton's first reaction was amazement. He began to laugh but quickly stopped when he realized his position.

"Gentlemen, I don't know where you got this supposed order, but it is incomprehensible that you would believe it. As rational beings, you cannot suppose that it is anything but a fabrication."

The people in front of him stared back blankly. Shelton's mind raced rapidly. "Perhaps you should all sit out here and calm down for a while. You're welcome to use the grass area for your comfort. And again I assure you this paper is a hoax of some sort."

115

The old man said reproachfully, "Colonel, we want a better answer than that. Please talk to someone inside, and meanwhile we will wait on the grass. And thank you for the offer."

Colonel James Shelton ducked inside the door and picked up a wall telephone. He spoke rapidly to E Ring and explained the contents of the document. While he spoke, the citizen army outside broke its ranks and sprawled in the grass. Thermos jugs of lemonade and Coke were distributed. Sharon and Tom munched the sandwiches from breakfast. The protesters continued to wonder openly about the origin of the document. Some were still unconvinced, but the majority were filled with apprehension.

Minutes stretched into a half hour, and Colonel Shelton had not emerged. The guards around the front door were quietly equipped with tear-gas guns handed out surreptitiously. At Fort Myer, several miles distant, the officer of the day was ordered to send two thousand combat-ready soldiers by truck to the Pentagon. They were to appear within one hour.

Someone in the crowd of resting marchers had waited long enough. He stood up and shouted: "We want an answer, we want an answer." A swell of voices chanted with him. Inside the Pentagon, hundreds of office workers went to the windows. The panes rattled from the concussion of angry words. Colonel Shelton was deep within E Ring, explaining the mood of the marchers to a confused general, who had just read the Stark directive. Shelton was losing his calm. "Sir, those people are really shook up over this thing. And they weren't at all mollified when I put it down as a crank job. We've got to find them some kind of reasonable explanation, or this place will be a battleground by nighttime."

The general said: "How the hell did they fall for this bullshit?"

Shelton said: "They're so bothered by the whole nuclear situation that anyone could turn them on with it. Since they spend half their waking hours wondering what the hell the world is coming to, a smart agitator could just plant a seed like this and watch it flourish. And I'm afraid that's what has happened today." The general said: "Wait until the television people get a hold of this one. No matter what we tell them, they won't be satisfied. And if there are agitators mixed up in the crowd, we'll catch hell one way or the other."

The general had made up his mind. "Look, Shelton, go out there and stall them until the troops get here. Then we'll tell them to disperse, and if they don't we'll go back to the old days and spray them with gas. But try to get them out of here peacefully."

Colonel James Shelton went out of E Ring to the upper level, where the SOUL marchers were shouting their indignation at the walls.

It was 11 P.M. in Peshawar, almost thirty-eight hours since the ultimatum had been sent, with thirty-four hours to go, when the giant C-135 rode over the darkened plain. Its engines quieted suddenly to just above a whisper. In the cabin, Karl Richter and half of his Operation Scratch team put seat belts on. Joe Safcek stubbed out his cigarette. The plane dipped to the left and came straight in at a row of blue lights running along the ground. The wheels touched and screamed, and the motors roared into reverse to brake the momentum. When the aircraft stopped, the three men unbuckled their harnesses and stepped to the door, which opened suddenly to admit a burly MP, signaling them to follow him. They descended into the darkness and, guided by flashlights, went to a jeep, which deposited them before an isolated and bleak barracks. These were the same barracks from which Francis Gary Powers had walked on May 1, 1960, to take off on a never-completed overflight across Soviet territory to Bodo, Norway.

President William Mellon Stark was about to sit down to lunch with Robert Randall. He was edgy, curt to the point of rudeness, but Randall did not seem to mind. The forty-year-old advisor had known the President too long. Besides, he continued to marvel at the way the man bore up under the strain. Randall knew he himself would be near to cracking in the same spot. When the waiter had left the room, Stark picked at his food and fretted.

"According to what Richter told me, Safcek should be on his way to Tashkent in an hour or so."

Randall made no comment.

"Good God, it's awful to think that we're reduced to relying on a handful of commandos to save the entire country." The President finished his consommé and pushed the dish to one side. The waiter came back in with the entrée, a chef's salad, and the two men ate in silence for a few moments.

"Bob, I can only give that team twenty-four hours to blow that building. Beyond that I must have some leeway. I've been thinking about General Roarke's idea of a nuclear strike by one plane. Maybe he wasn't so wrong. Maybe, just maybe, it would take the wind out of the Russians and scare them so much they wouldn't go to war over it."

Robert Randall munched a piece of lettuce reflectively and answered: "You know, if you combined it with a hot line to the Russians within a minute or so of the strike, it might work. You could tell them that it was just a one-plane operation, not

118

an all-out attack, and put the pressure back on them for the responsibility of starting a big war. The important question is: who's in charge there. Would cool heads really prevail?"

Stark retreated to a pessimistic silence. While eating vanilla ice cream, he suddenly spoke: "Tell Roarke to have a plane ready just in case. I've got to have another option."

Randall patted his lips with the napkin and excused himself. The President remained at the table, and did not look up as Randall left.

Secretary of Defense Clifford Erskine was lunching with General Roarke in the besieged Pentagon when Randall called with the President's message. Physically, Erskine was feeling worse. The pain in his left arm had become almost unbearable. He was intermittently nauseated and suffering from chills and sweating. Erskine and Roarke were discussing Operation Scratch, and the secretary had spent fifteen minutes defending the plan. Erskine was not inclined to like the tall Texan who worked for him. To him, Roarke was a boor, an insensitive man who irritated the brilliant administrator of the nation's defenses. Erskine had come to Washington from the presidency of Consolidated Industries, one of the Big Ten in American business. He had never liked the military mind. Now in close daily contact with it, he abhorred its ingrained insistence on the use of power in time of crisis. Erskine was appalled by any application of force to settle the world's problems. He had watched the country submerge into the morass of Vietnam and thrash about in it painfully for years. When he was asked to take the job, Erskine had told Stark that he would never allow himself to be associated with such a debacle during his term of office. He found Stark a sympathetic listener, a kindred spirit, who also seemed to have pacifist tendencies. Their years of association had not altered Erskine's opinion of the President.

General Roarke considered the secretary a weak person, unfit for the job. The two men had clashed frequently over strategy during Roarke's tenure as chairman of the Joint Chiefs, and their animosity was barely covered by a veneer of civility. On this day, Roarke had come to Erskine to complain bitterly that Stark was running scared, that Operation Scratch was doomed and so was the country unless the Joint Chiefs were allowed to act, decisively. Erskine listened patiently for a while but then cut the general short with: "The President thinks this is the best way to avoid a nuclear war. So do I. And that's the way it's going to be."

The phone on Erskine's desk rang shrilly. He picked it up and listened as Robert Randall relayed Stark's instructions. Erskine asked Randall to repeat the message. As he waited, his features turned chalk white, and his palms began to sweat. The secretary mumbled good-bye to Randall and put the receiver down. "Roarke, this is a happy day for you. The President wants you to get that plane ready in case Safcek doesn't make it."

The general's face expanded in a huge smile. He responded, "Yes, sir," and bolted out of the room.

Secretary of Defense Clifford Erskine made a decision. He ordered a car to take him to the White House immediately. He went down an elevator and into the underground garage. As the limousine poked upward into the noontime sunlight, Erskine heard the roar of the protesters in the distance. Out the window he saw people waving placards reading: "SAVE THE UNBORN." Clifford Erskine could not have agreed more.

Colonel James Shelton's renewed dialogue with the march leaders was an exercise in banalities. His instructions had been to delay, and he was succeeding. The wizened old man and the other spokesmen had fenced with him over the piece of paper. Shelton had repeatedly denied its authenticity, but they wanted proof from him. By 1 P.M., they wanted proof from the Joint Chiefs of Staff. Shelton told them that was impossible, that the Joint Chiefs would not consent to a confrontation in front of the Pentagon.

Thursday, September 12

When he saw troopers from Fort Myer arriving in half tracks, Shelton had had enough. He faced the five men and said: "Gentlemen, you may present any petitions that you wish. Other than that, I believe you have made your point that you are concerned about a possible nuclear war. For my part, for what it's worth, I share your sentiments. Now then, I must ask you to retire from these premises in an orderly fashion. In one half hour, you must be off the grounds."

Colonel Shelton looked out of the corner of his eye at the several hundred soldiers deploying across the entrance to the Pentagon with a feeling of relief. "Beyond that time, you will be considered as trespassers and dealt with accordingly." Shelton turned and walked back into the building. The old man and his friends stood irresolutely for a moment, then melted back into the crowd of chanters, who began to call, "We want Erskine, we want Erskine." Erskine was not there anymore. He was on his way to the White House to resign his job.

In the radio room in the sub-basement of the Pentagon, an operator sent a message in top secret Croesus code:

```
TO: ELLINGTON, GENERAL USAF
    INCIRCLIK AIRBASE, TURKEY
    PREPARE ONE SR-71 PLUS BACKUP PLANE
    FOR SINGLE MISSION. TARGET TWELVE MILES
    NORTH OF TASHKENT, SOVIET UNION. DETAILS
    TO FOLLOW
    ARMAMENT: TWO TWELVE-MEGATON NUKES
    PROJECTED STRIKE TIME: WITHIN THIRTY-FOUR
    HOURS
    FINAL ORDER WILL BE ISSUED BY STARK
    ALONE
                              ROARKE JCS
```

In the barracks at the edge of the airfield, Joe Safcek was meeting the rest of his team. Luba Spitkovsky moved across the room to him and shook his hand energetically. She was slight, just over five feet tall and barely one hundred pounds, yet there was nothing frail about her. Safcek was struck by her deepset eyes, her pale, taut skin, and high checkbones. Her golden hair had been cut short into a mannish bob, framing the girl's intent face. Safcek remembered now that the Pentagon briefing officer had described her as a cold-blooded killer. He found it almost impossible to believe.

Safcek felt vaguely distrustful of her, not because of anything obvious, but just because she was a woman. He had never worked with a woman agent before and could not imagine her being anything but a weak link in the chain. But her first remark forced him to smile broadly. She said: "Colonel, in Russian, Luba means love." The remark was outrageous in the context, and Safcek felt better about the girl.

Behind her stood Peter Kirov, who soberly confronted the colonel and extended his hand. Safcek examined him closely and saw a young man, with close-cropped hair like Safcek's, a broad Slavic face, and a slim moustache, His eyes were very dark, close together, and piercing in their intensity. Kirov was heavily muscled, obviously in excellent physical condition. Safcek said: "Welcome aboard," and Kirov bowed slightly and retreated from his new commanding officer.

Karl Richter observed the introductions with a benign interest, then asked: "Shall we go over the details one last time, folks?" The four members of Operation Scratch sat down with their mentor, and the briefing began. Propped on an easel was the same blown-up map Richter had taken Safcek and Gorlov over on the plane. It covered an area from Peshawar north to Tashkent and vicinity. A bull's-eye marked the airfield, another indicated the target area. A blue line marked the route of the helicopter out of friendly territory into hostile land. Richter pointed out the terrain and added: "We'd like to drop you in during daylight to avoid going through the mountains by night, but it would only give them a better look at you once you landed, and besides we're running short on time. You will leave here shortly before one A.M. local time—that's about three quarters of an hour from now. The chopper will hug the floors of the valleys through the mountains and out into the flat. Russian radar positions have been ascertained, and we'll be able to slip by them at a height of three hundred feet."

Boris Gorlov groaned at the thought of negotiating such a formidable obstacle in darkness, but Richter curtly asked: "Do you have any other way, Boris?" He had none, and the discussion continued.

Joe Safcek was warming to the task. His nerves had steadied after leaving the States, and he had pushed thoughts of Martha and Tommy into the recesses of his mind. It was imperative to deny his other life and concentrate on the job at hand.

Safcek studied his subordinates as they sat listening intently to Karl Richter, and he felt increasingly confident. They werc professionals in a rotten game, and he would not have to watch his flanks while they were along.

Richter showed a magnified picture of the target area.

"There it is. The building in the middle has to have the laser. Only a place that big could accommodate the weapon. Plus the Samos satellite has taken pictures of the roof, and it appears to be a rollback type, permitting the laser to poke through and fire."

"What are the other buildings?"

"Most likely workers' buildings, scientists' dormitories, and machine shops. The place is apparently a self-contained unit,

123

sealed off from the outside world. That partially explains our own failure to estimate their rate of progress over the past months. Few people came out or went in."

Karl Richter wanted to add: "But Grigor Rudenko found a way to get at the secret."

He continued with the briefing. Outside, Pakistani workers loaded supplies onto a large helicopter painted khaki and bearing a red star insignia.

Television mobile units had been drawn up around the White House since noon. The march had degenerated into a shapeless blob of dissident human beings, milling about in Lafayette Park. Tourists watched them indifferently at first, then with growing impatience as the protesters usurped their space and began badgering them with the news about President Stark's plan to start World War III. The tourists moved away, determined not to get involved. Only the curious stayed to listen, then to join the throng as it pushed across Pennsylvania Avenue toward the mansion on the opposite side.

The District of Columbia police had set up wooden horses to keep back the crowd that would be coming from the Capitol at the end of its march. But the police were ill-equipped to handle the vociferous thousands who now pressed toward the wrought-iron fence surrounding the Presidential mansion. From a guard post at one end of the grounds, an excited sergeant phoned in to the White House Secret Service room and told the duty officer that he needed help immediately. The Secret Service man hung up and ran to a window to gauge the extent of the emergency. He saw an unruly mass of people milling about just a few feet beyond the wooden horses in the middle of Pennsylvania Avenue. Two of the horses were already down. Police were clubbing back several protesters. The Secret Service man called for mounted patrols from the local city force. Then he sent word to Fort Myer for troops. As he talked, a policeman entered the room and handed him a pamphlet. He put down the phone and whistled in amazement. "Holy Christ, no wonder they're going wild." He ran down the hall to the Oval Room, where William Stark had just greeted Clifford Erskine.

The President had been surprised when the secretary had appeared in the outer office requesting an appointment. Erskine came in, tight-lipped and tense. He was barely courteous to the President, who asked about the demonstration over at the Pentagon.

"Mr. President, those people are sincere human beings, scared to death about losing everything we've built in this crazy world."

The President noticed the edge in Erskine's voice and replied: "I never said they weren't, Cliff. What's gotten into you today?"

"That phone call from Randall is what has gotten into me. I can't believe that you are even thinking of trying Roarke's way. And if you are, I'm here to hand over my job."

"Now wait just a minute, Cliff." The President was furious with his defense secretary. "Goddamnit, I won't allow you to go on this way. Jesus, with the whole world falling down, the last thing I need is men deserting me."

The buzzer on the intercom sounded, and a secretary announced the Secret Service man on urgent business. Stark ordered him in, and the man handed the President the pamphlet, while he explained the disorder outside. Stark's eyes opened wide in incredulity. "Where did they get this crap? he asked quickly.

"I don't know, sir, but they evidently believe it and are really looking for trouble."

The President was incensed. He jumped up from his chair and shouted: "Show them to me! Show me these people."

Erskine followed the President and the Secret Service man to an upstairs window in the family quarters. Stark pulled back the heavy white draperies and looked down on the SOUL protesters. He beheld chaos.

The guards at the White House had one overriding duty, to protect the President of the United States at all costs. When the mob had first surged up East Executive Avenue and remassed in Lafayette Park, the police had remained secure in the belief that violence was not intended. When the crowd spilled out of the park and up against the wooden horses, the police became frightened and summoned help. Before horse patrols and soldiers could appear, exasperated marchers had driven the police against the wrought-iron fence and wrestled with them at the entrances to the circular driveway leading to the front door of the White House. At that moment, the chief in charge of the White House detail ordered gas fired over the heads of the crowd. Inside the grounds, masked men had knelt, aimed, and lobbed canisters out into the street.

William Stark saw clouds of white vapor drifting across the lawn toward the mansion. In the avenue, hundreds of figures were running about madly, their hands to their eyes, handkerchiefs to their faces. Some were retching. Screams of anguish and terror reached the President's ears. He groaned: "My God."

Down below, the television networks were recording the scene. Alex Barnett of CBA News was standing on a bench in Lafayette Park commenting to listeners across the country on the extraordinary spectacle in front of the White House. Around him the battle ebbed and flowed. Barnett was describing the state of the marchers, choking and gasping on the grass. His own eyes were watering badly as the gas trailed across the street toward him. While he stood on tiptoes to get a better view, someone tugged at the cuff of his pants. It was Henry Fuller, his mouth puffed from the blow he had received earlier. Fuller was nauseated not from the gas but from the destruction of his dream. He had dragged himself from the pavement and gone back to the front of the line to restore order. But his pleas had gone unheeded. Most of the protesters had been swayed by the ugly implications of the Stark directive. The men who had first passed them out had disappeared. Their handiwork had been examined and accepted as the truth or at least as sufficiently alarming to need further explanation by the Administration. Henry Fuller, tears filling his eyes, had been cast aside.

Fuller had gone to a bench in the park and watched helplessly. When the gas came, he put a handkerchief to his face and retreated to the back edge of the green. Then he saw Barnett recording the event for millions. Fuller ran to him instinctively and grabbed at his leg for attention. Barnett looked down and asked: "Were you gassed by the police, young man?"

Fuller nodded but hastened to explain: "I'm a group leader in the demonstration. This morning we began the march, intending only to file by the White House and offer a silent protest against the Stratton-Seligsohn bill."

"And the police beat you up and gassed you?"

"No, well, yes. They gassed me, but you should know what brought it about in the first place." Fuller was struggling to be intelligible through his broken lips. The camera focused on them as the lawyer betrayed himself to the public gaze. "My name is Henry Fuller. I work for a government organization and came here today not to condemn my country but to condemn a bill which will lead to destruction of all freedoms."

Fuller was beginning to annoy Barnett, who wanted to concentrate on the frenzy eddying around them. He interrupted to ask, "Yes, and the Administration wouldn't allow a peaceful protest?"

"No, you don't understand. Somehow some radicals infiltrated us and passed out pamphlets . . ."

"Haven't you seen it?" A slim woman standing nearby, her eyes bloodshot and blinking, offered Barnett the handbill. Alex

Barnett read it aloud to the entire network while the camera closed in on a montage of clubs crashing against skulls and men and women lying in the middle of Pennsylvania Avenue, their heads seeping blood onto the roadway. When Barnett finished, he turned to the camera and said: "This is Alexander Barnett, reporting from Washington, where events of the past two days suggest that something cataclysmic is about to happen."

Six giant floodlights pinned the khaki-colored helicopter in their glare. Colonel Joe Safcek waited while his three companions boarded the craft. Luba, Peter, and Boris wore the uniforms of Soviet Army lieutenants. Their black boots were shiny with wax. Red epaulets decorated their shoulders. Safcek, impersonating a Colonel Dmitri Adzubei, put out his hand to Karl Richter.

"Karl, your briefings were superb. If we missed anything, it's our fault."

Richter's voice was low, controlled because he did not trust it. "Joe, use the radio when you can. We'll be listening in every minute."

Richter was fumbling for a final word. "And we'll be thinking of you. Good luck, Colonel."

Richter released his hand from Safcek's, and the colonel smiled and ran up the steps into the big Chinook helicopter. The door closed, and the blades whirred. Richter put his hands to his eyes to keep out the dust as the chopper leaped into the sky and disappeared to the north, its red lights blinking reassuringly.

Karl Richter watched it out of sight and suddenly the floodlights went off, and he was all alone on the runway.

Three hundred yards away, an American intelligence agent noticed a Pakistani worker at the base run furtively through the shadows to a car in the parking lot. The Pakistani got in quickly and drove to the main gate, where he showed identification and sped off toward Peshawar.

The intelligence agent eased his own car onto the road and followed the worker through the darkness. As the two cars entered the downtown area, the Pakistani slowed and parked across from a movie theater. The streets were crowded. In the crush of bodies, the agent nearly lost the Pakistani as he opened the car door and crossed the street. Then the agent saw a man standing just inside the theater entrance, staring at glossy photographs of coming attractions. The man wore European clothes. His trousers were quite baggy. The Pakistani reached him and spoke a few words. The man nodded and walked down the sidewalk. The Pakistani followed ten paces back. At the intersection the Westerner crossed and reached the other side. The Pakistani stepped out into the road.

The American agent shifted into first and pulled out sharply, twenty-five feet from the worker. He gunned the motor into second and bore down upon the startled man, who turned toward him in sudden terror. The agent closed his eyes as he hit the Pakistani squarely. An anguished scream lifted into the night, and the agent heard the sickening thud as the body bounced under his car all the way to the rear. He gripped the wheel tightly and raced around a corner. Behind him, the broken body lay mute.

The Westerner lit a small cigarette with trembling hands and puffed deeply on it while an ambulance siren moaned nearby. Then he strolled away from the murder scene.

The chopper pilot took the large craft directly north into the mountains. Beside him, a radar operator stared intently at the blue scope recording the topography. The pilot was nervous, terribly afraid of the forbidding land thrusting up at them in the stygian night. He tried to pierce the gloom with his eyes. The radar man, hypnotized by the light before him, wiped streaks of perspiration onto his fatigues.

Five feet to the rear, Joe Safcek huddled with his team in contemplative silence. The roar of the twin jet motors prevented him from speaking clearly to the Russians, who had curled up in the cramped space. Luba had her eyes closed. Pete and Boris strained ahead watching the pilot for any sign of trouble. Safcek lit a Camel and studied its ruby glow. He thought of Martha and Tommy and the neat house on the side street at Bragg. The colonel wondered what they were doing at that moment.

Like most American women, Martha Safcek was sitting in front of her television. She was aghast at the rioting taking place in Washington. Coverage had shifted from the White House briefly to the Pentagon, where tear gas and rifle shots created a scene now all too familiar to viewers.

Sharon McCandless and Tom Samuels had not wanted to get involved in any fighting. When the troops from Fort Myer formed a solid line in front of the building, they joined hundreds of others in chanting over them: "Send us Erskine. We want an answer." But that was all. The young couple did not expect anyone to come out and treat with them. If the pamphlet was a true copy, no one would admit it. If not, any denial would hardly have appeased the crowd. Sharon asked Tom to take her away. He told her to watch what happened when the time deadline expired. Thirty-one minutes after Colonel Shelton had disappeared into the Pentagon, a general emerged and asked the march leaders to disperse their people. The old man spoke through a bull-horn to the massed congregation and told them it was useless to demonstrate further. "Perhaps," he suggested, "we can go by the White House and lodge another protest." He was obviously unaware of the situation on Pennsylvania Avenue.

The crowd roared its disapproval and drowned out the old man's pleadings to disperse. The general held his hand up and pointed it straight out before him. The troops moved ahead in lock step, their bayonets thrusting at the first ranks. No one moved. The soldiers appeared irresolute, and the general shouted: "Use the butts." The soldiers turned their guns sideways and pushed forward. Someone pushed back, and the first marcher went down. Fists swung, and the general ordered: "Bring up the gas." Canisters fell into the close-packed mass, and Sharon McCandless felt pain and terror.

Like a wounded animal, SOUL dissolved into a mad stampede for safety. Rocks rained down on the soldiers. One of them, his nose broken, fired his rifle into the multitude. Sharon McCandless suddenly clutched her stomach and sank to the grass.

The girl moaned softly as Tom cradled her head in his lap. He called quietly to her, and she raised her head a little and said: "Tom, it hurts so much I . . ." The blond head fell back, and Tom Samuels hugged Sharon closer while blood soaked his pants.

A muffled cry of indignation spouted in a thousand throats: "They've killed her." The soldiers, stunned by the words, hesitated and slowed their drive. The general screamed: "Get the man who fired that weapon." It was far too late. Enraged men pounced on the troopers and wrestled them to the ground. While the dying girl's life poured out through her cotton dress, her avengers sought solace in pummeling the men who had caused

131

it. The general ran back inside the building, looking for an answer to the nightmare.

President William Stark thought he had found one answer. Profoundly shocked at the carnage out on the streets, he had called an immediate session of the elite group that had helped him in the past two days. He handed them a copy of an FBI report just delivered at the White House. It stated that five members of the Soviet Embassy staff in Washington had been followed that day, and each one had joined the march at varying points. Agents had been unable to follow them precisely after that, but all agreed that the men had carried with them large manila packages, which could easily have contained the deadly pamphlets later circulated to the demonstrators.

Stark handed his advisors soiled copies of the pamphlets. He said: "It's pretty obvious to me that the Russians are trying to cut my balls off with this. That Krylov has thought of everything."

When Martin Manson seemed not to understand, Stark continued impatiently: "He's done two things with this pamphlet. First, if we retaliate to his laser threat, he can tell the world, 'I told you so,' and I'm the worst bastard since Genghis Khan. Second, if he uses the laser on Washington and elsewhere, he can excuse it by saying it was a preventive strike against our decision to go to war." Stark pointed at the pamphlet in outrage. "This piece of phony junk will turn the world against me."

Secretary of Defense Clifford Erskine, who had already once offered his resignation and been sidetracked by the riot from pursuing the point, raised himself up in his chair and icily confronted his Commander-in-Chief: "Mr. President, that piece of junk, as you call it, may be forged, but isn't it true that you have issued an order today to prepare to bomb the Soviet Union within thirty-four hours?"

The others stiffened visibly. Unaware that Erskine and the President had had words earlier, they were unprepared for the direct challenge. Stark toyed with a pen for a moment, then glared down the table at Erskine. "Clifford, it's apparent to me that you no longer consider yourself part of the policy-making in this Administration. You made that quite apparent earlier this afternoon." Erskine stared back at him boldly.

"Therefore, I accept your resignation as of this minute."

Erskine rose from his chair, a defiant smile etching his mouth.

"For the record, Mr. President, I cannot be party to any plan to initiate a nuclear war. I would rather surrender this great country." He walked out of the room, his chin high.

President Stark did not know what to say. Sam Riordan looked at his shoes. Gerald Weinroth coughed self-consciously. Robert Randall broke the silence: "Has Safcek gotten off safely?"

Joe Safcek was riding through the most difficult terrain in the world. The Chinook helicopter was threading its way between mountains near the top of the world at an altitude of three hundred feet. Radar showed the danger clearly. Massive rock formations rose in sheer majesty on both sides of the frail craft. The pilot prayed that no violent wind drafts would throw him against them.

Safcek trusted his safety to the men up front. He smoked seven cigarettes one after the other. When he offered some to the Russians, they accepted gratefully.

Luba had never smoked before. She coughed badly on her first inhalation, and Joe pounded her back until she subsided.

She smiled gratefully and shouted above the motors: "Colonel, this is the strangest way to have a homecoming. But then I never thought I'd see any of it again, so it's better than nothing." Her smile was warm and childlike. Safcek patted her on the arm.

"Luba, did you have a boy friend in Chirchiz?"

Her face became solemn. "Avram Gurewitz and I were to be married. He was an engineer for a hydroelectric plant, and his prospects were excellent. We talked about having a large family, maybe four children. But he made one mistake. He wanted to go to Israel with me. When the authorities refused permission, Avram rebelled and started demanding freedom to do as he pleased. First, they put him in jail for a month, but he refused to give in. The next time they sent him to a labor camp for ten years. I have not seen him since."

She smoked the cigarette in quick, short puffs. "I could not stay in Russia after that. My heart was too filled with hate for those who stilled his voice." She stubbed out the cigarette and added, "Now I do what I can to bring them down." She laughed suddenly in a loud voice, which brought the other two Russians out of their restless nap.

"And what about you, Colonel? Tell me about your life."

Joe Safcek began to talk about Martha and Tommy. It pained him to think of them so much, but he talked nevertheless.

In front of him, the pilot turned sharply and said: "Sir, we have just crossed the Soviet border."

In a concrete bunker nestled into a hillside near the Volga River at Saratov, the Southern Soviet Fighter Defense Command plotted all activity in an arc from Greece to Pakistan. At a giant control map laid out on a table, a major nearing the end of his tour of duty monitored aircraft on the periphery of his country. Six American jet bombers had been recorded over

Ankara, Turkey, heading southwest, probably to Incirclik. Three Iranian night fighters were evidently practicing scrambles just north of Teheran. Nothing else had appeared on the board. The major yawned, glanced at his watch, and resumed his vigil.

In Moscow, it was a little after midnight, and Mikhail Ivanovich Darubin had retired for the night. A dispatch from the Soviet Embassy in Washington had reached him shortly before, telling of riot conditions in the enemy capital. Darubin had called Marshal Moskanko to tell him the good news, but the defense minister had given word to his secretary that he was asleep to all callers. Mikhail Darubin's last official act for the night was to order a cable sent to the embassy in Washington over Premier Krylov's name. The timetable called for it.

In his Kremlin apartment Premier Vladimir Krylov, however, was not asleep. He had put on a bathrobe and kissed his wife good night before going into the sitting room to do some paperwork. Krylov pulled a small box down from a bookshelf and took out a long-stemmed clay pipe and a compact mound of a brown substance. He flaked off several pieces of the mound with a knife and put them into the bowl of the pipe. Then he lighted it and lay down on a sofa to relax. As he sucked on the stem, inhaling deeply, Krylov began to feel light-headed. The room swam drowsily around him. The lamplight turned into a kaleidoscope playing in his head. He felt suddenly twice his normal size, and he was accepting the plaudits of a crowd in Red Square. They were waving their hands up at him, and he was acknowledging their adulation with sober dignity. To Krylov, the Presidium members standing beside him were midgets, obsequious and fawning. He did not like them.

The euphoric Krylov inhaled steadily on the pipe, and the sweetish aroma wafted through the room. His eyes glazed, and the pipe drooped in his fingers. Atop Lenin's tomb in his reverie,

Vladimir Nikolaievich Krylov did not notice when the pipe filled with hashish fell to the sofa and from there to the floor.

Mounted policemen had taken over Pennsylvania Avenue. The clouds of tear gas had been dissipated among the trees of Lafayette Park. For two blocks around the seat of government, men with guns barricaded all approaches to William Stark. Casualties had been taken to the hospital. Fourteen policemen had been badly beaten. One was given the last rites of the Roman Catholic Church. Henry Fuller had helped pick up some of the marchers. The priest who had earlier defied him had been found in a gutter, his skull fractured by a horse's hoof. At least fifty men and women had shed blood. Hundreds were gassed into violent sickness. A depressed Fuller had urged his people to go home and forget their crusade for the time being. Most laughed at him, but they wandered away from the arena, cursing the man behind the draperies in the Executive Wing. For his part, William Stark cursed their gullibility.

It had brought the wrath of millions down on him. Telegrams were flooding into the White House from irate Americans, condemning him for allowing the marchers to be beaten and demanding the truth about the pamphlet. The president of France had called, seeking Washington's position. So had London and Bonn. The premier of Japan had cabled for clarification.

At 4:27 P.M., four men emerged from the White House and were accosted by reporters. They were the leaders of the Senate and House of Representatives. Representative Jonas Ingram spoke for the group and said the President had assured them

136

that the pamphlet was the work of cranks, intent on spoiling the march. His face grave, Ingram refused to say any more. The white-haired statesman did not mention the awesome news he and the others had been told in the Oval Room. William Stark had shown them the Soviet ultimatum and explained the desperate mission Colonel Safcek had been sent on. Stark had told them the pamphlet was undoubtedly the work of Soviet intelligence trying to paralyze both the country and Stark. Jonas Ingram and the Congressional delegation went away from the besieging reporters with heavy hearts.

The chopper was out of the mountain passes and scudding low over a vast plain, almost desert, which rimmed the southern part of the Soviet Union. Here, in the cradle of ancient civilization, where Genghis Khan and Tamerlane had ruled for centuries with dripping swords, the pilot had no worry about flying into a natural obstacle. Though now at 150 feet altitude, he was more concerned about possible detection from nearby fighter bases. The radar operator tuned to frequencies supplied earlier by National Security Agency tapes. The frequencies were quiet. Only static filled the cabin of the helicopter. No lights appeared beneath the helicopter. The course had been plotted to avoid any settlements in the barren landscape. If a nomadic herdsman heard the rumble of the chopper it did not matter to the crew or Joe Safcek and his team in back.

The pilot checked his instruments, then his watch, and called: "Twenty-five minutes to landing zone, sir." Safcek checked his own watch and grunted in satisfaction. He leaned over to Peter Kirov and signaled. The Russians followed him to the rear.

At 5 P.M. in Washington, a cablegram was transmitted into the Soviet Embassy on 16th Street NW. Behind the tudor facade of the mansion, which fronted almost directly on the bustling street, a code clerk rushed upstairs with it to Ambassador Tolypin, who examined it and issued terse orders. Within minutes, the entire staff had dropped their ordinary chores and began packing embassy property into hugh cartons. Behind the building, men scurried to limousines to ready them for service. In the basement, several women threw documents into a vast incinerator roaring with flame. One of the packages tossed to the fire contained the last of the pamphlets bearing William Stark's bogus signature.

In an office building across the street, FBI agents noticed unusual activity as three employees of the embassy hurried out and trundled away lawn-cutting machines from the grounds. The FBI agent in charge trained his binoculars on the windows, usually heavily curtained but now wide open to his gaze.

At Fort Meade, Maryland, a cryptographer was handed the coded text of the Soviet cablegram received minutes earlier by a listening post. He stared at it and grinned: "Christ, this one's easy. We broke this baby five years ago, and they haven't used it since. They must be kidding."

In fifteen minutes he had the answer before him and, shaken, called for his supervisor on the double. The supervisor took one look at the text and called the White House. Robert Randall answered. He wrote down the message and asked for confirmation immediately by courier. Then he took the elevator to the new swimming pool in the basement, where Stark was doing the Australian crawl in solitary splendor. When Randall came to the edge of the pool, Stark asked; "What now?" Randall wasted no time on preliminaries. Glancing at the sheet of yellow paper he carried, he gave Stark the bad news. "NSA has intercepted this."

EVACUATE EMBASSY WITHIN NEXT TWENTY-FOUR HOURS. MOVE HEADQUARTERS TO UN MISSION. DESTROY ALL UNNECESSARY MATERIAL. BEYOND TIME PERIOD CANNOT GUARANTEE YOUR SAFETY.

KRYLOV

The chopper was just two minutes from the landing zone. In the cockpit, the pilot threw a switch and a brilliant light beamed down to the ground from one hundred feet. A ribbon of road was caught in the glare. No car headlights were visible in either direction. The light was doused immediately. Engine power was reduced, and the craft settled lower in the sky. At 3:47 A.M., Central Asian time, the pilot felt the wheels touch and landing lights flashed in the cabin. He raised his right hand and shoved his thumb upward. In the rear, Joe Safcek turned a key and backed a Russian Army car out the lowered rear ramp. Once clear of the large craft, he pulled up beside the cockpit and raised his left arm out the driver's window. Then he drove off a hundred yards to avoid the whirlwind of the chopper rotors. In thirty seconds, the craft vaulted into the sky and swung away to the southeast. Safcek wheeled the car onto the main road fifty feet away and headed for Tashkent, sixty miles to the west. Behind him the desert was empty of all life. In the sky, two twinkling red lights glowed for a moment, then were lost to view.

At Peshawar, Karl Richter was distraught. Informed that the intelligence agent had pursued and killed a Pakistani spy, Richter had to assume that he might have passed on information about the flight in his very brief conversation with the man at the movie house. Even a few words hurriedly exchanged could have given the enemy inexpert knowledge of Safcek's coming. Richter was doubly troubled because he should have heard from the pilot as soon as Safcek left the plane. Thirty minutes had gone by beyond the projected touchdown, and Richter went to the radio to inform President Stark of the problem.

At 4:18 A.M., the receiver crackled, and through the static Richter heard the phrase: "Troika, troika." Then the transmission abruptly faded. Richter had heard what he wanted. He told the White House that Joe Safcek was on the road to Tashkent.

In the Oval Room, President Stark thanked Richter and considered the wreckage of the day. His nightmare had been going on for forty-two hours; it could all be over in thirty more. The Russians had divided the country by inciting the marchers. Only the fact that Safcek was inside the enemy camp gave him any reason for hope.

Clifford Erskine had one last job. In his office on E Ring, the former Secretary of Defense called Steve Roarke to him and told the general he had resigned his job. Roarke, stunned, told Erskine he was sorry to see such a thing happen. Erskine continued cleaning his papers from a drawer while Roarke tried to think of something else to say. A lethal silence prevailed until Erskine looked up from his belongings and asked: "General, what were the casualty figures outside the Pentagon today?"

Roarke had the figures at hand. "One woman dead, twelve soldiers and civilians in critical condition, forty-five walking wounded."

Erskine shook his head sadly. "Christ almighty. All because one fool fired a gun into innocent people."

Roarke bristled: "Innocent, my ass. Those marchers are all alike, whether they're kids or middle-aged. They may think they're patriotic, but let me tell you something. Most of them follow a pattern. Going back to 1939 and the Russo-Finnish war, this type has rooted for the wrong side. Mannerheim of Finland was merely a fascist; Stalin's fight with them was legitimate. Only in World War Two, when the Russkies needed help, did certain of these people agree with the American government. After that we've had nothing but a pattern of marches, riots, and disorders. Most of them still believe Alger Hiss was bagged by the FBI. The Rosenbergs are still martyrs. And then the Vietnam thing was a disgrace. Just remember those Vietcong flags waving about in the breeze. They paralyzed Lyndon Johnson and ruined us in Southeast Asia."

Erskine had finished packing his papers. "Just a minute, Steve, I happen to agree with those people about Vietnam. Are you calling me a Commie?"

"Not at all. I'm not saying that. Many responsible Americans felt we were wrong in Vietnam, and I myself blame Lyndon Johnson for his handling of it. What I am saying is that most of these liberals are naive human beings. And a hard core of malcontents has always led them down the path of righteousness by conjuring up plots by whatever administration is in power. They're still trying to prove that Jack Kennedy was killed by a rightist plot, or the CIA, or by anybody except Oswald. And then today, that goddamn pamphlet. They were willing to believe that within minutes. I wonder what they'd say if they knew the other side was threatening to burn them up by tomorrow night. Probably that we brought it on ourselves."

"You know, General, you may have just hit on the truth. If we hadn't sickened the people over Vietnam and Asia, you might still have their confidence. If we hadn't been so hypocritical in supporting dictators and so ready to export democracy to the far corners of the earth, you'd probably still have enough money to keep even with the Russians on research. But no, we had to plunge in here and there to shore up the dams against communism, and the bulk of the American public finally got tired of the waste of lives and money and said 'Stop!'

"What made this country think we had any right to force our way of life on others? We can't even solve our own domestic problems, and we may be right around the corner from a bloody revolution. Who are we to act as policeman of the world? If we're in trouble today with that laser, it's quite possible that your way of thinking helped put us in that fix."

Incensed, General Roarke tried to interrupt, but the secretary waved his hand for silence.

"Don't bother to argue with me. We're worlds apart."

Clifford Erskine was suddenly very tired. He was sick of arguing with Roarke, sick of Washington. His breastbone ached. His left arm was riddled with pain. He rose from his seat for the last time, thought of shaking hands with Roarke but rejected it. Instead he said "Good-bye" curtly and stepped to the door. At the threshhold, he caught his breath sharply and staggered from the intense pain in his chest. Erskine tried to say something to Roarke, but the words were cut off as he fell dead in front of the General's polished shoes.

Only three trucks passed the Soviet Army car as it moved leisurely toward Tashkent. Joe Safcek was exhilarated, as he always was on such a mission. His mind was clear, his reflexes highly acute. Safcek had noticed that the other members of the team were also exhilarated, perhaps just because they were back in their native land. Though aware that they were facing instant death if found, they were nonetheless happy to return. Even Peter Kirov had become voluble. Withdrawn most of the time since Safcek had met him, Peter rode through the darkness telling of his youth in Volgograd, formerly Stalingrad, the site of the greatest German defeat in World War II. While Safcek watched the road for traffic, Peter told his companions of the many days he spent fishing on the Volga and of the ice floes that came down the great waterways in January to make a giant land bridge across to Krasnaya Sloboda. Peter's eyes sparkled as he dwelt on those days, and his white teeth flashed as he suddenly pounded Boris on the back. "We should have some vodka here to celebrate being home."

Gorlov winced from the blow but managed to smile warmly at his confederate. "Soon enough, Peter. When we blow that laser sky high."

Luba, sitting beside Joe, was suddenly grim. Her close-cropped hair neatly covered under a garrison cap, she turned to the window and stared at the impenetrable darkness. Safcek noticed a streak of light crowding the night sky and checked the mileage gauge. "Only twenty kilometers to our first stop. We should hit it just about dawn." Luba did not react.

In the President's sitting room, William Stark talked earnestly to Herbert Markle, Commissioner of Natural Gas Utilities. He had known Herb Markle for twenty years, since the time when both were freshman congressmen. When Stark became President, he appointed Markle to head the commission overseeing an industry spreading its pipelines under every major city in the United States. Stark spoke for nearly thirty minutes to the puzzled Markle, who listened raptly to his friend and took notes on a small memo pad. Finally Stark shook hands with him and cautioned: "Herb, no matter what happens, remember I know what I'm doing. Trust me." Herb Markle left the White House quickly, and jumped into a waiting limousine before reporters could guess his identity.

Upstairs, William Stark paused to change into a fresh shirt and tie. He combed back his graying hair and washed his face with a cold facecloth. Feeling slightly restored, he went to the elevator and rode down to the Oval Room. While the Bagman took up his accustomed position outside, Stark greeted Randall, Riordan and Manson. Weinroth was missing. His ulcer had finally hemorrhaged. Roarke was unaccountably delayed. Stark went to his chair and made himself comfortable. Martin Manson noticed that the President's hands were quite steady. The Secretary of State thought it remarkable how the President was holding up.

Stark began by exploring the previous hours. "We've had a helluva day, gentlemen, and I'm afraid it's going to get a lot worse. I'm happy some of you are still with me." The trio laughed quietly while he continued: "At ten A.M. tomorrow morning, I am going to begin evacuating the capital of all inhabitants not expressly needed to maintain vital functions."

Manson asked: "What in God's name for, Mr. President?"

Stark looked patiently at him. "Because I have to believe that the Russians will use the laser on us tomorrow night." And he added, "I'm not going to leave nearly a million people as sitting ducks."

Robert Randall broke in: "Why don't we go on the air and tell the people the truth about the Reds? Maybe we could condemn them in front of the world and force their hand."

"No. I've thought about that long and hard. All along we've tried not to rock the boat, not to do anything that might make that unstable government go crazy. That's why we sent Safcek

144

in instead of just blowing it up as Roarke said we should."
Stark was adamant. "For me to go on television now might
drive the Russians to all-out war. And their excuse could be
that they believed the story contained in that damn pamphlet."

Sam Riordan added: "Speaking of the Russians, my men say
they're pulling out of the embassy up the way as if the devil's
chasing them."

"It figures," said Stark. "Perhaps it's only a war of nerves,
but I can't take the chance they're bluffing. I've got to believe
they mean to burn the city."

"Mr. President, what reason will you give the people for evacuation? I mean, once the country gets wind of this, you might
have a general panic, especially after what happened here today
with the riots."

"Martin, it's all taken care of. Don't worry. We're going to
have a good gimmick for an official story that makes sense.
It should be enough to get the folks moving."

Stark spread his hands out toward his advisors. His voice
almost pleading for understanding, he said: "Look, we have
little more than a day left to work this out. I haven't told the
Israelis what happened to them, so they wouldn't try to retaliate.
I haven't told the Allies because what they don't know won't
hurt them. And I won't tell the American people for the reasons
I just gave you. We agreed days ago to stall for time until Safcek
could get there and eliminate the weapon. For God's sake, let's
hold on to our nerves for a while."

The men with him shifted their feet uncomfortably. Stark
mussed his carefully combed hair with his hand. "How about
a drink to our man in Tashkent?"

As they prepared to adjourn, General Stephen Austin Roarke
came into the room slowly and approached the President. The
general was unaccountably somber, almost in shock.

"Mr. President," he said, "I have some very bad news. Cliff
Erskine just dropped dead at the Pentagon."

145

Four men sucked in their breaths at the same time, and Stark reeled back from the general.

"Oh no, Steve, oh no." Stark sat down again and looked wildly about as he tried to assimilate the news. "How did it happen?"

Roarke told the group the main details, leaving out his argument with the secretary. "And his wife, does she know?" Stark asked.

"We just cabled the American Embassy in London to tell her. She stayed on there after Cliff left for Geneva. The Ambassador will take care of her."

Stark nodded absently. "God, I feel it's all my fault after what happened here today. I'd never had a disagreement with him before, and then this fight over the laser. Did he say anything to you about me."

"No, he didn't. He was just cleaning out his desk and never mentioned you as far as any personal feelings."

Stark murmured something about seeing everyone later and hurried out to tell Pamela the dreadful news.

Joe Safcek had arrived at his first destination. As the desert sky filled with an incredibly beautiful blend of rose and violet hues he turned the automobile off the main road onto a dirt trail one mile outside the sprawling city. Half a mile into the dusty plain, the members of Operation Scratch saw their rendezvous, an eleventh-century mosque, abandoned for hundreds of years and long fallen into decay. Two minarets rose from the roof. The circular dome was nearly intact, except for a small hole near the middle. The dome was a shimmering azure blue, which reflected the sunrise and lent an ethereal grandeur to the setting.

As Safcek approached it, he wished for a moment that Martha could share it with him. Then he turned off the road, pulled the car around to the rear of the building, and saw what he wanted. One of the basement rooms of the mosque had sagged outward, crumbling the wall and leaving a gaping hole leading directly into the interior. Safcek manhandled the car over several small rocks and jockeyed it inside. Only the rear fender remained in the sunlight. The colonel jumped out, rummaged inside a bag and took out shoe polish which he rubbed over the chrome fender to eliminate glare. He opened the trunk, urging, "Let's get this stuff inside and get ready for work." Kirov and Gorlov started pulling equipment out. Luba watched them carefully for a moment, then went over to a slim box. She took it by its handles and raising it effortlessly, moved toward the gloomy cellar.

Safcek rushed to help her. "Careful, Luba, that little devil is more important than all of us." She was carrying the atomic bomb.

As though struck dumb by the awesome material in her arms, Luba just murmured: "OK, OK." Safcek wondered whether her nerves were bothering her.

Sixteen miles due north of the bomb and its guardians, the Soviet police held a man at bay. Andrei Parchuk, the director of the laser center, was surrounded in his office by four state security men, specially sent from the Center in Moscow. He had been held under house arrest until they arrived at 2 A.M. They had now been badgering him for nearly four hours. Parchuk wanted desperately to sleep, but they would not let him alone. They had forced him to stand while they asked him

147

about Grigor Rudenko and the blueprints Parchuk had given him. Parchuk denied everything.

Andrei Parchuk was a member of the prestigious Soviet Academy of Sciences. He was also a controversial figure. Five years before, he had sent a letter to the Presidium demanding the release from prison of several Soviet intellectuals jailed for writing articles against the régime. For this act, Parchuk had suffered harassment from the state security police, who warned him that further protests would result in banishment from his chair at the university and possible imprisonment. Parchuk never again spoke out publicly against the Kremlin.

The elderly scientist was afraid. He knew they might beat him, and he was certain he could not stand up to it. Parchuk had heard of notorious methods used to elicit information from suspects. He realized that Rudenko must have broken and that Rudenko was a far stronger man than he.

The state security men had scrupulously avoided touching the director to that moment. Parchuk had sparred with them intellectually, feinting and stalling, trying to avoid any damning admission. As sunlight flooded against the window, the interrogators pursued him relentlessly.

"When were you last in Moscow, Professor?"

"Let me see, it was around the sixth of September, for two days. But you can check that easily by referring to my schedule here."

"And what did you do there?"

"I was summoned to a meeting of the Presidium. Marshal Moskanko wished to confirm some aspects of my initial report on the first test-firing of the laser. He conducted a lengthy seminar on the implications of the weapon in the struggle with the West."

"Where did you stay, Professor, while you were in the city?"

"At the Rossia. I have receipts from there if you want to see them."

"Did you get to do any shopping?"

Parchuk hesitated briefly. He looked at the grim-faced men before him and lied: "No, I didn't have any time for that."

"You didn't go to the GUM store at all?"

Parchuk was frightened as they tried to corner him.

"No, I had no free time."

One security officer rose from his chair, walked swiftly over to Parchuk, and slapped him on the cheek. The scientist covered himself with his hands, while his eyes filled with tears. The security man hovered over him menacingly. "You are nothing but trouble Parchuk. We have been watching you for years."

Parchuk shook his head while trying to compose himself. The security officer pried his hands loose from his face and with one powerful blow broke his jaw. Parchuk fell to the floor, unconscious.

"Pick the bastard up and take him to Moscow. We'll show him to Rudenko and see what he says then." Parchuk was dragged out of his office and hoisted into the back seat of a car.

In the compound of scientists' homes, several curtains parted to watch the abduction. Behind one, a man cursed as he saw Parchuk shoved unconscious into the black government car. The man clutched the drapes in his fist until the car drove off at high speed. He went to the kitchen table, put his head down, and sobbed in anguish at losing part of his life.

The man was Anatoly Serkin, a thin-faced, bespectacled, thirty-eight-year-old physicist. He was Parchuk's protégé, his prize pupil. They had met at Leningrad Government University, where Parchuk held a chair in quantum physics and optics. Parchuk liked the intense, volatile Serkin, partly because the younger man was struggling under the burden of supporting a wife and a child while attempting to earn his doctorate. Serkin and his wife, Nadia, lived in a one-room apartment with a bed in the middle of the floor and children's toys scattered everywhere. When Serkin invited Parchuk to dinner one night, the professor was deeply touched at the way the young couple tried to please him. He was even more impressed when he sat down at the pink table that served for every meal. His steaming bowl of soup fell off the shaky leaf onto his lap. After a moment's shock, Parchuk began to laugh uproariously while the embarrassed couple mopped the floor and his suit. The accident dissolved any social barriers between the hosts and their guest. After brandy, coffee, and Prokofiev's Symphony Number 3, played on Serkin's decrepit record machine, the professor left the dingy apartment happy for the first time in months. His wife had been a victim of the Nazi massacre at Kharkov, and Parchuk had been a very lonely man for all the long years since. Childless, he had only memories of a wonderful woman to sustain him in his twilight. It was not enough. Though he wrapped himself in a protective cocoon of books, music, and research, Parchuk needed people to talk with, to listen to him, and care for him. The Serkins provided that during the next years.

When, more in tribute to his scientific brilliance than his politics, the Presidium of the Soviet Union bestowed the leadership of the laser program on Parchuk, he took Dr. Serkin with him to Tashkent. All scientists were confined to a restricted area, but the authorities tried to make life there as pleasant as possible. Each family had its own home. Food was plentiful. Recreation, though limited, was available. The Serkins and their child, Galina, loved the desert and the very infrequent trips into the city of Tashkent, where they examined vestiges of the Mongol and Tartar cultures that had made Tashkent a world-famous capital.

Parchuk was absorbed in his work and rarely left the grounds. But nearly every evening he wandered over to the Serkins for dinner. He and Anatoly would talk of Dostoyevsky and Gorki and of the exciting advances being made around the world in their specialty. For each it was a safety valve from the pressures imposed on them by officials demanding results on the laser.

It was Parchuk and Serkin who solved the greatest problem connected with the laser, controlling the diffusion of the concentration of light once it encountered the ionosphere layer. When the two men worked out the theoretical approach to containing the intense beam, it was merely a matter of time before the Russians managed to test-fire a prototype into a forest in Siberia near Irkutsk.

Elated with the results, Parchuk went to Moscow to report progress to the Presidium. After that first trip, he came back to Tashkent deeply troubled. The Soviet marshals had indicated great interest in the offensive capabilities of the laser. When he was summoned to Moscow the next time, he took the blueprints and other data with him, not telling anyone, not even Serkin, what he was thinking of doing with them. It was on that second trip that Marshal Moskanko, the Soviet defense minister, had ordered him to annihilate the Israeli atomic center as a first step in world domination. The next target would be the United States of America. Parchuk and Serkin had never thought their creation might be used to enslave the world. They had believed the laser was just a defensive weapon, and had not reckoned with the Soviet military leaders. On his second day in Moscow that time, Parchuk got in touch with the only man he felt he could trust in such a situation, Grigor Rudenko, husband of his niece, Tamara.

He returned to Tashkent with equal feelings of grief and guilt. When they aimed the laser into the Sinai and killed more than a thousand human beings, Parchuk felt too ashamed to face Serkin. The younger man, too, was appalled at what they had done.

Now Parchuk was gone, and Serkin wept for him on the kitchen table. Nadia found him there when she came to make breakfast. She collapsed when he told her what had happened to their dearest friend. While Nadia tried to recover, Anatoly

Serkin went to his record player and put on Prokofiev's Third Symphony, Parchuk's favorite.

Joe Safcek liked his hideout. In exploring the mosque, he had found a subterranean vault, containing the remains of warriors and holy men from centuries past. They had been laid to rest in scooped-out caverns in the walls. Safcek unceremoniously moved fragments of bone to one side and tenderly placed the rectangular package holding the atomic bomb.

While he surveyed the rest of the building, Luba and Peter laid out their collection of handguns and automatic rifles. On the second floor, Boris set up the radio, which had an effective range of six hundred miles.

At 8 A.M., Safcek returned and said: "We couldn't have found a better place. No traffic outside. At about one we'll take a scouting trip. In the meantime, why don't we relax a bit? Anything to eat, Luba?"

Luba, who had not regained her former vivacity, busied herself getting cartons of rations from a knapsack. She handed them out to the men without a word and went back to a corner, where she eased down onto the dirt floor and opened up her breakfast. Joe Safcek munched his cold rations slowly and asked Luba for some coffee. She got up again and started to prepare it over a tiny field stove. When it was offered to him, Safcek smiled at the girl and asked, "Something on your mind I should know about?"

She hesitated for just a moment, then shook her head and went back to her position. Joe watched her settle down and then drank the strong coffee slowly. It burned his tongue but he liked it too much to care. Safcek tried to ignore Luba's moodiness while he mentally arranged the next hours in his mind.

Friday,
September 13

WASHINGTON

MOSCOW

TASHKENT

IN the Atlantic Ocean, the Soviet task force had not slowed its progress toward the east coast of the United States. For the first fifty hours of the ultimatum period, the twenty-two ships had maintained strict radio silence to avoid eavesdropping by American units shepherding them nervously westward. By a form of gentlemen's agreement, each force had left the other alone.

They were companions on a strange odyssey. Unwelcome, the Russians nevertheless plodded onward into the territorial waters adjacent to America's heavily populated seaboard. American officers on the shadowing escorts had no idea what the Soviet plans were, but strict orders from the White House forbade any interference with the invading host.

At 1:54 A.M., the Soviet cruiser *Kutuzov* broke radio silence:

> Arrival Montauk area 2000 hours tomorrow. Will be prepared to receive envoys any time after that hour.

The message, directed to Soviet Naval HQ, Kronstadt, was sent in ordinary Morse code.

Astounded American eavesdroppers forwarded the wording to the Situation Room of the White House for further analysis.

At 2:06 A.M., William Stark was awakened by the ring of his bedside telephone. He had taken two sleeping pills to allow him to get some rest before the frenzy of what might be his last day, but the phone intruded immediately on his forced slumber. When informed of the intercepted message, Stark was strangely cool. He thanked the duty officer and told him to pass the text on to Randall when he arrived at seven A.M. The bewildered colonel agreed and hung up. Stark lay back on the pillow. When Pamela asked what was wrong, he shrugged. "The other side is trying to ruin my catnap, that's all." He put the light out and went back to sleep.

On the other side of the world, in the dry heat of midday in the Uzbek Soviet Socialist Republic, the Operation Scratch team was about to move out on its first reconnaissance of the laser works. Joe Safcek sent Peter outside to bury evidence of their visit to the mosque. Luba rushed to help Kirov, and the two agents carried out the garbage of the first few hours—ration boxes, ammunition cases, and rifle cratings.

On the desert, in the shadow of the mosque, Kirov quickly dug a hole and dropped in the telltale signs of their presence.

When the last spadeful of earth was carefully smoothed over, Luba wandered away into the shimmering heat. Peter called to her, but she kept walking, and he ran to catch up.

She smiled as he came alongside.

"It's so beautiful out here."

"You lived nearby, didn't you?" he asked.

"Yes, to the north and east," and she pointed past the white-walled huts and the modern apartment buildings barely visible on the horizon. "My mother is up there now, and I can almost hear her singing as she cooks."

Luba had stopped smiling.

"It's so terrible not to be able to see her."

"I know just how you feel, Luba. I feel that way myself now and then, about my own home."

She brightened. "I know your city. My father took me there when I was sixteen. We stayed with my aunt in Beketovka."

"Beketovka, sure. I lived about three miles north of there in the suburbs of Volgograd. Did you ever climb Mamaev?"

"That's the memory I treasure most from that summer. I can still hear the funeral music in the rotunda of the mass grave."

"And the granite fist coming up from the floor and holding the eternal flame?"

"Oh, God, yes. It's so moving and yet so depressing. All those bodies in there, just wasted lives."

They had walked nearly a quarter mile into the vastness of the parched plain. Behind them the crumbling blue dome of the mosque stood serenely under the glare of the sun.

"One other place I remember well," she said, "is the grain elevator on the south side of the town. The guide told us that forty men had been holed up in there for weeks before the last one was captured. It's incredible when you see that place now to imagine that any such horror story ever took place. The grain is being stored as before. Workmen swarm around it. I could not really believe that so many died there."

Kirov shook his head. "You can tell, Luba, if you get up close. The bullet holes are everywhere in the cement silos. Some have been filled in, but I guess they got tired at some point and left the rest."

Luba stared at Peter in calculated appraisal. "You're right, absolutely right. I forgot about the holes. They really are the only clue."

She stopped abruptly and began to retrace her steps to the mosque. Surprised at this sudden move, Peter hastily turned and rejoined her. Luba had taken off her hat and was now combing her fingers through her short blond hair.

"I heard you talking to Boris about the winters in Volgograd," she continued. "What's it like when the Volga ices over?"

"Well, its funny. The Volga isn't like most of our rivers.

First, the ice comes down from the north in little chunks. Then bigger floes appear and make navigation almost impossible. But because the river runs so far south it isn't until January that the ice crashes together and forms a solid mass. From then until spring you can walk across and, if you want, even fish through the ice. It's very beautiful then."

"In January, it freezes?"

"Right. Up until that time the river is filled with dangerous chunks of ice moving south."

They had reached the mosque, and Luba had retreated once again into a moody silence. Peter stooped, picked a wildflower from the ground, and handed it to her. She took it without comment and re-entered the subterranean chamber, where Safcek waited.

The colonel had just finished marking an alternate route on a map, in case the primary road to the laser was unaccountably blocked. Safcek was furious. His blue eyes narrowed as he confronted Kirov and Luba.

"Where the hell have you two been? I sent you out to do a simple job, and it takes you nearly thirty minutes."

Peter rushed to explain, while Luba stood silent with the wildflower dangling from her hand.

"We just walked around a little bit, talking about the old days."

"Old days, my ass. Today is all that counts for us. What if someone had seen you? Or did that even occur to you?"

Safcek folded the map and stormed out to the car. Peter followed sheepishly, while Boris Gorlov snuffed out a candle and took it with him.

Without a word, Luba walked to the front of the car and got in beside Safcek, who rammed the car into reverse and backed out of the hiding place.

All wore their regulation Soviet Army uniforms. Each had forged identification papers, signifying name, rank, and serial number in the Soviet Army. On another paper was noted their general specialty in the army and their current assignments. Ostensibly, the four were on detached duty from a training camp near Bukhara to observe troop activities at a base forty miles north of Tashkent in the same direction as the laser works.

Safcek drove slowly, confidently, onto the main road into Tashkent. Only one car saw them pull onto the highway from the dirt trail. Its occupants did not slow to observe them.

The colonel's stomach rolled slightly as he headed into the sprawling metropolis. It was his first view of Tashkent, capital of Uzbekistan. Richter had filled him in briefly on the plane about this almost legendary city of more than one million people drawn from all over the Soviet Union. Only twelve percent were European Russians. The rest were a mixture of ancient races, the Kirghiz, Tajiks, and, like Luba's mother, the Uzbeks, descendants of Tamerlane and Genghis Khan, who once ruled the circle of their world from this hub.

The city was an oasis surrounded by cracked and scorched desert. Here in the Chirchiz River valley, the Soviet government had brought to flower a green carpet on the arid earthen floor of Central Asia. They had constructed apartment houses, government buildings, cotton-harvester plants, and tractor factories, even a huge stadium and a museum of history. Because of earthquakes, no building was higher than five stories, but there were thousands of them rising in the midst of forested parks and giant lanes of rose bushes.

The tension of being out in the midst of an enemy host gripped Safcek, but he remembered his days in Hanoi. He had survived that encounter, he told himself, and could survive this one. He reached his hand out to Luba and squeezed her arm softly. "Act like a tourist, young lady." For the first time in hours, she smiled back at him.

The streets were suddenly congested with vehicular traffic. The old Tashkent and the new Soviet society blended swiftly into a blurred montage of incredible Oriental beauty and stark modern architecture. Citizens mingled in western and eastern dress. From the desert, men and women in flowing robes and burnooses brushed against their countrymen from European Russia. Safcek maneuvered through this mainstream, calculating from memory the route he had been given at Peshawar. He kept watching for Soviet Army roadblocks or checkpoints, but guessed that in the bustling center of Tashkent he would not have to pass any inspections or close scrutiny. He was right. In thirty minutes, Safcek had gone through the city and reached the northern highway leading to the laser works and beyond.

Six miles southwest of Washington, D.C., a station wagon drove slowly through the dead of night along a side road. Inside, a man dressed in coveralls was using a pencil flashlight to read a map. He spoke rapidly to the driver: "Frank, according to this, we should stop about fifty feet ahead."

The driver nodded and edged to the side of the road near a clump of trees. The men stomped through tall grass until they came to a dip in the ground. "Here we are, Frank." The flashlight roved over the map one last time as he made sure. "Put the stuff right in the middle of the hollow."

Frank bent down and dug into the soil with a spade. He scooped out a hole eighteen inches deep and placed a satchel charge in it.

The men went on in a straight line another fifty feet, and Frank dug again. He put another satchel in the second hole. Then the two men walked casually back to the station wagon. They drove toward Washington until the driver spoke: "Mr.

Markle, we're far enough away now." Herbert Markle, the Commissioner of Natural Gas Utilities, pulled a small black box out from under the seat, checked it for a moment and then pressed a red button. Behind them the sky filled with fire, and in seconds, the sound of an awesome explosion rocked the car. More explosions, bigger than the first, followed with triphammer velocity. The night was suddenly daylight around them.

The commissioner growled: "Hurry, Frank. I have to go home and check in with the boss."

The desert still surrounded the Operation Scratch team, but the flat plain had given way somewhat to grassy rolling hills dotted with occasional trees and patches of wildflowers. Joe Safcek watched the mileage gauge carefully, and from time to time he glanced through the right side of the windshield. Eleven miles north of Tashkent, Boris Gorlov pointed suddenly and exclaimed: "Off there in the valley." Then they all saw the cluster of brick buildings nestled between two low hills that nearly shielded it from a casual passerby.

Safcek drove on until a following car passed him. With the road clear in both directions, he suddenly pulled over, jumped out, and shouted: "Follow me, Luba." Nodding to Boris, the colonel added: "Make it look good, fellas," and he plunged down the embankment to a culvert beside the road. He made a mental note of it as a good place to leave the car that night.

Peter Kirov immediately went to the right rear tire, knelt down, and unscrewed the air-pressure covering. Then he put the eraser end of a pencil against the valve and held it there while the tire slowly flattened.

161

Boris opened the trunk and took out a spare, jack, and nut remover. He put them down beside Peter and sank onto the grass to have a cigarette. Peter looked up and down the road once more, saw no one approaching, and joined his partner.

Safcek and Luba had reached a low hillock two hundred yards in from the highway. They lay side by side inches from the crest. The colonel peered over. "Give me my glasses, Luba." She reached into a bag and pulled out a pair of field binoculars. which Safcek trained on the valley floor a mile and a half away. The laser complex leaped up at him.

While Luba wrote furiously on a small pad, Safcek analyzed the enemy before him.

"The main road circles up to the gate from my left. The gate itself has three men on it, all armed with AK-47s. There's a fence maybe ten feet high running around the camp on all sides. Probably electrically charged judging from the wires on the top. Let's see." Safcek shifted his gaze. "The big building has forty or fifty soldiers walking their posts. To the left are a row of homes, the scientists', Richter figured. It looks pretty peaceful in that section at least."

The colonel focused away from the camp to find further security measures. Under a clump of trees he saw two trucks with SAM surface-to-air missiles on their backs. In front of the gate, he noticed a gully running perhaps two hundred yards out toward the highway. It was the bed of an old stream, dried up years before. Safcek examined the gully for several minutes, noting the natural cover it seemed to afford anyone approaching the installation. Then he whispered: "Luba, they have dogs out on patrol." He was following a guard walking carefully along the gully floor while holding a hound of indeterminate extraction on a leash. The guard stopped finally, turned, and went back up the gully toward the main gate. Luba grabbed Safcek's arm and pointed.

The roof of the big building was swinging back from its

162

moorings. A siren began to moan in the distance. In two minutes the black interior of the laser works was exposed, but Safcek could not see clearly into the depths. As he cursed his luck, the enormous barrel of the secret weapon emerged and probed the sky. At least fifty feet of it was naked to the colonel's inspection and he scanned it carefully. "There's a line of concentric rings spaced a foot apart all the way down. The gun is made of some sort of silver metal. And the aperture at the front is approximately fifty feet in diameter."

The siren sounded again, and the laser slowly retreated into its lair. The roof slid back into place, and Joe Safcek was finished with his observations. "That's a dress rehearsal for tomorrow's firing, I imagine." They dropped back from the crest and started toward the car.

Boris and Peter were hard at work. Seeing a car bearing down on them from the north, they had begun fixing the tire. Peter was unscrewing the nuts from the wheel, while Boris stared diffidently at the automobile, which slowed and suddenly pulled over to the opposite side of the road. Two policemen got out; one was unbuttoning his hip holster.

Boris looked up at the visitors who came straight to the side of the car.

"Trouble, Lieutenant?" one asked.

"Just a damn flat. My friend here is the mechanic."

Peter smiled at the strangers.

"May we see your papers, please."

"Of course." Boris and Peter handed their forged documents to the officers, who read them carefully.

Joe Safcek and Luba were only fifty feet away and in the culvert when they heard the voices. They fell to the ground immediately and listened as Boris talked with the police.

"Can you tell us where we can get something to eat farther on?"

One of his inquisitors frowned over the documents and then

163

smiled: "In Leninskoye, you'll find a great little restaurant called Vanya. And it's cheap, too." He handed back the papers, saluted, and walked back to his car with the other policeman. Boris waved once as the auto sped down the highway toward Tashkent.

When it was just a speck, Boris whistled, and Joe and Luba climbed into view within seconds. Peter threw the tools into the trunk, kicked the new tire, and got into the car with the others. Safcek drove north two hundred yards past a sign that read, "Unauthorized personnel not admitted." He noted the side road leading to the main gate, made a U-turn, and began the return trip to the sanctuary of the mosque. He warned Boris and Peter to keep low in case the police came back along the same road, but nothing out of the ordinary happened. In twenty minutes, the car was swallowed up in the traffic of Tashkent, and the members of Operation Scratch resumed their roles as fascinated tourists in the heart of Soviet Central Asia.

Inside the laser complex, Professor Anatoly Serkin, now the acting director, finished checking data on the weapon after the test run. His fellow scientists continued to avoid discussion with him about the abduction of Andrei Parchuk as he wandered through his last inspections. It had been that way all day. A heavy, almost mournful silence pervaded the laboratory area.

At 5:15 P.M., Serkin went home for a brief, quiet supper with Nadia and Galina. He spoke little, and only Galina's insistence on playing with a toy roused him to any enthusiasm. He finally tucked her into bed and joined his wife for coffee on the porch. Sensing his deep depression, Nadia tried to get him to talk about Parchuk's kidnapping. She put her arms about his neck and whispered tenderly to him, but he pushed her away abruptly.

"Nadia, Parchuk is a dead man." There was despair in his

voice. "When State Security gets its hands on you, you're already at the grave. And how he looked when they drove off! That was just a sample."

She broke down at the remembrance of his description. Serkin stroked her hair softly.

"Just pray for him, Nadia. Pray for his soul."

Serkin could not continue. He stumbled off the porch and back down the road to his office.

In the radio room at Peshawar, Karl Richter had time on his hands. Richter was now only a bystander. He had given Safcek and the others all the information the United States intelligence community had at its disposal. He had been satisfied that no other team had ever gone on an assignment with such a wealth of hard facts about the enemy. Yet he was fearful for the people he had seen leave by helicopter. That they could actually accomplish a mission so hazardous deep inside the Soviet Union was almost inconceivable. Richter had watched Joe Safcek during the briefings and been completely impressed with the man's calm professionalism. At times, he found himself believing that Safcek and his group had a chance. Then he would remember Grigor Rudenko, who defied the odds for years but finally was unmasked and destroyed. And Joe Safcek was facing obstacles far more formidable that Grigor had faced. Richter was convinced the Russians would trap him as they had trapped Grigor, who was now probably buried in an unmarked grave.

Grigor Rudenko lay on his cot at Lubianka. His mouth was a constant aching void, crusted with blood, and oozing pus from infected wounds in the gum. But he was alive by grace of his inquisitors. In the past twenty-four hours, they had brought him to the interrogation room twice and forced more sodium pentothal into his arm, and Grigor had dreamed more beautiful dreams and told the man in the white coat about his contacts with the British Embassy and the materials he had passed to American intelligence for many years and about a man named Karl Richter who was his best friend and original espionage drop. The interrogators were fascinated with his long rambling stories and intended to keep him alive to dredge every detail of his Jekyll and Hyde existence from him. They were ecstatic at having found a master spy in their midst.

They even began to feed him a light soup, which he forced past his torn lips and swallowed gratefully. A nurse came to his cell and bathed his tortured body with a cooling sponge. In his waking moments, Grigor thought about his wife and children. In his induced dreams, he always reverted to his carefree boyhood in the United States. There Grigor could laugh and relax while he confessed heinous crimes against the Soviet state.

Now, at 1 P.M., Moscow time, on the afternoon of September 13, they came for him again. The man in the white coat was waiting in the antiseptic hospital room, but he had no needle in his hand. Vassili Baranov, deputy director of the state security police, was there too, and he nodded pleasantly to Rudenko, who refused to acknowledge him. Baranov told Rudenko to sit on a chair in the corner. A bright light was switched on over his head, and it shone directly into his battered face. Rudenko sat there for fifteen minutes, wondering when his interrogation would begin.

Then the door opened, and two secret police officers entered, supporting a man between them. Rudenko squinted to recognize him. But the light blinded him. Baranov spoke sharply, and the man was brought directly in front of Grigor, who could see that the victim had a broken lower jaw, which hung loosely away from his face. Blood masked his mouth.

"Grigor, this is your old friend, Parchuk."

Rudenko stared into the man's terror-stricken eyes.

166

"He's my wife's uncle. Why is he here?" Rudenko mumbled.

Parchuk was bent forward, his head down. One of the secret policemen tapped him lightly on the broken jaw, and the old man groaned loudly and raised his head to stare at the form under the light. Parchuk began to wail. Baranov ran to him and screamed: "Stop this, Parchuk. Look at him and see what stubbornness gets you."

The old professor sobbed: "Grigor, Grigor, I am so sorry I did this to you."

Baranov said: "That's all I wanted to know." He took his pistol and placed the barrel in the professor's right ear.

"Say good-bye to Grigor, traitor." As the professor tried to swing away from the gun, Baranov pressed the trigger, and a bullet ripped into Parchuk's head. He crumpled into a heap.

Grigor Rudenko stared at the body, but felt too numb to utter a sound. Baranov ordered the corpse taken out and said calmly to Rudenko, "Let's you and I have another chat." He led Grigor to the table where the man in the white coat waited with the needle.

Grigor Rudenko was listening again to Tchaikovsky's *Swan Lake*. He now looked forward to his visits to the antiseptic white room at the end of the hall because he could hear his favorite ballet in the brief intervals when he was not under the influence of sodium pentothal. That pleasure combined with his visits to Sheila and Karl during his reveries made Grigor eagerly anticipate the moments when Baranov summoned him for friendly chats.

As Dr. Senski plunged the needle into his vein, Grigor tried to keep time to the music with his hand but he floated slowly away from Lubianka.

Baranov's voice was calm and quite pleasant.

"Grigor, I never mentioned this before, but did you ever have any dealings with other embassies in Moscow?"

Karl Richter interrupted Baranov, and Grigor was happy.

"Grigor, you drive, and I'll be in the back seat with Maureen. And don't keep turning around with wisecracks."

"What about the French, Grigor?"

"I knew Maurice Debran there very well."

"Hasn't he been transferred back to Paris?"

"Stop driving so fast, Grigor. You'll kill us all." Sheila was very nervous but suddenly laughed gaily when Grigor pulled into the lovers' lane near the lake.

"Yes, he went back last Sunday."

"Did you see him off?"

"No, but I was at his apartment on Saturday night."

"Did you give him anything?"

Grigor kissed Sheila's lips. Her eyes were closed and her honey-colored hair tickled his nose.

"I gave him the other set of blueprints and notes about the laser."

"The other set?"

"Yes, Parchuk gave me two in case one was lost . . ."

Baranov's voice had changed. He was tense, rough in his pursuit of Rudenko.

"The same as the set that Brandon had?"

"Exactly."

Baranov groaned audibly. "Bastard! I should have known he'd be too smart to trust it all to that American teacher."

Sheila lay looking up at him, her head in his lap, and he was murmuring: "Will you wait for me?" She reached for his mouth with her lips.

"Grigor, who was supposed to be Debran's contact?"

"I don't know. Someone in the CIA."

"In Paris?"

Grigor's hands moved on her back.

"In Paris?"

"Yes, yes, but I don't know who."

"Are you sure you don't know?"

Sheila was breathing rapidly, and Grigor looked quickly into the back seat, but Karl and Maureen had gotten out and walked down to the lake.

"Are you sure, Grigor?"

"Yes. You know that I'm telling you the truth. Debran has friends in the CIA who pay him for different jobs."

"Did he know what was in the package you gave him?"

He could feel her mouth against his ear.

"Did Debran have any idea what he was delivering?"

Grigor crushed Sheila against him.

"Answer me, Grigor." Baranov was relentless. "Answer me."

Sheila put her arms around Grigor and tried to hold him to her. "Don't go away now," but he had drawn back to quiet the insistent questioner.

"Debran knew nothing. Are you satisfied?"

The exasperated Baranov said: "Take him out of here. I have to report this to Moskanko right away."

Fire trucks from fourteen communities had been called in to try and contain the explosion of the natural gas pipeline feeding into Washington. Two enormous breaks were allowing millions of cubic feet of gas to escape into the atmosphere. The billowing fires had advanced hungrily on a huge forest, which blazed quickly. By 7 A.M., the area was a holocaust, consuming virgin timber and threatening to spread into populated areas.

In the White House, President William Stark heard the news on the morning TV show from New York. He picked up the phone and called Markle at his home. When the commissioner came on the line, Stark knew he was totally depressed by his night's work. "Herb, in one half hour, initiate phase two. Correct?" Markle sighed wearily and agreed.

"And Herb, after that I'll take over. You just agree with everything you hear. OK?"

"OK, Mr. President. Don't worry about me. But I just hope this doesn't get out of hand." Stark reassured him and hung up.

At 8 A.M., a thunderous explosion rocked the Washington suburb of Bethesda, Maryland, north of the city. Two miles beyond the city limits, on a deserted hill, another natural gas pipeline burst in two places, creating a tremendous fire through the heavily timbered land. Fire-fighting equipment was called in from forty miles distant to contain the inferno.

Stark heard this news within minutes from Robert Randall, who met him in the Situation Room. Stark listened to a description of the explosion and then asked Randall what Safcek was doing. "He's not supposed to report in to Richter until ten A.M. our time. By then he'll know what he's going to do about the laser."

"By the way," Randall said, "Ambassador Tolypin and the entire Soviet Embassy staff flew to New York from National at eight A.M. When reporters asked them what was going on, they refused to talk."

Randall picked up the transcript of the Soviet cruiser's conversation and handed it over to Stark: "The duty officer says you've heard this one. What do you think?"

Stark shrugged. "It's just an attempt to rattle me, I'm sure. They're trying to stampede us in these last fifteen hours."

A phone call came in for the President from Markle.

"Mr. President, the explosions we've had this morning north and south of the city have caused possible breaks all along the lines through the city. We may have as many as fifty from the stresses caused by the blasts. I wanted to warn you about seepage."

"What does that mean, Herb?"

"Well, there's a strong possibility that escaping gas can destroy life, and also the fires from further explosions would make the old Chicago blaze seem like kid stuff."

"In that case, Herb, perhaps we should evacuate the vicinity affected."

"The problem, there, Mr. President, is that the entire city is in trouble. The pipelines go right through the center of it."

"OK, thanks, Herb. I'll do something about it."

Stark turned away to Randall and said: "Call the Civil Defense Director and tell him to begin an evacuation of all of downtown Washington. Tell him I ordered it and explain why. And Bob, tell him to treat it with the same urgency he'd use in time of war in order to make this thing work right."

Randall went to the phone, but before dialing he suddenly asked: "This is your little gimmick, isn't it?"

Stark pointed at the phone: "Just call that man, Bob, and get the ball moving."

Arndt Svendsen, Secretary General of the United Nations, sat in his spacious office overlooking the East River and thought this mild mid-September morning one of the most beautiful he had ever seen. Tugs rode lazily past him on their way up to the Harlem River. Loaded barges made barely perceptible headway down the ribbon of water toward the ocean at the foot of Manhattan Island. Smog was for once absent from the blue sky. A brilliant sunlight crinkled his face as he gazed out on the city he had come to love as much as his own Oslo.

Dressed in a light brown suit, his fingernails manicured, hair trimmed, Svendsen was ready to preside over the opening session of the General Assembly of the United Nations. For once, the world situation seemed reasonably stable. No major wars were in the offing. Only in the Middle East had the conflicting powers failed to reach a state of total truce. As Svendsen enjoyed the view, his secretary announced the arrival of Yuri Zarov, chief Soviet delegate to the United Nations.

Surprised at his sudden appearance, Svendsen invited the Russian to sit down before the magnificent picture window. He ordered coffee and then asked: "Well, Zarov, to what do I owe the honor of this visit?"

The impassive Zarov took a piece of paper out of his briefcase and thrust it at the Secretary General. "This is the reason. This threat to the security of the world."

Svendsen looked at the paper and scoffed: "Surely, Zarov, your government doesn't believe this is true. The United States has no intention of beginning a nuclear war, and your country should be the first to know that."

Svendsen laughed: "You know, Zarov, I don't like to seem non-neutral, but the Soviet Union has more spies per square inch in this country and around the world than anyone else."

Zarov bristled, but Svendsen continued. "From all the information gathered by you, you have to know that William Stark has no intention, and never did, may I add, of blowing up the world."

Zarov smiled broadly. "Are you finished maligning my government, sir? Because if you are, I want to add proof to my charge. We are willing and, in fact, insist that you call a special meeting of the Security Council this evening. There I will prove our case and expose Stark as a fraud and potential mass murderer."

The suddenly concerned Secretary General agreed to convene the council at 6 P.M. right after the first session of the General Assembly ended. When Zarov left, Svendsen went back to the window and stared unseeing at the panorama. He was shaken by the Russian's demand and Zarov's demeanor, and began to ask himself if William Stark could possibly have lost his senses and plotted what Zarov said.

Maurice Debran had not proved to be a reliable courier. After he left Moscow, he stopped in Copenhagen to meet his mistress, Inga Holdens. They stayed at the Royale Hotel across from the Tivoli Gardens, and Debran forgot about the package Rudenko had given him. He walked the streets of the Danish capital with his friend and shopped for presents for his wife and children back in Paris. On Tuesday, September 10, Debran and Inga made love for the last time, and he went out to Kastrup Airport and caught the direct flight to Paris.

When he got home, Debran was seized with guilt and spent two days being attentive to his family. On Friday, at noon, Paris time, he went to the Café St. Laurent, ordered a Campari, and waited for the daily appearance of Michael Macomber, resident American CIA agent in the city. Under cover of being an author, Macomber coordinated all activities of his agency in France and the Low Countries.

Debran saw him instantly and signaled Macomber to join him. Attired in a velvet jacket and bell-bottomed slacks, the American threaded his way through the noontime crowd and put out his hand to the Frenchman. Macomber knew that Debran sometimes engaged in clandestine activities for the United States while carrying on his normal duties as a diplomatic courier for his own country. It gave Debran extra money to finance his personal clandestine activities.

173

The two men talked animatedly for a while, the American patiently waiting for Debran to come to the point of his visit to the café.

"Grigor Rudenko gave me something for you."

Macomber was startled. He had not seen Rudenko for years, not since he had been in Moscow as part of the embassy staff. Macomber had briefly acted as Rudenko's channel to Richter in Washington, but soon having to assume other responsibilities, he had lost touch with the Russian. When Debran mentioned Rudenko's name, Macomber instantly wondered whether the Frenchman was baiting some sort of trap. He wondered whether Debran had now added the Communists to his list of employers. It would not have surprised him.

Debran was not subtle. "Rudenko says these are very important to your country and you should pass them on to Washington."

Macomber did not acknowledge that he even knew Rudenko. "What's in the package?"

"I don't know, but here it is."

Debran held it for a moment in front of Macomber's face.

"My expenses in this case have been quite high, Macomber."

The American sighed and asked, "How much, Maurice?"

"Five thousand American dollars."

"You're not serious!"

"Oh, but I am! The way Grigor was acting, it's worth all of that to your people."

Macomber looked at the envelope and Debran's mocking smile.

"Why don't we go for a walk, Maurice, and talk this out?"

"By all means, let's do that."

Debran swallowed his Campari, and the men went out into the late summer brightness of the Left Bank.

Macomber took him to his home in the 16th Arrondissement. In the living room of the third-floor suite, the American poured

Chateauneuf du Pape into glasses and handed one to Debran. "To your continued health, Maurice."

Debran drank slowly, eyeing the CIA man, who smiled over his drink.

"Now may I see this very important letter of yours?" Macomber asked. "I can't tell how much it's worth until I read it."

Debran sipped thoughtfully, then handed over Rudenko's message. When Macomber tore it open, a cascade of blueprints and memoranda fell out onto the coffee table.

The American sat down to examine his treasure. Macomber was no physicist, but he was reasonably fluent in nontechnical Russian. The blueprints were incomprehensible to him and the notes on them almost as impossible.

The memos were a different story. One from Andrei Parchuk told of the initial Soviet test firing and described the extent of the damage inflicted on the Siberian target.

Another from Parchuk told of the Presidium meeting where Moskanko had told him he would destroy the Israeli atomic center and later use the weapon on the United States.

Macomber tried to hide his own feelings from Debran as he read these stunning words. His heart was pounding furiously in his chest, and he wanted to get rid of the Frenchman before he betrayed his excitement.

Macomber got up and went to a desk, where he pulled out a cigarette box and reached inside.

"You said five thousand, Maurice."

"Correct."

"It's worth three to me."

Macomber waved a packet of money at Debran, who tried to fathom the American's concealed reaction to the contents of the envelope.

"Three, Maurice, and keep up the good work. Perhaps next time we can do even better by you."

Maurice Debran hesitated, thought of his financial burdens, and accepted the proffered payment. Macomber saw him to the door and asked: "Does Grigor Rudenko use you often in his work?"

Debran shrugged: "Once in a while, but never have I seen him so insistent on my getting this to the proper channels. He seemed very disturbed, very upset."

Macomber nodded and said good-bye.

When he was sure Debran was in the elevator, Macomber called his assistant, Jim Perkins, out of the next room and pointed to the documents. "Jim, unless these are fakes, we've just uncovered the worst mess since Pearl Harbor."

Michael Macomber left Orly Airport one hour and forty minutes later, bound for Washington. In his briefcase he carried Grigor Rudenko's bombshell. In Langley, Virginia, it was 10 A.M. when Sam Riordan hung up from talking to Jim Perkins, who told the director why Macomber had left in such haste. The elated Riordan immediately dialed the White House. He was anxious to tell Bill Stark his first good news in days.

But William Stark was not there. The President had gone to a wake. The vault was cool and dark except for a tiny light burning in the ceiling. Stark sat alone beside the flag-draped coffin. Outside, in Arlington National Cemetery, Secret Service men and the Bagman waited while the President of the United States paid his last respects to a fallen comrade, Clifford Erskine. Because of the evacuation now beginning, last rites for the Secretary of Defense had been delayed and the President had flown by helicopter across the river to be with his friend for a final brief moment.

Stark sat beside the man who had quit on him the day before and thought of the many happy times they had shared together in Washington. He had enjoyed Erskine's dry humor and intellect immensely. The two had frequently played golf or ridden down the Potomac on the White House yacht, discussing affairs of state or talking about subjects they found mutually stimulating. It was Erskine who had introduced Stark to the *Federalist* papers written by Madison, Hamilton, and John Jay. It was Erskine who had sharpened Stark's ability at chess. They had shared many hours of contemplative relaxation, and William Stark had found them to be among the most pleasant aspects of his Presidency. Erskine had become like a brother to him. Their views of people and the world had been surprisingly alike, and Stark found it difficult to believe that the first man to defect from his cabinet had been Clifford Erskine. Now his friend was dead, and Stark blamed himself.

The President reached out to touch the flag, mumbling, "Forgive me, Cliff." His eyes were moist, and he caught himself on the verge of a sob. His chair rasped on the cement floor as he stood. Hastily, he brushed his hand across his eyes to erase the tears and stepped out into the blinding light. The Secret Service men trailed him down the path past thousands of white markers from other wars and other crises. Stark began counting them absently and reading the dates. He thought, "Maybe next time nobody will be left to bury the dead." The President stopped reading the stones and hurried back to the White House.

In the ancient mosque south of Tashkent, the Operation Scratch team was preparing for the assault on the laser complex, checking equipment, cleaning weapons. Peter and Boris had not been able to sleep even for a moment. They had spent several hours criticizing the current Soviet leadership. Peter Kirov was convinced the overtures made by Smirnov in past months were a sham, part of the plan to lull the United States into a false security. Boris Gorlov argued strongly that the premier was well-intentioned and might be in serious trouble with the other members of the Presidium. Neither man had evidently been briefed on the coup that had replaced Smirnov with the figure-head Krylov.

Joe Safcek had not joined the conversation. He was more concerned with the night ahead. From the scouting mission just hours earlier, he knew that it would be almost impossible for his group to storm the bastion. That left him with the option of using the atomic bomb, and he was deliberating how to do it most effectively. As he mulled over the route and strategy, Luba appeared on the stairway, and Safchek called up to her: "Luba, did you rest?"

She stretched luxuriously and said: "At least two hours. I'm ready to go anytime."

Safcek looked at his watch. It was 9:45 P.M. He broke in on the dialogue between Gorlov and Kirov.

"Boris, it's time for our report to Richter. Write this down: Arrive laser area 2245 hours Tashkent time. Using fissionable material. Expect detonation approximately 0100 hours Tashkent time, allowance one half hour for local conditions. Rendezvous chopper at 0300 hours. Got it?"

Boris read it back, and Safcek told him to get upstairs imme-diately and send.

Gorlov moved quickly up the crumbling stairway to the set propped against a window. From it an antenna ran to the roof of the ancient mosque.

He sat down and quickly encoded Safcek's message.

Gorlov adjusted the frequency knob, depressed the sending key and spoke softly into the microphone:

"This is Laika, this is Laika . . ."

In Peshawar, Karl Richter heard him instantly.

178

"Eagle here, Eagle here . . ."

Gorlov smiled in the dim light and continued with the message from Safcek. He spoke in fluent Russian and alerted Karl Richter to the plans for the night. After one minute and two seconds, Gorlov signed off.

As he got up to strike the antenna from the outside wall, a sudden noise on the stairway startled him, and he whirled. A hand locked over his mouth, and a knife cut into his throat from under the left ear across the Adam's apple. The hand released him, and Boris slid gurgling to the floor.

In Peshawar, Karl Richter was already speaking to President William Stark, who was back in the Situation Room with Robert Randall.

"Yes, sir, Gorlov just told me the blast should occur within the time period one thirty to two thirty P.M. in Washington. He made no mention of any trouble so far."

"Thanks, Karl. Let me know right away on any news."

Stark turned to Randall and said: "Richter says they're about to make their run for the laser, and so far it's gone smoothly." Stark looked at his watch. "About three hours to detonation, I figure." He thought a minute. "On that idea of yours for a standdown, tell Roarke to order everybody away from the missile silos and to keep the bombers on the ground for a while. Maybe we can lull the Russians a little until Safcek has his chance." He paused. "Also, better tell him to put a couple of satellites up over Tashkent right away."

Less than thirteen hours remained until the ultimatum deadline.

Outside the White House, civil defense officials wearing armbands had appeared on the streets. They headed to assigned posts, where they advised people about the gas danger and ordered personnel away from the city.

On radio and TV, listeners were bombarded with orders to evacuate because of the danger of gas seepage, explosion, and fire. All were advised to take the barest minimum of clothing and food for several meals in case of delay in repairing defective pipelines.

Huge downtown office buildings disgorged men and women, who found their cars and headed for the suburbs. Lines of buses appeared as if magically at major intersections to take all passengers normally dependent on metropolitan transportation. Many of the younger evacuees were in an exceptionally good mood. Relieved at getting time off, they clambered into their vehicles and rode off toward Virginia and Maryland.

Army troops had appeared, some directing traffic, others standing before empty stores to prevent looting.

On Capitol Hill, senators and representatives heeded the plea to leave without question. They sent their staffs away and quietly, dutifully, moved on. In his office, the venerable Jonas Ingram packed his papers in a worn briefcase and stepped to the door. Having heard from the President's own lips what the Soviet Union had in mind for America, the elderly congressman had no illusions about the real reason for the evacuation. He put on his panama hat and walked into the corridor. As Jonas Ingram came out into the daylight, he stood for a moment and looked up at the white dome of the Capitol; then he stumbled down the steep steps to his waiting limousine.

In the mosque, Boris Gorlov's killer moved to the radio, sat down, and quickly adjusted the frequencies. The killer depressed the key and called urgently: "K-422, K-422 calling from Tashkent

. . . come in, come in . . ." A swirl of static answered. "K-422, calling from Tashkent . . ."

"We have you, K-422 . . . where are you exactly?"

I'm in a—"

Luba Spitkovsky smashed the receiver with the butt of an automatic rifle, and all reception ended.

American intelligence gatherers were moving their chess pieces on the board. A Samos camera satellite circling the globe at an altitude of one hundred and two miles received instructions through its on-board computer and acted immediately to comply. Jet thrusters in the tail were activated for four seconds, and the silver capsule veered off its prescribed course to a new orbit, eighty-four miles high and farther to the west. At a point near the city of Tashkent, reverse thrusters were activated, and the satellite slowed and hovered over the laser works just north of the city.

Over the north Italian Alps, a Midas-sensing satellite received a new set of directions from its brain on the ground and swiftly reacted to the programmed data. It moved across the Balkans, across the Black Sea and the Caucasus to slow and stop forty miles west of the Samos satellite. The Midas heat-sensing devices were tested once and then trained far below to the area covering Tashkent and thirty miles north. The probe was centered directly on the laser complex.

In the United States, technicians sat by their recording instruments waiting for tangible evidence that Operation Scratch had succeeded. Beside them were phones linking them with President William Stark at the White House.

181

The fires north and south of Washington were still raging. In Bethesda, the order to evacuate took on a more urgent tone as the spreading holocaust began to eat at residential tracts. At least fifteen homes had been destroyed before 11 A.M.

In the Oval Room, William Stark heard this news with a deep frown. Herb Markle had worried that the situation would get out of hand. Stark had reassured him it would not. And now Bethesda was a battleground between the devouring flames and exhausted firemen.

Beyond the south lawn, he could see the traffic jammed on the approaches to the Potomac bridges. While horns beeped and drivers sweltered in the heat, the exodus from the city proceeded at a snail's pace.

The television stations had canceled regular programming for special reports on the disaster. There on the screen were the uncontrolled fires in Virginia and Maryland and gas company personnel painstakingly searching for gas leaks along the lines.

Stark and Randall watched the reports, and then Randall said, "The city should be empty by tonight." Stark grunted his agreement and added: "I want them moved at least ten miles out of town. Weinroth told me the effective kill range of the Soviet weapon is probably six square miles. Of course, we can't know for sure whether they'll be accurate, but we have to assume they can get within a mile of their target."

Randall had another problem to discuss. "What do you think of Carlson's report from the UN that the Russians have demanded a Security Council meeting for later today?"

Stark retorted: "What do you think?"

"Probably another attempt to lay blame at our door for increased provocations around the world. It's just going one better on what they did with that pamphlet yesterday."

182

Stark stretched his arms above his head and yawned. He shook himself briefly to ease his tired body. He had had very little sleep since the arrival of the Soviet ultimatum, sixty hours ago.

"We'll wait and see what they do," the President said at last. "I can't tip our predicament to anyone yet. They're just aching for the chance to use that goddamn laser. And if I tell the world that it's the Russians who have gone mad, half the people won't believe me anyway."

Stark leaned back in his chair, then looked up at his advisor. "You know something, Bob? I'm amazed to find *myself* in this predicament. Me, the peace President. For Christ's sake, I've spent the past year preaching peace to the whole goddamn world, trying to work with the Russians and the Chinese and generally pulling in our horns on the perimeters. God, when I think of the mess I inherited in this country. Strikes, race riots, absolute chaos in the streets. And now, look at how little it takes for people in this country to start swallowing the same old line, that this 'imperialistic' régime is bent on taking over the world. We're always to blame, rarely right, while somehow, the other side comes off as well-intentioned and reputable. I know that the people who believe this stuff are well-meaning, most of them anyway, but for years now they've been convinced that we're the bad guys in the world. And there is no way, no way, to convince them otherwise."

As so often before, Randall found himself in agreement with Stark. "It reminds me of the Cuban missile crisis," he said now. "In the middle of that mess, Kennedy got a telegram from Bertrand Russell, condemning him for attempting to plunge the planet into total war. Russell never mentioned Khrushchev, who started it all. At the time, Kennedy said it was the first instance he'd ever heard of where a man whose house was being burglarized was blamed instead of the burglar."

President Stark chuckled appreciatively. "That's exactly what I mean. I must sound like Steve Roarke when I talk this way, and I'd say this is one of the few times I've ever seen eye to eye with him on anything. God knows, the extreme right in this country is just as dangerous as the extreme left, but somewhere in there I've got to sympathize with the general. These radicals want to tear down the system, and they drag along innocent moderates, who honestly want to correct inequities—and I'd be the first to admit we have plenty of those. But, damnit, so has the rest of the world. They see most of the faults right here. Then the radicals whisper in their ears, and they follow like sheep." Stark slammed the desk in frustration.

Randall sat quietly, observing the evident strain on his President's face.

Stark rubbed his eyes. "Christ," he said, "I'm so tired of it all. This situation's got me down, especially the waiting, knowing there's a timebomb ticking down for all of us. Right now, Joe Safcek is the key. If that guy can pull it off, all this won't mean a thing. If he can't, well . . ."

Luba Spitkovsky held the end of the gun barrel directly under Peter Kirov's left eye and said: "Downstairs, pig." Kirov got up slowly, carefully. Luba prodded him in the back, and he lurched down the stairs to where Joe Safcek stood. "What the hell's going on?" the colonel asked.

Luba's voice was harsh. "He just killed Boris and tried to contact his friends in Moscow. I stopped it."

Kirov stared coldly at Safcek, who hit him once on the bridge of the nose. The sound of breaking bone was accompanied by a rush of blood through Kirov's nostrils and onto his shirt. Kirov staggered but held his ground. Safcek pounded his fist into Kirov's stomach, and the Russian groaned as he fell to the floor.

Safcek looked at him with loathing.

"Luba, did he get anything off before you caught him?"

"No, Colonel. He did make contact with someone in Moscow, but I kept him from giving the exact details of our position. He used the call letters K-422."

Safcek seized the terrified Kirov and pulled him upright. "Who are you, you sonofabitch?" Kirov's face was a crimson mask; his nose was spread flat, and his eyes were filled with terror. But he did not speak.

The perspiring Safcek stood up slowly and went over to Luba.

"How did you find out about him?"

"Remember the conversation on the ride here last night? He was talking to Boris about his childhood in Volgograd. Well, in the middle of it, he mentioned the ice forming a land bridge across the Volga in January. Anyone who has ever lived in Volgograd or near it would know that the ice starts coming down in November and is a solid sheet by the first part of December at latest. His remark ate at me, but I couldn't be sure.

"This morning, I deliberately went out to walk with him so that I could draw him out some more. Everything he said added up, except for the ice. But he seemed so positive that I began to doubt myself. After all, I never lived on the Volga myself, and what I had heard could have been wrong, too."

"That's why you were so moody, wasn't it?"

"Yes, Colonel. All I had was a feeling that Peter was not what he said he was. And now this."

"Forget it, Luba. Someone back in Washington or Germany failed years ago on this guy, and he slipped through our security checks. It's as simple as that."

Luba smiled gratefully and asked: "Shouldn't we just dispose of him? We're running out of time."

"Not yet, not yet."

At 11 A.M., Ambassador Tolypin entered the United Nations press room. Flanked by aides, the Soviet diplomat posed dutifully for photographers and television cameramen. Usually gregarious and smiling, Tolypin remained grim-faced all during the picture-taking. After five minutes, he waved his hand for them to stop and went to the podium. For a moment only the hum of cameras intruded, and then he began to speak:

"Under instructions from my government, I have just removed all diplomatic personnel from Washington. Tonight we will leave for the Soviet Union from Kennedy Airport. Because of recent provocations and disclosures, the Soviet Union considers the next days filled with peril for the entire world. As a result, all of our missions in this country are being sent home for their own safety."

Tolypin paused, and reporters rushed in to question him.

"Mr. Ambassador, are you implying that war is imminent?"

"Gentlemen, I am merely stating the obvious. You are aware of the Stark order exposed yesterday during the march in Washington. My country has ascertained that it is true beyond a doubt and will prove that charge later today. Under such circumstances, we have no alternative but to prepare for any contingency."

Tolypin picked up his notes, thanked the newsmen for coming, and walked out the door. Behind him he left frantic men fighting for precious phones.

Hands on hips, Joe Safcek stared down at his prisoner. Kirov was stirring, trying to breathe through his mutilated nose. Seeing

186

Safcek over him, he shrank back. Safcek grabbed a fistful of Kirov's hair and yanked him upright.

"Kirov, this is your last chance. Answer my questions now, or I'll start breaking you up into little pieces. What is your organization?"

Kirov's lips tried to form a word but failed. Safcek asked him again. Kirov was silent.

Safcek was getting desperate. He looked at Luba, who showed no emotion.

Joe Safcek took Kirov's left arm, bent it over his own knee, and began to wrench excruciatingly.

"Talk, Kirov!" he snarled.

Kirov cried out: "KGB. I'm a captain!" Safcek eased the pressure.

Safcek nodded. "And you infiltrated the NTS in Germany?" Kirov had slipped into the dirt. "Yes, to spy . . . report back to Moscow."

"What about this trip?"

Kirov lay quiet for a moment. He was slipping to the brink of unconsciousness, yet he struggled to answer.

"No idea," he snorted through his swollen nostrils. "No idea until Pakistan."

"Did you tell anyone there or since then?"

"Yes, yes."

"Who?"

"Earlier at the laser place. The policemen who stopped us."

"How did you tell?"

"When Gorlov . . . talking, I wrote on my papers . . . warned police not to try to take us there . . . we'd be back."

Joe Safcek wanted to rush at Kirov and hit him again, but he controlled himself and asked: "What does K-422 mean?"

"My number . . . organization."

"That's all?"

"Yes, yes."

Safcek was suddenly very tired. Sick of looking at the evidence of his savagery, he turned away from Kirov.

"Luba, I can't tell if he's lying or not. I suppose he could have slipped something to those policemen this afternoon."

He suddenly whirled on Kirov.

"What else did you tell those men?"

Kirov pulled his face out of the dirt. "Just said spies . . . coming back tonight."

Joe Safcek walked away.

A light summer rain beat against the Soviet army car as it sped toward Vnukovo Airport in the Moscow suburbs. In the back seat Marshal Moskanko, ignoring the presence of the chauffeur, spoke forcefully to his companion, Marshal Bakunin.

"Just keep a grip on your emotions, Pavel Andreievich, and in twenty-four hours, you will congratulate me for being a genius. When you get to the laser works, keep in close touch, and I will inform you of the American reactions right away. With Parchuk a traitor, I want you down there to make sure my orders are carried out with precision and dispatch."

The thin-faced Bakunin nodded glumly as he watched the rain streak the window in the dark. "You will give the Americans enough time to surrender before you use the laser?"

"Of course I will. But we will hear from them long before we have to use it. Stark will collapse well within the eleven and a half hours remaining."

Bakunin took out a handkerchief and wiped some mud off his boots. "Remember, Viktor Semyonovich, what I said about rats. They are vicious when all is lost."

The car had stopped in front of the terminal. Bakunin slipped out, and Moskanko called after him. "Why don't you think of Stark as a koala bear instead? When faced with disaster, they curl up and die of fright."

Bakunin went through the glass doors without a word.

Moskanko picked up the car phone and put through a call to Marshal Fedoseyev, commander of Soviet land forces, in the Defense Ministry. "He is on his way," Moskanko said. "No, he did not complain. And we can keep him out of the way until it is over. Maybe I should have given him some books to read to keep him occupied." Moskanko chuckled as he hung up and ordered the driver to take him back to the city.

The bone in Peter Kirov's nose had fractured in three places, blocking both nostrils. He was forced to gulp great drafts of air into his mouth while he watched Luba furtively. His left arm hung limply beside him, and the pain in his body brought tears to his eyes. Luba hung menacingly over him. There was no question that she would kill him on a word from Safcek. Whenever Kirov shifted to get into a more comfortable position, she brought the rifle up and fingered the trigger.

Kirov knew his situation was hopeless. Safcek could neither take him along on the mission nor leave him behind alive. Kirov's own training in the KGB denied him any further attempt at optimism. He was a dead man, but his hasty fabrication about the police might still stop the mission. He regretted having been unable to warn his superiors about this operation inside the Soviet Union. The fact that he was able to mention Tashkent in his radio dispatch did not pinpoint the peril. If he had succeeded, he could have asked for and been reassigned to some safe post in the Communist bloc and allowed to pursue a more reasonable life. Peter's solitary existence as an agent behind enemy lines had never given him the time to form any permanent attachments. Now he was glad that he had no worries about leaving someone behind. His family had been among the 25 million in the Soviet Union killed by the Germans, and his dedication in life was to the Party and the system, which had neither time nor heart to mourn him.

He groaned, and Luba hissed: "Suffer, Kirov, for what you did to Gorlov. I'd like to cut your throat myself."

Kirov wiped his bloody face with his right hand and sniffed through the bubbles in his nostrils. When Joe Safcek approached him and looked down, he tensed.

"Luba, we haven't much time left, and it's pointless to try and beat anything more out of him. I'm not sure he told the other side anything, and even if he did, we have to go ahead."

Safcek had regained his composure. But he was increasingly disgusted with himself for brutalizing the Russian lying in the dirt and wanted no more of what was to follow.

"So eliminate him."

Kirov received the words almost as if he, too, were being given instructions.

Safcek did not look at Kirov again. He strode to the stairway and called back to Luba: "Only don't use a gun. It might attract some attention."

She nodded and put the automatic rifle up against a wall. Then she came to Peter Kirov, who suddenly twisted away from her reaching hands.

Luba seized him by the throat, and Kirov felt her thumbs pressing in on his windpipe. She just looked at him and relentlessly forced his life away. Kirov was conscious of a terrible pain in his lungs, and his head exploded in lights and black circles that whirled and whirled him into darkness. He fell back into the dirt of the ancient mosque.

Luba went to find Safcek, who was packing equipment in the trunk of the car and did not look up as she approached.

"It's done, Colonel," she said softly, and he continued arranging the supplies. At his feet was the box containing the atomic bomb. He carefully put it in a corner away from the handguns and other paraphernalia.

"Let's take care of the bodies in there."

Inside the gloomy mosque, the dead Boris Gorlov lay on his back. In the candlelight, Safcek saw Gorlov's open mouth and glaring eyes. Luba stared at the remains of the KGB man who had defected to the West.

"He must have known it would happen someday," she murmured.

Safcek knelt down and went through Gorlov's pockets. He found forged papers and a few rubles. "There's nothing else, I guess. I thought perhaps he might have something more personal we could bring back with us." Safcek looked up at Luba.

"It's not much, is it, for a man to leave behind?" The colonel seemed to be searching her face for an answer, a reaction to his question.

Luba shrugged and walked over to the body. She pulled Boris's eyelids down over his sightless eyes and stepped back.

They carried Boris Gorlov down the stairs to the dusty cellar floor and laid his body beside his murderer's. Safcek went to the wall where the bones of ancient men rested, and knocked dust and bits of bone back into the farthest recesses. Then he returned to lift Boris to his final resting place. Blood dripped steadily onto Safcek's wrists, as he carefully placed Boris in the makeshift grave. He pulled Gorlov's tunic up under his chin to hide the ghastly effects of Kirov's knife, then stepped back and went to the other corpse. They searched the double agent. He also had left nothing behind. Luba grabbed Kirov's legs, and Safcek grabbed him under the arms and hoisted him to the grave just above Gorlov. Peter's head lolled back and forth as they dumped him into the cavern. Joe Safcek could not look at the broken face.

He sat down on a box of rifle ammunition.

"We'll have to make a few changes now that there's only two of us. We can't carry too much. You can manage the AK-47. I left six satchel charges in the trunk instead of twelve. We wouldn't be able to handle more and still move quickly. They should be enough to get us through any kind of interference before we're as close as we need to be for setting up the bomb."

They made one last equipment check. Luba stuffed ammunition into her pockets, and then the agents passed by the crypt for the last time. Safcek hesitated a moment, reached up and tried to straighten Peter Kirov's bent left arm. He could not. He let it flop onto the body and snapped. "C'mon, Luba. We're running out of time."

It was 11 P.M. in Tashkent, one hour later than they had told Richter they would be leaving the mosque. The last phase of Operation Scratch was already well behind schedule.

Zero hour was eleven hours and eighteen minutes away.

Helicopters from the D.C. metropolitan police department hovered over the avenues leading from the city and reported on the congested traffic.

The blaze in northern Virginia had eaten its way nearly to the Potomac. Its smoke had blown across the river and onto the clogged highways. Motorists were nearly blinded by the billowing clouds, which obscured the sun and caused a premature twilight.

In Bethesda, the fires had finally been contained but only

after sixty-five homes had been consumed in the inferno. Traffic was detoured northeastward into the Baltimore area.

In the White House, William Stark could see the mountainous clouds of smoke drifting toward him from the Potomac. Herb Markle had called shortly before, deploring the extent of the damage, but Stark had quickly silenced him, warning him to keep his nerves under control and his story straight. Markle reported that there were indeed several leaks in the pipelines and that his men were sealing them off as rapidly as possible. Markle did not think there would be any further trouble in the downtown area.

Stark had brought his executive committee together for a hasty working lunch. Roarke reported on the requested standdown and confirmed that all stations had retreated from a war footing and were practically defenseless. Manson said that all friendly nations were besieging the State Department for further information on Tolypin's charge at the UN that the U.S. was provoking a war. Randall announced that the Soviet naval task force was now one hundred miles due east of Montauk and slowing down to keep its proposed rendezvous at exactly 8 P.M. that night. Sam Riordan said Macomber was due in by suppertime. He also had a gruesome postscript on the blueprints story—Perkins had just called again from Paris to say that Maurice Debran had been found dead on the Métro tracks. Riordan had one other item. He mentioned that Krylov had not been seen publicly for two days. Perhaps he was holed up inside the Kremlin itself.

"Sam," the President commented, "Krylov may be staying put, but I think it's about time *we* made plans to get out of town. I want all necessary personnel at their assigned places in the mountain by nine P.M. tonight. It's imperative we have a working organization in case the Russians push their timetable ahead and let go before the deadline." Then he added: "Or in case we have to go to war with them."

General Roarke pursued this issue. "Incirclik has the two SR-71's ready to go. They've hidden them in a special hangar at the end of the field and posted armed guards around the perimeter. General Ellington says they can take off with fifteen minutes' notice."

Stark acknowledged this information with a grunt, and changed the subject.

"Now that Clifford Erskine is dead, you will not bother to report to John Dunham. Though he's acting Secretary of Defense, I'm not going to delegate anything to him until this thing is over. Understood?" Roarke nodded happily, and Stark went on to discuss the state of evacuation. Randall estimated that by 8 P.M., the vast bulk of citizens would be across the river into Virginia and as far north as Baltimore. So far, the operation had gone quite smoothly with only minor traffic accidents.

In the darkness, Joe Safcek and Luba drove through Tashkent. Because nighttime traffic was nearly nonexistent, Safcek realized his presence in the streets was unusual and drove accordingly.

Luba watched the occasional pedestrian warily. On Navoi Street she noticed a policeman lounging on the corner. Out of the side of her mouth, she mentioned him to Safcek, who nodded and kept his face forward. The policeman ignored them, and they moved slowly past the Opera House and the islands of roses in the middle of the street. It was oppressively hot, and Luba rolled down the window and breathed deeply. They passed the Uzbekistan Legislature Building, where a huge statue of Lenin stared back at them.

"Colonel, do we have to use the atomic bomb?"

194

"I'm afraid so, Luba. It's impossible for us to break completely through their screen by ourselves. It would take a task force with tanks to get into the compound and lay charges in that building. This way we can set it off in the gully that runs up to the main gate and neutralize the whole area."

"Well, why can't we set it off here along the road instead of running the risk of being caught near the plant?"

"We could, Luba, except that I have to be absolutely sure that the explosion will get the weapon. An atomic bomb is a very unpredictable thing. At Hiroshima and Nagasaki, some people who were only eight hundred yards from Ground Zero survived. Buildings remained upright at the same distance. So, the closer in I can get with this one, which isn't as powerful as those were, the surer I'll be that the place will go up completely. There are a lot of hills around here, and I can't afford to let them deflect the blast away from the laser."

"But what will be the effects of the bomb?"

"I'm not sure. Back at the Pentagon, they said the total destruction by fire and blast should not exceed an area of eight square miles."

"I hope you're right," Luba groaned. "My mother lives in Chirchiz, and that's only ten miles east of here."

"Oh, God, I forgot that!" The colonel tried to think of something to reassure her. "I do know this is a very clean bomb. The radiation effects are almost totally negligible."

Luba thought about it and then sighed. "If anything did go wrong, she'd probably never know what hit her, and I'm sure if I told her what I was doing and why, she'd tell me to go ahead. I think my mother hates the state worse than I do, if that's possible." Luba stopped, and Safcek said: "I'm sorry it has to be this way, but I have no choice. You know that."

Luba reached across to him and squeezed his right arm tightly. "Please don't think of it again."

He looked at her hand, and she pulled it away suddenly.

195

In the silence that followed, Joe Safcek busied himself with the road ahead and the mileage gauge, which had clicked off three kilometers beyond the city.

As car headlights loomed out of the darkness, Safcek's hands tightened on the wheel. They came up in a blinding rush, bathed the interior with a bright light, then passed swiftly away to the south. Safcek's hands relaxed.

They tightened again quickly when he saw a revolving ice-blue light beckoning him in the distance.

"Goddamnit, a roadblock," he said. Luba strained forward and saw the beacon at the side of the road about two hundred yards away. She saw two cars stopped and policemen walking around them inspecting the occupants.

"What do we do, Colonel?"

"Let me think." Slowing down in response to a policeman's waving hand, Safcek pulled up behind the stationary vehicles. Safcek shifted into neutral and left the motor running. "Take it easy, Luba." He was watching two security officers as they ordered the driver out of the first car. "Let's see how they act before we do anything."

The driver of the first car had produced some papers, and the questioner trained his flashlight on them. He apparently asked the man for further identification, and the motorist after a few moments produced more documents. With what seemed agonizing slowness, the security men looked inside the car, front and back. Next, they took the keys to the trunk from the man. They lifted the lid and poked around in it deliberately. After they had finished their fruitless search, they slammed the top down and gave the driver back his papers. He waved to them, and drove off past the patrol car with the revolving light on the roof.

Safcek was reading his watch. "Jesus, we're losing time fast."

The security police were at the second car, and three people were coming out of it and fumbling for their papers. Luba said,

196

"The trunk again," as one of the policemen moved to the rear and opened it.

"I know, I know. We can't let them near ours." Safcek was trying to think of a solution.

The three people ahead were now being searched by the police.

"Is the AK-47 loaded?" Safcek asked.

"Yes, but it's in the trunk."

"If they ask us to open it, make sure you grab the gun and use it on them. Kill them both."

The second car was moving away. A policeman was at Safcek's window, shining a flashlight on Safcek's uniform. "Good evening, Colonel. Sorry to bother you, sir. Would you mind stepping out of the car for a moment and giving us your papers, please. It won't take long."

Safcek and Luba got out and handed over their forged identification papers and travel orders.

Safcek smiled at him. "What's the problem, Sergeant?"

"We have a little scare around here about enemy agents."

"Here in Tashkent?"

"All we know is Moscow got a fragment of a radio report from somewhere around here. We're just playing it safe."

Luba was smiling at the other sergeant, who was leaning against the hood.

"Aren't you a little late on getting to your next assignment, sir? These orders say that you must report in by midnight."

Safcek spoke in a low voice as the sergeant examined the papers with his flashlight. "Well, my friend over there," he said, jerking his head toward Luba, "and I stayed a little longer than we planned in Tashkent. She wouldn't let me out of the hotel room." Safcek snickered, and the sergeant chuckled appreciatively.

"I understand, sir." He moved suddenly toward the trunk and said, "May I have the keys, please?"

Joe Safcek began to shout. "Sergeant, I think you have enough proof of my identity in your hand. Your comrade has not complained of any discrepancies in the lieutenant's papers, and you are just delaying me now."

The sergeant kept walking to the rear. On the other side of the car, Luba casually moved down to meet him at the trunk.

"Sergeant, I'm speaking to you. If you don't give me back my documents and let me pass, I'll put you on report with your commanding officer."

The security man hesitated at the rear bumper and said: "I have my orders. Please give me the keys."

Safcek pursued him and said: "Your name and unit? I'll have you broken."

The sergeant looked over the top of the car at the other security man, who shrugged back. In the reflection from the blue light, the sergeant's face was a blend of resentment and doubt. He stared at Safcek, who was poised in indignation.

"Here are your papers, sir. Please forgive the inconvenience. I was merely doing my job."

Safcek sagged as he accepted them. Without another word, he returned to the driver's seat and waited for Luba to join him. The sergeant hurried up to the window and added, "Colonel, please accept my apologies for the delay." Safcek slammed the car into gear and sped away. In the rear-view mirror, he saw the two security men talking animatedly. The sergeant Safcek had bullied was spreading his hands in the air in dismay.

Safcek shifted his gaze to Luba. "Close, huh?" She was pale and her hand fluttered as she asked, "Can I have a cigarette?"

He laughed in a low voice as he handed her one. "I hooked you on these, didn't I?"

She nodded and dragged deeply. Safcek watched her out of the corner of his eye. The strain appeared to be getting to her. Luba's eyes darted right and left as she watched the road. Her cheekbones seemed to bulge out of her face. She smoked the

198

cigarette down to the end, and Safcek did not interrupt her attempt to compose herself. He himself was not immune to fear. Out there in the darkness, the enemy was waiting for him. His stomach was churning but his mind was operating at maximum efficiency. He had been to the mountain before and looked down at the land beyond. It no longer terrified him. He only wanted to get the job done.

"Okay now?" he asked gently. She nodded and threw the butt out the window.

They were now an hour and thirty-five minutes behind schedule.

It was not yet 1 P.M. when the IL-62 parked at the regular commercial gate for deplaning passengers at Kennedy Airport. Only six men got off the huge jet from Moscow. Because of their diplomatic passports, they passed swiftly through customs and entered a long black limousine for the ride into New York City. In the rear seat, Mikhail Darubin was reading a copy of *The New York Times*. He finished the story of Clifford Erskine's sudden death at the Pentagon and poked one of his companions in the ribs. "This could not be better for our purposes."

Darubin was in great good humor. So far, everything he and Moskanko had planned had been going right.

As the car passed over the Triborough Bridge, Darubin looked for a long moment at the sharply etched New York skyline and said: "Tonight all that will be ours! Stark will never have the nerve to unleash a big war. And then I will quietly ease poor Krylov into retirement and give him a year's supply of his favorite hashish to dream with."

His companions chuckled appreciatively.

"The premier lost something, I think, when the Egyptians let us down in the Six Day War. He never regained his spirit. Now all he can do is dream about the old days when he was full of ideas and guts. But at least he did what we wanted in backing the army. Now we can let him graze in a pasture until the drugs sap his brain."

Darubin patted the newspaper against the upholstery reflectively. "Ten hours more." His serene face gazed out the window as the limousine pulled off the FDR Drive and eased into the heavy crosstown traffic on its way to the headquarters of the Soviet Mission to the UN on East Sixty-Seventh Street.

In Washington's sprawling black ghetto, hundreds of yellow buses moved up and down the streets picking up families and individuals waiting on street corners. Government cars roamed side streets. Drivers spoke through bullhorns urging residents to leave the danger zone.

Few balked. Leaders of the militant African Nationalist Movement had held a council of war in the morning and discussed defying the Administration's request to evacuate. After a vote, they had decided to obey the edict, since if any explosions did occur in the ghetto, the African Nationalists would be saddled with the blame. At noon, the council had driven off to Baltimore in a convoy of private cars. Behind them they left a padlocked office and a Doberman pinscher to protect their records and arsenal.

Workers at the Pentagon began to leave by 1 P.M. Only absolutely essential personnel remained to direct the military affairs of the country. In huge underground working areas, men and women kept their hands on the pulse of the strategic and tactical units around the world.

200

Friday, September 13

Cabinet officials had quietly told their families to seek safety elsewhere. Martin Manson's wife flew off to Miami; her husband told her she might as well take the excuse of the evacuation to have a vacation at the same time. Sam Riordan called his wife in Georgetown and suggested she visit the family estate in upper New York.

National Airport and Dulles witnessed the departure of an increasing number of important people. Mary Devereaux passed through at 1:15 P.M. Bob Randall had met her at lunch and given her the money for a week in Acapulco. When he told her he would join her in a few days, she went away happily.

Randall went on to his home briefly, packed two suitcases, and took them with him to the White House.

On Embassy Row, the order to leave the city had caused no great alarm. But in almost every beautiful mansion, skeleton staffs remained in residence to oversee the affairs of their respective governments. Stark knew this would happen and did not make a fuss over it. Aware that some people would always manage to stay behind in the forced departure, he was satisfied that most residents would be gone if the Russians carried out their threat.

In the Pentagon, General Stephen Austin Roarke sat in conference with the acting Secretary of Defense, John Dunham. Roarke was much more comfortable with the new man than his predecessor, Erskine. Dunham never had cause to argue directly with the head of the Joint Chiefs and did not share Erskine's jaundiced view of the military. He was convinced the American people had been continually misinformed about their government's activities in Asia and that the armed forces in particular had been held up to ridicule.

Roarke was a satisfied man on the eve of the ultimatum deadline. When Stark had given him the signal to prepare a mission from Incirclik, he had ceased his criticism of the Safcek operation. Now he merely awaited the order to launch the preventive strike at Tashkent.

"Dunham, when Stark says go, we'll call the Reds' bluff. How long has it been since we did that? It's incredible how we've let them bamboozle us over the past twenty or thirty years. Remember in Korea when we gave the Chinese their privileged sanctuary across the Yalu? And everyone agreed that the next time we would go all out. Then came Vietnam and Laos, and the Commies had their privileged sanctuaries in Cambodia and on the Ho trail. It was utterly fantastic that we could get sucked in again. There was no way to win there with them coming down the trails and sneaking back and forth across the borders whenever they wanted. And, of course, when we did something about it, the army got blamed for the mess. We were inept, war-mongering, and finally just butchers of innocent people.

"And those goddamn liberals in this country, those myopic bastards refused again and again to see the menace for what it was. Jesus Christ, they forced us to cut back, strip our defenses, cut our research and development programs. I'd like to go on the air and tell those creeps that this whole business of the ultimatum came about strictly because of their blind stupidity, their absolute refusal to recognize that the Russkies and their friends intend to blow our brains out as soon as they get the chance. But if I did, they'd have me committed for being Dr. Strangelove. They're incredible people, so goddamn self-righteous and humanitarian. They actually think the Reds have no aspirations for anybody else's territory!"

Dunham agreed and added: "It's the same right here on the homefront. The radicals, black and white, have been telling them straight out for years that they're going to destroy the country, bring the war to the suburbs, and take everything. And they don't believe it, just play the fool to these people who are fascists masquerading as defenders of morality. Nothing but fascists."

Roarke sighed disgustedly and turned to some papers on his

desk. "To hell with them. Any word from those Russians in Cuba who are supposed to come here after the ultimatum?"

"No, but I suspect they'll be chiming in shortly with a little psychological muscle. The Soviet ships in the Atlantic are directly east of Montauk and heading for it at ten knots."

"I know. I can't wait to nail them too."

Roarke looked hard at the acting secretary. "By two thirty Stark has to know if Safcek made it. After that he's got to give the word to Incirclik. I'll be waiting right here by the phone. With great pleasure, may I add." He smiled at his newfound friend.

On the horizon to the right, a dull glow appeared, and Safcek remarked: "They're busy tonight, that's for sure. Must be floodlights all over the grounds."

Checking the gauge he saw only one kilometer left to go. Slowing the car, he began searching for the culvert they had found in the afternoon. When he saw it, he pulled the automobile over and checked the road carefully in both directions. No lights marred the highway.

Safcek maneuvered the car down the slight slope and onto an even stretch of ground hidden from view. He shut off the engine and lights. In the darkness that engulfed them, the two agents heard only the rustle of the desert wind and an occasional insect. Safcek read his luminous watch: "Twelve thirty. We'll have to hurry.

"Let's go over this one last time. I'll carry the bomb; you cover me with the automatic rifle. We'll walk through the underbrush about one mile and aim for the gully. Watch out for the guards and the searchlights. Also don't forget to keep the mines checked out. The detector should keep us out of trouble on that score."

She listened carefully. "How long do we have to clear out before the bomb goes off?"

"It'll be on automatic once I set it. Thirty minutes."

"Ready?" he asked gently. She nodded, and they went back to the trunk, where Safcek handed Luba the automatic and a small hand-detector for mines. He strapped on a Walther PPK pistol and picked up the bomb container. "To hell with the satchel charges," he muttered. "We're running so late now that it will have to be the big bomb or nothing." Then he closed the trunk lid and whispered: "You go first."

In the bright moonlight, Luba picked a path down the slope and across a meadow running about five hundred yards toward the light in the northeast. Safcek carried the bomb case in his right hand and cautiously walked in her footsteps. She was picking her way very carefully, acutely aware of possible land mines. The moon kept hiding behind the clouds, and Safcek lost Luba twice in the sudden gloom. It was taking much longer than they had expected. She moved slowly, the rifle in her left hand, the detector sweeping back and forth in her right. At the top of the first rise, she stopped, and Safcek caught up to her. They looked down and saw the laser complex a mile distant, bathed in bright lights from six searchlights probing relentlessly over the perimeter, touching down in narrow swaths and crossing one another now and then in their constant vigils. Beyond the searchlights, the buildings were themselves almost darkened. The main structure, totally windowless, as Safcek had noted during the afternoon, loomed darkly above its neighbors.

The gully Safcek had picked for the detonation point lay in darkness, too, except for moments when the searchlights found it and examined it for intruders.

As Luba started to work cautiously down the hill, Safcek

whispered to her to hold, and he watched the searchlights closely to establish whatever pattern they might have in the gully area. It was irregular, obviously hand-manipulated by guards in the watchtowers. Safcek cursed audibly, and Luba turned to him.

"What's the matter, Colonel?"

"Those damn lights are unpredictable. I can't get a fix on them, and we need one in order to make our run into the gully." He hesitated and watched them for a time, hoping to find he was wrong. He was not. From the trees, the guards sent random probes into the gully, directing their beams in a careless, infuriating manner.

Safcek nudged Luba and said, "We can't wait." He pointed toward the shadowy gully and added: "Let's make straight for there. When I touch you again, stop. Don't speak in the meantime."

She headed down the slope without a word, and he followed with his container. She was going even slower now as they came closer to the danger zone. Her detector moved ceaselessly over the ground as she placed her feet down gingerly. At each step she halted to consider the next.

Six hundred yards from the fence around the laser complex, Luba heard the first noise. She dropped to the ground. Safcek fell behind her. The voices of two men drifted to them on the warm air, and a man laughed. Luba looked back over her shoulder to Safcek and pointed into a clump of trees just outside the fence and off to their right. Safcek felt his breath coming in short gasps. The voices seemed to come closer and then suddenly faded and were gone. Only the labored breathing of the two agents broke the stillness. After some minutes they got up and inched forward again.

The maddeningly slow pace continued. Luba was ten feet in front, probing the ground with the detector, when Safcek looked one more time at his watch and did some quick arithmetic.

He trotted ahead to her and touched her on the shoulder.

"Luba, all the delays," he whispered. "It's one twenty now. The only way we might make the rendezvous with the chopper would be if we started back this minute. And even so, we'd have trouble going through that block on the highway again."

As she waited for him to continue, she stood still beside a tree. Her face was shadowed by the limbs, which blocked out the moonlight.

"So I want you to take the chance to get away. Take the car and keep heading north. You can melt into the countryside. You're a native here. And your mother will hide you."

He saw her teeth suddenly as she smiled at him.

"Colonel, I can never see my mother again. It would mean her death if I did. And I have no other life that I care about."

Joe Safcek looked down at the tiny girl. "You're sure?"

"I'm sure, Colonel. Please believe me."

"OK, then, let's keep moving." He pushed her forward.

It was 10:25 P.M. inside the Kremlin walls.

Marshal Moskanko appeared enraged with the man before him. Vladimir Krylov leaned against the desk as he tried to focus his mind on his benefactor. Why was Moskanko glaring at him? Why didn't he go and glare at someone else? Krylov decided to bring great powers of concentration upon the formidable face of the man who was directing his nation's government.

"Vladimir Nikolaievich," Moskanko said disgustedly, "you are a disgrace. Look at yourself. You are nothing but a dope addict. And you call yourself Premier of the Union of Soviet Socialist Republics!" The defense minister's expression had changed to a mocking grin.

Krylov drew himself up. "Comrade Moskanko, I cannot stand the thought of what you intend to do to the people of America." He felt he had put that well and forcefully. "So I"—he paused, feeling time flowing by him on all sides as he searched his mind— "so I have no intention of being available for consultation on what to do in the next hours." His hands, at least, would be clean.

The defense minister laughed loudly as if from a great distance. "Vladimir Nikolaievich, we never had any intention of seeking your advice. We knew you were a coward."

The premier of the Soviet Union flushed. "I am no coward, Marshal, but I do have a conscience and could never live with myself if I was part of a plot to kill millions of people." Again he paused for he did not know how long. "I've done some bad things in my life but never have I contemplated the cold-blooded deaths of half the inhabitants of the world." Krylov stood straight before his master. "Your group has gone mad."

Moskanko was not offended. "Vladimir Nikolaievich, you may say whatever you want. You do not matter anymore. You are just excess baggage to us now. When we are ready, we will give you a nice little dacha out in the country, where you can brood and smoke and rot. In the meantime, stay out of my way. It will all be over in nine hours."

Vladimir Nikolaievich Krylov was not finished. He sat down heavily and waved his finger at the bemedaled soldier. "Comrade Moskanko, you will bring desolation to our land. . . . The Americans will fight in the end. . . . Stark may be torn, but he will finally face you down and send his missiles against us." Rarely had Krylov felt so confident of himself, of his words.

Yet Moskanko replied. "You are wrong, Vladimir Nikolaievich. His position is hopeless. He will be lucky not to lose his job before the ultimatum expires."

Krylov disdained to reply. He gave his attention instead to the music of balalaikas playing only for him.

"If he fights," the defense minister was now saying, "he will have to be a completely different man from the Stark we know. He has always been eager to make accommodations with us. First in the Middle East, where he left the Israelis more or less on their own. Then in Asia, where the United States has lost much of its influence. No, my dear Vladimir Nikolaievich. Stark is a compromiser, an appeaser who takes the course of least resistance. That is why we will win."

The marshal rose from his chair. "So you see, Comrade Premier, you have no guilt to worry about. And after this, you will have nothing else to worry about. You are quite finished."

He stared at Krylov, whose hand rubbed his two-day growth of beard in a rhythmic movement. The premier's face was furrowed in concentration, looking as if he were about to say something portentous. But Krylov said nothing to his tormentor, who was now moving rapidly toward the door.

Moskanko issued an order to the guard in the next room: "Don't let him out. Make sure his phones are disconnected." The defense minister strode briskly out of the building where Vladimir Nikolaeivich Krylov was now a prisoner listening to distant music.

The searchlights continued to probe unrelentingly around the perimeter. Safcek and Luba were now only 250 yards from the entrance to the gully. She was being even more careful as she made the final approach. Her hand counter swept in a wider arc, and she moved more hesitantly.

Safcek checked the luminous dial of his watch. It was 1:37 A.M. When he heard a low whistle off to the left behind a group of saplings, he knew they might soon stumble upon a dog patrol. It was enough to make up his mind. Safcek ran to Luba and whispered: "This is OK."

"But it's out in the open!"

"That's all right. It won't take long."

She crouched beside him while he pulled the box handles apart and lifted the lid. She looked inside and saw hundreds of tiny Styrofoam pellets. Safcek reached into them and drew forth a Colt .45 automatic pistol, which the Styrofoam had cushioned from buffeting. He took the gun out and held it gingerly by the barrel. In the moonlight, it glinted dully. Even in his haste, Safcek had to marvel at the sophisticated weapon. In the butt of the gun, a marble-sized ball of Einstinium 119 particles rested inside a thin coating of plastique. Above it was a transitorized battery; two wires ran from the battery into the plastique cover. Attached to one of the wires was a tiny vial of prussic acid. On the outside of the butt was a single black button. When forcefully pressed it would break the vial, causing the acid to eat into the wire. In thirty minutes' time, with the electrical contact broken, the plastique would implode onto the transuranic particles, forcing them into a precise density. In a millisecond, the resultant nuclear explosion would obliterate the laser works.

"You just press the button, Colonel?" She took it in her hands.

"That's all, Luba. And then run like hell."

Peter Kirov's message to the Center in Moscow had put the state security forces at the laser on special alert. Inside a concrete blockhouse within the compound, a sharp beep echoed off the walls at 1:39 A.M. as infrared body-heat sensors signaled the presence of intruders. The duty officer rushed to a television monitor while a sergeant pushed a button to focus a camera on the violated sector.

The officer saw two badly blurred shapes standing just at the edge of a line of trees. He could not further identify them except that they seemed to be wearing uniforms. One of the strangers was holding something and examining it closely.

"What is their range?"

"Two hundred yards beyond dog-patrol boundary, sir."

The duty officer nodded. "Take them now."

Joe Safcek had wasted enough time. "Give it to me, Luba," and she held the pistol out to him. As he reached for it, the gun began to dance away, and Luba slowly sank into the grass. Frantically, Safcek grabbed again at her hand, but it was gone, and the pistol had disappeared. The frustrated colonel was suddenly dizzy and nauseated. Struggling desperately to plant his feet firmly, he started to curse at Luba for falling asleep when he needed her. But he realized he, too, wanted to rest for a while, and his body went down onto the lush softness of the clearing, and he lay beside Luba.

Four men wearing grotesque gas masks approached the forms in the clearing. They moved slowly, warily. Their rifles were trained on the trespassers.

In the blockhouse, the duty officer watched the monitor while he spoke to the patrol by walkie-talkie.

"Be careful with them. They may not have gotten enough gas. We have a malfunction in the lines out there."

The bodies had begun to move. One of them staggered to his feet, and looked wildly about for something on the ground. The other one was moving about on hands and knees. Both were shaking their heads as if to clear them. The one standing suddenly lunged toward an object on the ground, and the duty officer shouted: "Shoot them."

Joe Safcek felt a terrible pain as a bullet hit him, and he fell onto Luba's riddled body.

The masked men came up and one of them prodded Safcek with the tip of his rifle. He toppled over and lay face up in the meadow.

The patrol leader reported: "A colonel and a lieutenant. The lieutenant is a woman. The colonel has a bullet in his right shoulder. The woman is a mess, but she's still alive."

"Any weapons on them?"

"The usual, a Walther pistol, an AK-47 rifle. It is too dark out here to tell if that's all"

"Bring them in. We will pick up any other equipment when it is light."

The duty officer switched off the radio and noted the time in his log: 2:05 A.M.

In the Oval Room, Stark sat with Randall. The President was on the intercom to the Situation Room.

"Any news from Safcek?"

"No, sir."

"How about the satellites?"

"Midas Twenty-Six reports nothing. Same for Samos Ten."

Stark punched the button off and returned to his foreign-policy advisor.

"We're already running late on the detonation, right?" Randall asked.

"I'm afraid so. It should have gone up by now, and the chopper will soon be at the rendezvous, a good two hours' drive from the laser. Maybe he ran into trouble but is still in a position to set it off even though he may never get out. He'd do it that way if he had to." Stark spoke with more optimism than he felt. After all the hours of waiting, the President was losing hope in Operation Scratch. For a fleeting moment he damned himself for ever putting so much faith in it. He felt foolish for okaying it, for having counted on it to solve his problem. Stark caught himself and told Randall, "Get ready for a long night."

The time was 3:18 P.M. The ultimatum period had entered its final eight hours.

At 3:45 P.M., Washington time, the thing Herb Markle had feared happened. At an intersection in the Anacostia Flats, workmen had just started checking the natural gas pipeline. One of them dropped a tool on the pavement. It sparked, and great puffs of flame burst around the men and rose seventy-five feet into the air. Two of the workers were engulfed in the fire. While some of their co-workers tried to reach them and smother the flames, others ran about shouting at pedestrians and those in cars to get out of the area. It was too late. A monstrous explosion lifted the street four feet in the air, and fire erupted from the ground. One explosion followed another as buildings in a two-block area fell and burst into flame. Cars were melted down. Hundreds of witnesses to the disaster scurried back and forth looking for an escape route. Sirens sounded in the distance, and soon fire engines came charging into the holocaust. Hoses were quickly run out. Some hydrants had been destroyed, and the fire department had to splice lines in from working pumps many blocks away. Flames from the burning neighborhood reached into the sky to join the billowing clouds from Virginia and Maryland.

Herb Markle heard the news almost instantly. He buried his face in his hands, crying: "Oh God, what have I done?" His secretary heard him and wondered what the remark meant.

Markle called the White House and insisted on being put through immediately to the Oval Room. Randall answered and heard the hysterical Markle demanding to talk to Stark. Randall would not let the distraught man talk to the President in his condition and told him Stark was in a meeting of the Joint Chiefs of Staff. When Markle said he would not accept any further responsibility for the deaths, that it was Stark's fault, Randall snapped: "Listen, Markle, you keep your mouth shut. Someday, you'll know what this is all about, but in the meantime, you'd better get a hold on yourself and protect the President of the United States. I'm warning you, not asking you. For Christ's sake, shape up!"

Almost incoherent by this time, Markle nevertheless haltingly agreed to maintain silence.

The last two agents from Operation Scratch were brought inside the compound they had tried to destroy. Luba Spitkovsky was placed on the table in the infirmary. The doctors examined her multiple wounds, conferred, and ordered her taken immediately by ambulance to the main hospital in Tashkent. Then they moved on to the unconscious Safcek. His single wound had bled profusely.

The doctors worked swiftly, removing the bullet and cleaning the gaping hole.

Two hundred miles to the southeast, a khaki-colored helicopter raced toward the Soviet border at an altitude of one hundred feet. In the cockpit, an anxious radio operator tapped out a message to Karl Richter in Peshawar. It began, "Dear John, Dear John." At his desk, Karl Richter decoded the fateful words and transmitted them immediately to President Stark in the Oval Room of the White House:

"Mr. President, Safcek did not make the rendezvous. The chopper waited as long as it could—until three fifteen A.M.—and there was no sign of him on the road."

Stark asked: "Nothing further from Safcek himself?"

"Nothing, sir. He must have been discovered."

Richter waited as Stark put his hand over the mouthpiece and told the grim news to Robert Randall and Martin Manson. Then he cut back to Richter saying: "I'll be waiting right here."

In Peshawar Karl Richter poured a double Scotch, added an ice cube, and sat back, waiting for the remote possibility that the radio would come to life.

The streets around the United Nations were jammed with pickets and the curious long before the Security Council meeting was due to convene. By 5 P.M., extra police details had been brought in to control the swelling masses who materialized from the caverns of the city to promote their own causes. Ambassador Tolypin's 11 A.M. press conference had already had its desired impact on the American people. Worried families in the eastern time zone rushed through dinner in order to be at the television set when the fateful debate began at 6 P.M. Some network commentators had begun to make a connection between the forced evacuation of Washington and the Soviet intimation of a fatal breach among the world powers. A terrible uneasiness had filtered out to the suburbs and the prairies, to the high-rise apartments and country towns where parents wondered what tomorrow would bring for their children. Some people went into their bomb shelters, dug years earlier, to check stocks of canned goods and survival gear. Others cursed the fact that they had neglected to provide one.

Friday, September 13

Everywhere, anxious anticipation was an almost tangible presence, for no word had come from the White House about the Soviet allegations. President William Mellon Stark had issued no response. His press secretary, Edwin Rast, continued to declare that Stark would not deign to reply to such gross insinuations. The American people could only wait for the debate to shed light on the menacing dialogue.

Inside the UN the delegates' lounges were filled with frantic diplomats trying to get concrete answers to their own governments' frenzied cables. The British representative, Lord Harkness, an elegantly dressed, pinch-faced veteran of countless crises, had cornered the chief American delegate, Ronald Carlson, and was badgering him with less than subtle demands for information. Carlson had been able to parry most of these searching queries so effectively that the British statesman was losing his aplomb.

Carlson's greatest problem was his own lack of information. His only orders from the White House had been given that morning after Zarov announced his intention to expose the United States. Carlson, a former president of the World Bank, had been sent to the UN by Stark as a reward for his financial support during election campaigns. Unfortunately, Carlson found himself completely outside the mainstream of politics and policy-making in his new post. He was not called into cabinet meetings. He was merely handed directives to carry out. While he and Stark were still on the best of terms personally, Ronald Carlson intended to resign his position and go back to Kansas at the end of the General Assembly session. He had become tired of being an errand boy.

Carlson was as mystified as anyone else and found it difficult to fend off impassioned delegates such as Lord Harkness, whom he had admired for years. Yet he had no choice. Stark had told him to remain mute and evasive, to deny the Soviet claims, whatever form they took, and to stall any Soviet attempts to censure the United States by vote of the Security Council. Ronald Carlson, faithful to his oath of office, had agreed to these conditions and now braced himself to meet the challenge.

Lord Harkness was completely exasperated. "Carlson, I've known you a long time and always had excellent feelings toward you. And yet now I find myself disbelieving your words. You're deliberately hiding something from me, and I resent it.

"Lord Harkness, I've told you the truth. The United States has no designs on the Soviet Union. Stark has already said the pamphlet yesterday was the work of cranks. And you know him better than to suppose he would ever intend to annihilate anyone. What more can I tell you?"

Harkness was not so easily rebuffed. He looked reproachfully at his friend and said: "Why doesn't Stark go on television and tell the whole world the Reds are playing their dirty rotten game again? His silence only makes people wonder what in God's name is going on. I must tell you that my government for one is highly nervous over the situation. Stark has told the prime minister that nothing is amiss in the world. We are not children, you know, and you cannot treat us this way."

Ronald Carlson felt truly pained for Harkness, who stood with his Scotch and water in the middle of the lounge and begged for some morsel of hard information. He put his hand on Harkness's shoulder.

"I understand your predicament and your prime minister's sense of outrage. But I have to repeat my earlier remarks. The Soviet machinations are just that, an attempt to put us in a bad light. They've been doing that for years and nothing has really changed, has it?"

Harkness shook his head in impatience and abruptly walked away. While Carlson watched him leave, the chief delegate from Japan, Eisaku Ono, confronted him with the same questions. Sighing, Ronald Carlson repeated his defense of the American position.

At the doorway, Ambassadors Zarov and Tolypin were immediately besieged by a flurry of diplomats who asked them the inside story of the pending council meeting. Both maintained grim faces while they urged patience until the actual debate. Zarov added: "Then you will see the extent of the conspiracy."

Commissioner Herb Markle had been unable to stay in his office. He went to the scene of the pipeline explosion and walked through the two blocks of misery. He saw the firemen digging in the rubble and began to weep. He was noticed by a policeman, who gently patted the distraught man's shoulder.

Wrenching away, Markle continued his anguished inspection past smoldering cars, until he suddenly turned and went back the way he had come.

At Lafayette Park, he stood glaring across at the windows of the White House. He stayed there for a long time, smoking one cigarette after another. Then he moved swiftly toward the Presidential mansion. When the guard at the West Gate stopped him, Markle identified himself and asked to see Stark.

Unaware of Markle's previous encounter with Randall, Sam Riordan authorized him to enter.

Stark shook hands warmly with his friend and asked immediately about the awful situation in Anacostia. Slumped in a chair, Herb Markle told him the gruesome details. When the President seemed too preoccupied to pursue it, Markle lost control and shouted: "How in God's name can you sit there so calmly while the dead are in the morgues because of you? How can you be so callous?"

Stark kept looking at the phone beside him. His thoughts

went to Joe Safcek, lost and unaccounted for in the desert, to the Security Council meeting minutes away, to the laser that threatened to burn down the city in five and a half hours. He forced his attention back to Markle.

"Herb, please calm down. I care very much about those people who died today. And I want you to stop tearing yourself into little pieces because you followed my orders. It's not your fault."

The phone rang, and Stark grabbed for it.

"NORAD, sir. Nothing yet from the Tashkent area."

Stark carefully replaced the receiver and, in what had become a nervous mannerism over the last three days, looked at his watch: 5:45. He turned back to his guest.

"As I said, Herb, stop torturing yourself. I'll explain things soon, and it'll make some sense, believe me."

Markle exploded: "Some sense, for Christ's sake. Can you make sense out of murder and blasted homes? Can you? Well, I can't, and I won't accept any of it. I'll be goddamned if I'll be saddled with this outrage for the rest of my life."

He was towering over Stark, who sat motionless, taking the verbal battering. In the next room, Robert Randall heard the uproar and rushed in.

The Commissioner had not finished.

"I walked through that place just now and saw what your orders have done to I don't know how many families. And you keep on acting as though it was merely a regrettable error. Well, let me tell you something: you've changed a helluva lot since you got in that seat. Is it power that's done it? Power?"

Randall spun Markle around and said in an angry undertone: "March out of here, Herb. How dare you do this to the President?"

At the door leading from the Oval Room, Markle laughed scornfully and shouted: "Who are you planning to kill tomorrow?"

218

William Stark had no answer. He turned away from his friend and looked out at the landing pad, where a helicopter carrying Michael Macomber was due momentarily from Dulles International Airport.

The fifteen members of the Security Council were in their seats at 5:55 P.M. Some smoked pensively, others stared up into the television room where correspondents from the major networks supplied a colorful commentary to over 90 million watching Americans. In other parts of the world, satellites carried the broadcast live to other millions of anxious people trapped between the two major antagonists in the continuing cold war. In the Soviet Union, television programs did not carry any of the drama emanating from the UN.

At precisely 5:59 P.M., Arndt Svendsen entered the chamber and went quickly to his seat. The Secretary General was not in his usual happy frame of mind and ignored greetings from old friends as he shuffled papers and peered over his spectacles at the council members. At 6 P.M. he rapped his gravel, and all noise subsided.

Svendsen adjusted his spectacles and began: "Gentlemen, we are here tonight in reference to a rather unusual request from the delegate of the Union of Soviet Socialist Republics. This morning he came to me urging that I call a special session of this body to discuss a most serious matter. We are here assembled, and I now propose to allow the distinguished Mr. Zarov to present his case for your consideration. Do I hear any objections?" Hearing none, he asked Zarov to speak.

The television cameras panned in on the short, well-fed form of Yuri Zarov, the sixty-two-year-old bearer of orders from the Kremlin. Zarov had survived the frequent convulsions of power in the Soviet Union for the past twenty-seven years. A totally humorless man, he was well-known to Americans. Like an angry neighbor, he had frequently complained to them about U.S. indiscretions and ambitions. He scolded, threatened, and lied to the American people about its government's chicanery and belligerence. His audience had come to enjoy his presence in their living rooms, anticipating his diatribes with a benign humor. The Russian provided a pleasant diversion from the ponderous debates that normally emerged from UN crises. Zarov was an enemy but surely not a bore.

He sat at ease in his accustomed spot just to the right of the chief United States delegate, Ronald Carlson. Zarov began to speak in a soft voice, and the translators rushed to pick up his words and relay them in several languages to listeners.

"Mr. Secretary General, esteemed members of the United Nations Security Council, I have asked you to come here to listen to a tale of perfidy so outrageous as to defy precedent. It affects all of us because it concerns an attempt by one of us to enslave the world."

Zarov reached for a glass of water and drank deeply while the amphitheater buzzed with an astonished reaction. Ronald Carlson, at his left, doodled with a pencil.

Zarov put down his glass and continued his attack.

"Perhaps it would serve everyone's best interest if I explained the background to this treachery. The whole world knows that the Soviet Union has been attempting for decades to stabilize the various conflicts that have threatened to envelop us in total war. In the Middle East the reactionary forces of the state of Israel have fomented aggression against the peoples of the Arab world. We have tried to help the Arab nations by supplying Egypt and its neighbors with the proper means to protect their freedom."

Several of the members smiled self-consciously at Zarov's statement. Ronald Carlson grinned widely and stared at the ceiling in amazement. Arndt Svendsen tried to conceal his absolute disbelief by studiously wiping his glasses with a Kleenex.

Zarov ignored the amusement and continued: "In Southeast Asia, imperialist forces have made a shambles of the region between the Mekong and the sea in their ceaseless pursuit of resources and territory. For our part, the Soviet Union looked on in horror while innocents were being slaughtered and land devastated by the 'democratic forces of liberation.' Since we had no desire to plunge the world into war over this issue, we could only send supplies to our beleaguered friends who calmly withstood the fascist hordes."

Ronald Carlson was now wondering whether Zarov would have the temerity to include Czechoslovakia in his list of good deeds. Zarov did not disappoint him.

"Even in one of our own socialist countries, we had to act to prevent a deterioration of the status quo. When imperialist reactionaries tried to subvert the government and inhabitants of that wonderful ally, we were forced to correct the situation by rooting out the enemy and exposing his deceits to the world. As you remember, the forces of the Soviet Union entered that country only at the request of true patriots who desperately sought our help. And as you know we neither murdered nor burned as Western nations have done countless times in recent history."

In the White House, Robert Randall switched off the set and went down the hall to the Oval Room, where William Stark sat in his big swivel chair. Stark was staring at a phone on his left which connected him with the tracking stations in California.

Stark looked up as Randall entered and asked: "Has Zarov started to speak yet?"

"Yes, but so far it's the usual baloney about our imperialistic excesses. I couldn't concentrate too much on him. Has Macomber arrived from Paris yet?"

"He's landing on the pad now." Stark waved toward the window facing onto the South Lawn behind him.

The two men went directly to the Cabinet Room, where the special Committee waited. Gerald Weinroth was there, too, brought from Walter Reed Army Hospital by ambulance to be present when the documents arrived. Sitting up on a hospital stretcher, Weinroth, though uncomfortable, was anxious to get a look at the material that would unlock the mystery threatening the lives of the entire population of the world.

William Stark shook hands with Michael Macomber and thanked him for his timely arrival. Then he asked Weinroth to study the blueprints. The professor propped himself up on the cot and studied the plans carefully for several minutes without a word. He turned the pages one by one with what seemed agonizing deliberateness. The other observers dared not interrupt his concentration. General Roarke paced up and down the thick red carpet. Stark himself sat in his swivel chair and stared intently at the scientist.

Weinroth seemed about to speak. But he plunged again into the mass of technical details and ignored the waiting group. Robert Randall spoke softly to Macomber, asking him again how he came to possess the documents. Sam Riordan listened carefully to Macomber's story, then passed on the news from Perkins about Debran's death. Macomber appeared shaken. Riordan asked, "Did Debran mention anything Rudenko said the last time they met?"

"No, sir, except that he seemed quite nervous and agitated."

Riordan said: "I can imagine he was."

Weinroth interrupted: "Mr. President, I believe these blueprints are genuine. They are a complete description of the weapon itself.

"The gun is three hundred and fifty feet long and has a bore of, let's see, sixty-six feet; it has semireflective mirrors at either end. The power comes from a nuclear generator plant that's six stories down and about a quarter mile away. That must be the place Intelligence pinpointed from the photographs. The en-

ergy is piped to the weapon through massive conduits into elec-
trodes and then thick supercooled cables that run the length
of the laser. When the energy is built up to the required level
of intensity, the scientist just presses a button, and the beam
fries a city like an egg.

"Oh, and one other thing. Sam, you caught the fact that the
Russians sent up a whole series of satellites in August. Well,
they were all part of this operation. The Soviets set up a string
of grapefruit-sized spheres in orbit, and these act like navigational aids for the laser. It can bounce off one of these balls
at exactly the angle needed to redirect it to a target on earth.

"That's about all we need to know at this moment. Our program is amazingly similar to theirs in most details. The only
problem is they are operational right now, and we aren't, thanks
to lack of money."

William Stark rushed to him. "That's fantastic, Gerald! Just
fantastic! Can we adapt this information to our own gun right
away?"

Weinroth looked away, cast his gaze around the room for
a while, and then met his President's eyes again.

"I can say positively there is no chance. Our contraption is
only slightly different from theirs, but the biggest problem is
that they have their nuclear generators working, and we won't
have ours going for three months. Without them, we can't get
any power to the weapon. Besides that, we don't have the spheres
in orbit to direct the beam back to earth."

Stark was crushed. "You mean having this material doesn't
really help us at all?"

"I'm afraid not."

"Goddamnit, to have these plans and not be able to use them!"

"Maybe we can," Randall said. "Why not let the Russians
know we have the blueprints and have worked out an operational laser? It's a bluff, but maybe they'll buy it and hold off."

Gerald Weinroth weighed the suggestion. "It depends on what

they know of our progress on the gun up to now. If they're in the dark, it might work."

Randall scribbled a brief hot-line message and handed it to Stark for comment. The president read it and said: "Go ahead, Bob. It just might set their clocks back for a while."

It was 6:45 P.M. in Washington. The deadline was four hours and thirty-three minutes away.

Joe Safcek opened his eyes and saw bright early-morning sunlight streaming in through the window. A nurse in white starched linen was at the foot of the bed.

Safcek wondered who she was and where he was, and then she spoke in Russian, and he knew. When he tried to move, the pain hit him, and he remembered the field and Luba. Safcek thought of the pistol and wondered whether he had ever reached it and pushed the arming button. But the sunlight warned him he had not, for hours must have gone by and he was still alive.

The nurse went to the door and spoke to a uniformed man, who then peered in at Safcek. The man's eyes were watery, almost friendly, as they examined the wounded man. In Russian he called: "Good morning, sir."

Joe Safcek just stared at the man looming up before him. He wore the uniform of a colonel in the KGB. Built like a fire plug, squat and lumpy, he was impeccably dressed, and his face, seamed and generously streaked with the ravages of good liquor, was affable and reassuring. Safcek noticed the Soviet colonel wore a walkie-talkie strapped to his right hip.

He pulled up a chair beside the bed. "I hope you're feeling well enough to talk for a moment or two."

224

Safcek was fully awake now. The realization that his mission had failed broke through the sedatives and anesthetics and left him alert and wary.

"What time is it?" Safcek asked.

"Six o'clock, Colonel. It is colonel, isn't it?"

Calculating swiftly, Safcek knew that it would be 7 P.M. now in Washington, which in just a little over four hours might be burned from the face of the earth. He decided not to waste any time on sham. "I'm Colonel Joseph Safcek, U.S. Army, Serial Number 0-1926112, on detached duty from Fort Bragg, North Carolina."

The Soviet colonel slapped his knee loudly. "Well sir, my compliments on your forthright attitude. It saves us all a lot of unnecesary effort. Would you mind telling me the details of your mission? We have sent your unfortunate comrade to a hospital in Tashkent, and I regret what our guards did to her. But I am sure you realize the methods we have to employ at this location."

Safcek shifted his position and winced at the effort. He ignored the officer's reference to Luba.

The colonel lit a cigarette and blew the smoke up to the ceiling. "Colonel Safcek, the details, please."

"We came here to destroy the laser. As simple as that. You caught us infiltrating before we could accomplish our task."

"You must be an amazing man, Colonel, for your country to trust you with such a tremendous chore. To think they believed you could single-handedly eliminate our most secret project! Incredible!"

Safcek tried to smile. "I've had some experience, sir. In Vietnam, I made a career out of living behind enemy lines and doing roughly the same kind of thing."

The Russian was properly impressed. He smoked the cigarette for a minute and then repeated his request.

"The details, please."

Safcek sighed through his pain. "Once inside the perimeter we could make our way to the laser, plant charges around the building and burn down the laser. The charges had timers on them, giving us thirty minutes to clear the area. At three o'clock we were supposed to meet a helicopter east of Tashkent and go home."

The colonel looked quickly at his watch.

Safcek reassured him. "The chopper's long gone now, Colonel. It could only wait fifteen minutes for us."

"Where was home?"

When Safcek did not answer, the Russian went on to another point. "We found no dynamite with you, Colonel. We did find six charges in the trunk of your car, though."

"They're still out there in a clump of trees," Safcek lied. "We only took six of the twelve we had because I felt that would be enough. They should be near where you found us. All our weapons are out there. I had two pistols and a knife. The woman had a knife and an AK-47 rifle."

The Russian smiled affably as he looked around for an ashtray. "Are there any other teams operating against us now? It's hard to believe the United States would leave its fate to just one group! No offense intended toward you, by the way. I must say I admire you tremendously on both a professional and personal level."

Safcek summoned his strength and accepted the compliment.

"Thanks very much. But I failed, and there's no one else around to help me out. You can rest easy on that."

The Russian was not convinced. As he rose from the chair, the ash fell from his cigarette to the floor. He smoothed it into the rug with the polished tip of his boot and excused himself.

"I'll be back later, Colonel Safcek. Please rest and ask the nurse for anything you want. Within reason, of course." The Russian laughed as he went out the door.

Safcek lay back exhausted. Helpless to control events further, his only hope was that someone would search for the pistol, pick it up, and play with it. Safcek asked the nurse to close the blinds.

Colonel Lavrenti Kapitsa had gone back to his office, where he found his distinguished visitor from Moscow. Sitting behind the desk, Marshal Pavel Andreievich Bakunin was leafing through the log detailing the capture of the intruders outside the perimeter. Bakunin was curt with Kapitsa.

"Colonel, have you talked yet with the wounded man?"

"Yes, sir, and I was quite successful."

"How so?"

"He just confessed to being a colonel in the United States Army Green Berets." Referring to notes, Kapitsa added, "His name is Joseph Safcek, serial number 0-1926112."

The startled Bakunin reached quickly for the phone to inform Moskanko when Kapitsa continued, "He was going to destroy the laser."

"With what?"

"Plastique. We found six charges in his car, and he says there are six more out in the field somewhere."

"Plastique? Could that do the job?" Bakunin sounded incredulous.

"Yes, sir. He could have done it *if* he had gotten through my men," Kapitsa said with a certain smugness.

Bakunin was suddenly agitated. "Colonel, you have had long experience with intelligence matters. What does this attempt tell you about the mind of the enemy?"

Before Kapitsa could reply, Bakunin rushed on. "Would the American President send these two this far on the slim chance that they could break our security screen and get up close to the laser? No, I think not. There must be something else that we do not know yet. What do you think?"

He looked searchingly at the KGB officer, who seemed deflated in the presence of the interrogator from Moscow. Kapitsa fumbled for an answer. "It is possible Safcek is only a decoy for some other move by Washington."

The marshal nodded. "That is just what I think. And it is the worst thought of all, because it means that Stark is not the man I was told he was."

Grimly, Bakunin reached for the phone again.

In Moscow, it was after 3 A.M., but the Kremlin was not asleep. The hot-line operator was startled by the insistent clatter of the teletype machine. He waited while a message appeared, then handed it to the duty officer, who ran to an adjoining room and thrust it at Marshal Moskanko, who had just finished his conversation with Bakunin about the Green Beret officer in Tashkent. The defense minister put down his coffee and asked: "From Washington?"

"Yes, sir."

Moskanko read it quickly and bellowed: "Put me through to Serkin!"

While he reread the message he lighted a huge cigar with trembling hands.

Professor Serkin came on the line and Moskanko said: "Serkin, I need your advice. Listen to this. It's a note I just got from the White House."

WE HAVE YOUR BLUEPRINTS. WE ALSO HAVE OPERATIONAL LASER WEAPON. IF YOU PERSIST IN YOUR ULTIMATUM, WE WILL REGRETFULLY PROCEED TO DESTRUCTION OF MOSCOW. EXPECT ANSWER BEFORE EXPIRATION OF YOUR ULTIMATUM OR EVENTS WILL TAKE THEIR NATURAL COURSE.

STARK

Moskanko's hands were clammy as he realized the impact of Stark's words. The gamble was lost if the Americans were indeed in possession of the same weapon. The defense minister said: "Is he bluffing or not, Serkin? Can they actually have one ready?"

Serkin tried to think through the defense minister's persistent questioning.

"I just do not know the exact state of their development, Marshal. If your intelligence people could help me there, then I could make a more calculated assessment."

"Fair enough. I'll have a conference call set up so we can discuss this more logically. By the way, is everything ready?"

Serkin was silent for a minute.

"Serkin, is . . ."

"Yes, Marshal, the laser is fully operational. We need only ten minutes lead time to carry out a firing."

"Good, good. I'll be back to you shortly."

Moskanko hung up and called for a battery of intelligence experts to be brought to him within a half hour. He looked once more at Stark's hot line and cursed the President of the United States of America.

Four men joined Moskanko in twenty minutes—Omskuschin and Fedoseyev, who had been awakened from a few precious minutes of sleep, and two civilians. They sat on a long couch while the defense minister took off his khaki tunic and unbuttoned his regulation shirt. He threw his tie onto the desk. A waiter came in with vodka and mineral water, and the men poured tiny glasses of the colorless liquid. They drained them at a gulp and reached for the mineral water to wash it down. While they munched black bread, the glasses were filled once more.

The florid-faced Moskanko smacked his lips. "Gentlemen, we have come up against a thorny problem. President Stark has told us two things: one, he has those damn blueprints Rudenko smuggled out, and, worse, he claims he has an operational weapon ready. Now, what I want to know beyond a shadow of a doubt is whether he is lying." The four men were silent. "Because if he is not lying, and I go ahead with my plans, Moscow will be gone in seconds."

The two marshals tried to speak at the same time. Moskanko waved his hand and said: "Brukov, what do you have to say?" Sergei Brukov headed North American espionage operations for the KGB. It was to him that all agent's reports from the United States and Canada were routed; it was from him that all agents were sent out. Brukov was a brilliant man, fluent in six languages, a poet, a chess master. He was also an extraordinary spy himself. For six years he had lived in the United States as an Illegal and spied on research in nuclear weapons. The unusually talented Brukov was totally unprepossessing. At the age of fifty-two he was gaunt, sallow-faced. He wore horn-rimmed glasses, and his teeth were mottled by years of accumulated tobacco tar. He smiled easily and now turned his pleasant gaze toward the defense minister.

"Dear friend and comrade, I do not believe you have reason to worry. Of course, I cannot be positive, but our latest reports indicate the Americans cannot possibly catch up to us in so short a time. As you know, we have access to their test facility through Raymond Darnell, the scientist. He has faithfully transmitted progress reports to us by way of our consulate in Chicago, and he has declared flatly that because of money problems the U.S. has gone ever so slowly on the gun. In fact, because their Congress was so pressured by all the dissension in the country, scientists there were prevented from having the gun maybe a year before we did."

Omskuschin interrupted: "But with the blueprints could they have worked out a quick solution and leapfrogged the time needed to fire a prototype. That is what really worries me. I do not underestimate the American technical capability one bit."

Brukov frowned and shrugged his shoulders. "That I cannot tell you. But as for their progress up to, let us say a week ago, there is not a chance they could be prepared."

"What about your end, Shumilov?" Moskanko asked.

Konstantin Shumilov, the Soviet director of intelligence for space activities, controlled the observations of all Soviet spy satellites. The forty-two-year-old Shumilov was quick to reply.

"We have had absolutely no emissions from the American sector. Either from Lincoln Lab or anywhere else on the continent. Absolutely none."

"Could they have tested it out in the Pacific or down range in the Atlantic?" Fedoseyev asked.

"No possibility. We would have seen it or sensed it. The Cosmos groupings have orbits that cover the areas mentioned on a continual basis. No place is left unattended for more than five minutes."

"Yes, but could they not have allowed for that and fired within that five-minute period?" Moskanko snapped.

"It is possible, Marshal. Let us say they shot out of Lincoln Lab and we missed it there; I am sure we would have picked it up at point of impact. Besides, the wide eye of the cameras and sensors would have caught the trajectory at an off angle regardless of where it impacted."

Moskanko was not convinced. "Get Serkin in on this now." A conference call was arranged, and Serkin announced his presence at the laser works.

The defense minister outlined the conclusions reached up to that point and asked: "Professor, could they alter their own weapon to accept our improvements?"

Serkin replied: "It depends on how closely it approximated ours to begin with."

Brukov broke in: "Essentially the same. In fact, much of our design is based on information we received about theirs from one of their scientists."

231

Serkin asked: "How about the nuclear generator?"

Brukov referred to some notes and replied: "Our informant told us on August twenty-fifth they were three months from test fire. The generator was far from ready."

Serkin's voice was crisp and sure now. "Then I see no way the blueprints could have brought them even with us. No matter how great the emergency, it would be impossible for them to fire without the power from the generator. Then, of course, they have to be sure the laser itself functions correctly, too."

Moskanko had heard enough. "Thank you gentlemen. I think I know what to do now. By the way, Serkin, Marshal Bakunin, who is at the complex now, is there only as my special observer. You take all orders directly from me." The conference call was ended.

In Tashkent, Anatoly Serkin plunged back into his work. He paused fitfully to drink coffee. Though he had not smoked for five years, he now puffed cigarette after cigarette as he tried to concentrate on the technical details of his job. He answered the questions of his assistants perfunctorily and in between conversations sat at his desk thinking of the gentle Andrei Parchuk.

Parchuk had worked in the next room, and Serkin had used the connecting door many times as he sipped coffee with his friend and discussed the day's work load. Serkin was intensely conscious of the emptiness nearby and could not keep his mind off it.

The calls from Moskanko had also been unsettling. Serkin was convinced the Americans were bluffing, but he was impressed with the audacity of the American President. He marveled that the man was still capable of resisting the enormous pressures being brought against him.

Had Parchuk, too, resisted? Was that why they took him away? Round and round his thoughts went. If Parchuk, who asked only friendship and gave only the love of a lonely man in return, could resist, what should Serkin think of himself?

In three and a half hours he would have to be ready to fire the laser at Washington.

The Security Council meeting had been recessed for nearly an hour. While weary delegates talked in the hallways or slumped in their seats, television commentators tried to fill air time by speculating on the Russians' next move. Clement Dawson of United News Broadcasting had as his guest the distinguished correspondent of *The Toronto Globe and Mail,* Henry Pinkham. The venerable Pinkham, an increasingly cynical witness to the futility of the international body, had watched Zarov emote for an hour, giving a Soviet view of recent history. Like many of the bored spectators and delegates, he tried vainly to fathom the latest Soviet tactic. Pinkham was convinced that Zarov was stalling for time, but beyond that he could not imagine what was going to happen. When Clement Dawson asked him to predict, Pinkham shrugged and replied: "I've seen them all here, Vishinsky, Zorin, Gromyko, at times when the world was about to go down the drain, and it always seemed you knew their battle plan. The Russians have never been masters of subtlety. And yet this time I must admit I'm stumped by all this. Zarov hasn't said anything new. In fact, he's just parroted the party line for an hour. After getting the whole world in an uproar the past two days over the diabolical ambitions of the United States, he's managed to let us down badly so far. As a reporter, I'm baffled."

Down below, Ambassador Zarov had suddenly returned to

his seat, and other delegates moved quickly to their places. A rumble of noise in the spectators' gallery was muted by the gavel of Secretary General Svendsen, who reconvened the meeting and asked Zarov if he wished to continue to hold the floor. Zarov said he did and glanced at his watch. It was exactly 8 P.M.

"At this time I am prepared to submit incontrovertible proof that the United States of America has cold-bloodedly planned to initiate hostilities against the socialist countries. I am prepared to show that President William Stark, despite his constant protestations of peace toward all men, has, in fact, ordered an offensive war to be waged shortly against peaceful nations." Zarov paused while delegates moved up in their chairs for his next words. Ambassador Carlson stared at his Soviet accuser with a bemused expression, a mixture of disbelief and curiosity. He even seemed to be smiling at Zarov, who ignored him and continued: "I have the honor of presenting the distinguished Second Secretary of the Soviet Presidium, Comrade Darubin."

The double doors to the chamber parted, and Mikhail Ivanovich Darubin swept into the room, across the soft carpet, and straight to the Soviet section. He did not look right or left as he took a seat next to Zarov. Darubin grimly looked down at his notes, while delegates and spectators erupted in a babel of conversation at this extraordinary turn of events. In the television room, Henry Pinkham sat stunned at the entrance of the Soviet leader. Dimly aware that the Presidium had been rearranged in the past weeks, Pinkham swiftly tried to place Darubin in his memory bank. He remembered Suez and nothing more.

Secretary General Arndt Svendsen felt a chill as he too attempted to recollect the background of the stranger in his midst. In the kaleidoscope of impressions that assailed him, one fact emerged clearly. Mikhail Darubin was trouble, a man with a sinister drive to place the Soviet Union in a pre-eminent position.

To Svendsen, Darubin signaled a reckless pursuit of Soviet aims in the world.

He gaveled the noisy delegates into silence and, in the ensuing quiet, looked at Zarov to continue. Zarov's face was triumphant.

"Mr. Secretary, I relinquish my chair to my esteemed colleague, Secretary Darubin."

The Second Secretary of the Soviet Presidium rose slowly and faced the rostrum. Dressed in an expensive Savile Row suit, gray with an almost indistinguishable pinstripe running through it, he looked like a prosperous Wall Street broker.

"Mr. Secretary, I beg you to forgive my intrusion into the deliberations of this august body. I have flown from Moscow to present the Soviet Union's answer to a situation so appallingly brutal as to defy comparison even with memories of Hitler."

Across the nation, some television stations had ended their coverage of the Security Council session to resume their regular prime-time fare of Westerns and situation comedies. But most of the audience remained for Darubin's speech.

In Washington, President William Stark was sitting with Randall and Sam Riordan as they fitfully watched Mikhail Darubin continue his indictment.

"The final proof of our suspicions came to us only a few days ago and in a strange way. I was called to Geneva to meet with a representative of the present American government. Ostensibly, he came to discuss further stages of the disarmament negotiations, which, as you know, we have been pursuing zealously. Instead, the man told us a story that confirmed our worst fears and has brought me here this evening. I would like to have you share now in that conversation. Because of a prior agreement with the man, we were able to record his words so that no doubt would linger in anyone's mind as to the veracity of the charge we make against President William Stark. His own subordinate's words will convict him before the world court."

Darubin turned and nodded to an aide, who pulled a tape recorder from under the desk and carried it to the desk of Secretary General Svendsen. The aide pushed a button and then retired to the Soviet section.

The tape whirred for several seconds, and then the voice of the dead Clifford Erskine filled the room.

"I am sure you realize, Mr. Darubin, I am a devoted American, but I am sickened at the thought of my country's diabolical plan."

Darubin was very pleased with his handiwork. It had been his idea to tape Erskine's voice secretly in Geneva and then splice words and phrases into an incriminating statement. Delegates who had known Erskine were sitting in bewildered silence, listening to every syllable issuing from the machine. Even Ronald Carlson had dropped his attitude of feigned indifference. He stared at the instrument in dismay.

"I have come to Geneva to warn you. President Stark and his advisors plan to destroy the Soviet Union, using atomic weapons on your cities and missile sites."

In the oval office, William Stark just stared at the television screen in amazement. When Randall tried to speak, the President waved him into silence.

Clifford Erskine had come to life again.

"As a sane man, I could not live with the thought that I had not tried to prevent the deaths of millions of innocent people."

It was over. The machine turned for a few seconds and then clicked to a sudden stop. The chamber was silent. Darubin rose once again from his seat and addressed Arndt Svendsen.

"And now, for the last measure of proof that the Americans are plotting against us. Once before, in May of 1960, my government was forced to expose publicly an infamous act by the government of the United States. At that time, Comrade Khrushchev revealed to a shocked world that he had in custody an American

U-2 spy plane and the spy plane pilot, Francis Gary Powers. I have just been informed by my colleagues in Moscow that we have foiled an attempt by American spy personnel to infiltrate and destroy one of our defense centers. We have the leader of that group, Colonel Joseph Safcek, Green Berets, serial number 0-1926112. Safcek has confessed everything about his mission and has directly implicated the President of the United States."

The gallery erupted. The delegates stared at the United States ambassador whose face was in his hands. His eyes were riveted on the tops of his shiny black shoes. Ronald Carlson was reminding himself to resign the next day for allowing William Stark to strand him out on the limb of ignorance.

"In conclusion, Mr. Secretary," Darubin was going on despite the clamor, which quickly subsided now. "In conclusion, I would like to state our position on this matter. We have no intention of being caught by surprise by the imperialist forces. If we detect the slightest sign of further hostile action toward us at any time within the next twenty-four hours, we shall retaliate with maximum power. This is not a threat. It is merely a statement of fact. We cannot be held responsible for what might happen since the burden of guilt lies heavily on Washington. The decision for war or peace lies in the White House."

Darubin inclined his head slightly toward Svendsen, gathered up his papers, and strode away from the desk. Followed by Zarov and others, he marched determinedly through the opened door and disappeared, leaving bedlam in his wake.

The Security Council degenerated into an impassioned scramble for attention. Ronald Carlson tried to get the floor but was surrounded by a milling throng of officials, demanding his private response to the charges.

In the streets outside the United Nations Building, pickets carrying transistor radios had heard the news from inside and instantly organized a raucous demonstration before the gates on First Avenue. Screaming "Impeach Stark" and "Fascist Pigs," hundreds of men and women walked back and forth in the humid night air. The police firmly held the crowd to the narrow path they had been assigned on the sidewalk, and the parade was kept within bounds. Television cameras brought the scene to the millions who had witnessed the confrontation. Most Americans were still dubious about the Russians, but they had been stunned by the spy revelation after being shaken by the voice of the dead secretary, who had persuasively condemned the President of the United States.

Washington, D.C., was free of crime for the first time in years. Except for a few government employees and embassy officials, the only pedestrians were army troops patrolling in mournful silence. Under the street lights they looked like a ghost battalion, seeking comfort in one another's company, smoking cigarettes, and listening for footfalls in the night. They prowled empty avenues in pairs looking constantly for signs of looters. But no one roamed the streets. The city was truly deserted, a tribute to William Stark's planning and the specter of further catastrophe.

Near the Union Station, firemen had finally left the two-block area where the pipeline had burst. Only the scars of the disaster remained.

At the White House, the President had not fully recovered from the Soviet stratagem at the United Nations. Staggered at the audacious use of the doctored Clifford Erskine tape almost as much as at the irrevocable news of Safcek's failure, Stark felt increasingly like the fly caught in the spider's web. The more he maneuvered, the tighter the enemy drew the net around him.

He finally excused himself from his advisors and walked into the bathroom. When he poured a cup of water, the liquid spilled over his coat, and he had to hold the cup in both hands to get a drink. In the mirror, his face was chalk white and beaded with sweat.

The President sagged down onto the edge of the bathtub and put his head down onto his arms. His stomach quivered, and his body started to shake uncontrollably. He suddenly knew why. It was simply fear, fear of the next hours and the decisions he had to make. He remembered Korea and the same reaction when the Chinese caught him in the open and laid in fifteen rounds. He had clawed with his bare hands into the dirt to escape the terrible noise and the screaming scraps of metal that searched for him. When it was over, he had begun to shake, and it was hours before he could function again.

Stark sat on the edge of the tub and thought of Harry Truman, who said, "The buck stops here." He thought of his responsibility to the people—the farmers and the South, the liberals, and even the radicals. The President thought of them and wondered whether they were all worth saving, whether the human race wasn't just a collection of muck dredged up from some prehistoric sewer to pollute the planet. The President recalled his continuing problems with the polarized society, consumed by its insecurities and prejudices: the peace-and-love people who held their fingers spread out in their special salute and were fully capable of ramming those same fingers up your ass if you didn't agree with their ideas, and their smug and equally righteous opponents who professed great morality while clawing their way to affluence. They were all flawed and unable to recognize it in the mirror.

William Stark thought of the nation he was supposed to save from the barbarians. "Christ, we're all barbarians."

The voice of Sam Riordan broke into his reverie. The CIA director was calling him out to the teletype. Stark splashed some cold water on his eyes and stepped out to face his duty.

By 9 P.M., New York time, the one hundred and seventy-six

Soviet Embassy and consulate officials who had assembled around the Darubin visit had not left for Kennedy International Airport. Instead, they had gathered to celebrate at the building that housed the Soviet Mission to the United Nations, there to wait the remaining two hours and eighteen minutes until the ultimatum expired. Mikhail Ivanovich Darubin was jubilant over his success at the UN. He patted the tape recorder beside him and offered a toast: "To Mr. Clifford Erskine, our Number One spy—and to Colonel Safcek."

Loud laughter accompanied the remark, and Darubin leaned back to savor his spectacular triumph. He knew Stark would be unable to rebut the charges. With the laser facing him down, Stark would be forced to surrender without a fight. The Soviets had boxed him in, and the President could not accept the onus of guilt for launching a nuclear war that would kill millions.

Darubin made his way to the building's communications room and ordered a message sent to Moskanko. The radio operator hesitated: "Sir, this channel will be monitored. Do you want me to code it?"

Flushed with success, Darubin wrote down a few words. "Send this in the clear. They'll never know what I mean." Addressed to Uncle Vanya, it said: "Dinner party a success. Chicken plucked skillfully."

His cup of mischief running over, Darubin weaved back to the celebration, which looked more and more like an election-night party for a landslide winner. Sinking into his chair, he reached for champagne to wash down his black bread and caviar.

In the Kremlin, Marshal Moskanko's forehead furrowed as he read the cablegram. Darubin may have performed brilliantly at the UN and plucked the chicken skillfully, but Moskanko could not share his effervescence, nor did he really approve of it.

The capture of the officer Safcek had made the defense minister uneasy. He had not thought the Americans would send in a ground team to destroy the laser works, and the marshal had begun to wonder whether Stark was finished. Nor had the hot-line bluff about the American laser given him any comfort. Perhaps it was Stark's final gambit, but the defense minister was no longer sure. He unbuttoned his tunic and began to write out a hot-line message for transmission. When he finished, he sent another message to Serkin in Tashkent.

The hot line gave William Stark the answer he feared. Moskanko had not believed his bluff about the laser:

> . . . WE WOULD ADVISE YOU TO CONCENTRATE EFFORTS ON COMPLYING WITH ULTIMATUM IN TWO HOURS. THE TIME HAS COME FOR SERIOUS CONSIDERA-TION OF REPERCUSSIONS IN THE EVENT YOU FAIL TO RECOGNIZE IMPOSSIBILITY OF YOUR POSITION.
>
> V. KRYLOV

Stark went to Pamela and told her to join him at the helicopter pad on the South Lawn in fifteen minutes. She did not ask what had happened in the past few hours. His face warned her that her husband was reaching the limits of his endurance. With Safcek's failure, with Darubin having laid the groundwork for the Soviet attack, the President was coming swiftly to the decision he had hoped to avoid. On the runway at Incirclik, Turkey, the SR-71 was fueled and armed, the pilot waiting word from General Ellington to take it across the Soviet border. Stark knew he had only one other choice: surrender. All this was in his eyes as he smiled at Pamela sadly and left for the Oval Room and a last-minute check.

Robert Randall gripped a suitcase in his right hand as he walked briskly into the nearly vacant press room. Morris Farber of *The New York Times* was curled up on a couch and did not hear the foreign-policy advisor approach. Randall called gently: "Morris, up and at 'em." Farber came up with a start, shaking his head. A little sheepishly, he offered: "Got pretty dull around here. No one will talk to me."

Randall came to the point quickly. "Where's your family, Morris?"

"My wife's in New York visiting the folks, and the kids are in school in Virginia. Why? What's going on?"

"We want you to come with us. The President's going on a little ride, and we'd like you as a witness to the next few hours. Sort of our own historian. OK?"

Farber was wide awake. "Sure, let's go. But I have to call the bureau to let them know."

"No, you can't. Sorry, but that's the way it has to be. You'll understand later when we fill you in on all the sad details."

The mystified and apprehensive newspaperman followed Robert Randall from the press room through winding corridors and rooms to the South Lawn, where a Marine helicopter sat, its lights blinking. Another chopper was making an approach from the direction of the Capitol. William and Pamela Stark hurried out from the White House and ran up the gangway. Sam Riordan and Martin Manson followed. Randall waved his hand for Farber to come along, and the two men joined the passengers in the cramped quarters. At 9:35 P.M., an hour and forty-three minutes before the end, the helicopter lifted into the sky and headed northwest over the city. Down below, very few headlights marred the blackness of the main streets. The lights at the base of the Washington Monument burned brightly, but no one was there to look up at the shaft's grandeur. The massed

242

flags surrounding the shrine waved listlessly in the warm air. In Lafayette Park, across from the White House, there was no one to see the figure of a man hanging by his own belt from the limb of a stout tree. His neck broken, Commissioner Herbert Markle had stilled the voice of his conscience.

In the helicopter, Morris Farber stared at the people with him and wondered what the hell was going on.

In Tashkent, Dr. Anatoly Serkin was by now a desperately unhappy man. He had spent much of the night beside the laser gun going over the final checklist of components. There had been a flurry of excitement on the grounds just before two, but no one had bothered to inform him what it was about. Even the director learned from the state security police at the complex only what they wanted him to learn. Then, between 6 and 7 A.M. had come Moskanko's calls. Now at 8:35 A.M., he held in his hand the latest message from the Kremlin.

CHANGE TARGET FROM WASHINGTON TO LOS ANGELES. WITH WASHINGTON EVACUATED, DEMONSTRATION NECESSARY OF EFFECT ON LARGE POPULATION. INITIATION ORDER WILL COME FROM ME ALONE.
MOSKANKO

Serkin was sickened. The men who directed him had already broken Parchuk. They had made Serkin a murderer of Jews in the Middle East. Now he was being ordered to incinerate several million people half a world away.

Serkin sat immobile. Then with a jerky motion, he reached

243

into his desk and pulled out a Beretta. For a long moment, he looked straight into the pistol's short barrel. He was startled by a knock on his office door. Hastily, Serkin slipped the gun back into a drawer.

"Come in," he called, and one of his assistants entered. "What do you want, Glasov?"

"Sir, you rang for me ten minutes ago."

"Oh, yes, I'm sorry. We'll need new coordinates—for Los Angeles in the state of California."

Glasov left. Serkin reached again for the drawer. He was not afraid to die, but he wondered how his family would survive. Could Nadia manage?

The physicist remembered how difficult it had become for him to face his family since the weapon had been turned upon human beings. The Presidium was using him as a puppet, to kill in its name. The death of an American city would make Serkin equal to Hitler in his own eyes, and for that he would have to answer either to his fellow man or his God.

He looked steadily into the barrel of the automatic and moved his finger over the trigger. Bringing the gun up to his face, he steadied it between his eyes. The muzzle was cold and impersonal; the bullets inside merely waited to be unlocked and sped on their mission. It was so simple. The master bending the slave to his will. Serkin thought of the deadly comparison between himself and the gun. Once an explorer, an adventurer into new realms of pure science, he was now merely the tool of earthbound masters.

"That's our curse, my dear friend," Parchuk had said one memorable night during those happy years when they would sit after dinner, listening to music and talking of books and science. "Every time we have the exquisite pleasure of discovery, we become victims of the basic lusts of man, which warp and defame our achievements. I could never be a party to such a calamity."

Parchuk had been unusually animated that night as he talked about an exciting development. At the latest conference of the International Physics Society in Paris, French researchers had disclosed that they had been able to initiate a controlled explosion and energy release of the plentiful isotope, tritium, a by-product of hydrogen that is distilled from water. By concentrating an intense laser beam on a tiny bottle containing the isotope, the Frenchmen had managed to release its energy for a brief instant.

Parchuk's face had beamed as he explored the implications.

"Just imagine, Anatoly, man will be able to drive his cars on minute quantities of tritium. Homes can be fueled with it. It's so abundant that we can revolutionize the daily life of every human being."

Serkin had agreed, but he cautioned: "You know the dangers, too, though. Any fool can rig up a distillery in his backyard and convert water into this isotope. Sooner or later, he can have the equivalent of an atomic bomb hidden away in his cellar."

Anatoly Serkin put the Beretta back in the drawer. He got up and walked toward his private bathroom. From the medicine cabinet he took down his shaving mirror and slipped the six-inch disk into the pocket of his smock. As Serkin left his office, he was humming the melody of Prokofiev's Third Symphony.

In the laser center's infirmary, it was 8:50 A.M. when Colonel Kapitsa returned to Joe Safcek. He inquired solicitously about the American's wound. The colonel had brought Safcek a gift, a freshly cut bouquet of yellow roses, which stood in a slim white vase beside the bed. Now the Russian offered Safcek a cigarette, which he accepted gratefully, and the two smoked without further conversation. Safcek enjoyed it greatly. He had almost forgotten his pain in his desire to inhale tobacco again.

Though Martha had been after him for years to give it up, he would not. In his business, life was short enough and he had no intention of denying himself a pleasure so simple. When he thought of his present position, he was glad he had not. At best, he would spend years in a Soviet labor camp. At worst, he would be killed either by a firing squad or . . .

Safcek wanted to ask the Russian if they had found his pistol, but he dared not show any undue interest. The Soviet officer finished his smoke and smiled at the American. Safcek stared into the weatherbeaten face and smiled back. "In your country, what do you do with agents who bungle missions?"

The Russian laughed: "We give them one last chance. We send them to America and make them sell drugs. If they fail at that, we abandon them to the FBI."

Safcek had to laugh in spite of himself, and the Russian seemed pleased at his little joke. He scratched his ear while the laughter rumbled and died, then suddenly said: "Colonel Safcek, we have a problem. My men have scoured the fields and have not come up with your explosive material. We did find their container with that ingenious packing material but not the charges themselves. Now, would you mind going over the situation one more time with me? It's important, as you can gather, that I find these little things as soon as possible. Our people are becoming very nervous wondering where they are."

He offered Safcek another cigarette, and Safcek noticed for the first time the shiny gold case he carried. The colonel seemed to have expensive tastes.

Safcek blew smoke through his nostrils and wrinkled his brow. "I told you what I remembered, Colonel. Let's see, we were near the lip of the gully. She had her rifle and knife with her. I had two pistols. Then I fell. The charges must have been somewhere between us." Safcek sought for plausible details. "I remember," he continued, "that she picked them out of the box while

246

I went ahead to have a look. Colonel, they must be out there, near where she was."

"Are you sure you had twelve charges? Of course you are. I'm sorry I asked such a silly question. We found everything else you said was out there, and your story checks out except for the explosives. Annoying, isn't it?"

Joe Safcek was breathing heavily now, assured that the deadly pistol was somewhere within the perimeter and capable of being handled. He had to know more.

"If I'm really lucky, Colonel, one of them will go off and set a fire here that will burn down the whole complex."

The secret police officer laughed uneasily. "I hope I can disappoint you on that score, my friend. But I do have the beautiful pistol in safe custody."

Safcek willed his face into expressionlessness.

"As a connoisseur of firearms, I was immediately attracted to it. It's a Colt .45, correct? I have seen one of those before. I think it is the type of weapon your police departments in the United States use as standard equipment. A very efficient tool, is it not?"

Safcek nodded diffidently. "It's all yours, Colonel. I guess I'll have no further use for it."

The colonel continued: "Don't worry about it. I take care of guns better than I do my own children. I have a special case in my office where I keep my collection. It will rest there as a memento of our friendship. When things settle down here, I intend to polish it and put it on a velvet cloth for all my aides to admire."

The colonel abruptly got up. He left several cigarettes on the bed, waved, and went out to look again for the missing plastique.

Joe Safcek lit another smoke while he tried to figure out how he could get to the officers quarters and find the atomic bomb.

247

By 10:10 P.M., the entire cabinet of the United States was inside the mountain in Maryland. Dug years before to protect the leaders of the nation in case of nuclear war, the enormous cavern was now the nerve center where the President could continue functioning while fully protected from enemy weapons. In his new Situation Room, William Stark kept abreast of the latest information from Intelligence.

The Soviet fleet had been anchored fifteen miles east of Montauk since eight o'clock, and the lights of some of the vessels had been turned on as if celebrating a holiday. The fleet commander was evidently waiting for guests to arrive.

In Cuba, a report had just come in that the members of the Soviet delegation had left their hotel and driven to the airport in Havana. The plane's pilot had received clearance from airport officials for a course taking him directly north toward Florida and the American mainland. The same informant at the airport stated that several Soviet officials were talking openly about shopping for their wives and girl friends on Fifth Avenue.

The situation map showed the disposition of every American unit in the world. It also showed those of the Soviet bloc. Nowhere on either side was any element in a Red Alert condition. Stark examined these unreal bits of data before he went into his office to weigh the decision to begin a nuclear war.

In a corner of the room, Morris Farber sat writing furiously in a stenographer's pad. On the brief flight from Washington to the mountain headquarters, Sam Riordan had revealed details of the past days to the astounded reporter. Riordan handed Farber the original of the Soviet ultimatum and detailed the subsequent Soviet actions to discredit Stark and pave the way for the use of the laser. The rest of the passengers in the helicopter had listened thoughtfully while Farber tried to write the story precisely as he heard it. He realized as a newsman that he was being given the most momentous story in history, but at the same time he wondered whether he would ever get a chance to print it. Later in the sanctuary of the underground White House, Morris Farber continued to record the nightmare. He would watch President Stark wrestle with the decision to kill millions of human beings.

Stark could not sit still. In shirt sleeves, he wandered up and down the floor, pausing now and then to sip Scotch and soda. The drink was having no effect on him. He knew it would not. His tolerance for great quantities of liquor was already a legend in Washington, and alcohol never clouded his judgment.

Riordan and Randall sat studying the latest intelligence reports.

Martin Manson was down the hall, briefing the rest of the cabinet on the depressing chronology of events. The members were aghast at the knowledge they now possessed. Some asked openly why they had not been consulted earlier. While Manson tried to heal wounded spirits, in the President's office, Stark suddenly asked: "Should we let Terhune in on this now?"

Randall responded quickly: "What the hell for? The Vice-President's in Manila. He can't help us, and you know he's argumentative in a conference situation, even long distance. He'd only get in the way."

"I know, but if things go downhill, he'll be the last one to know."

"If things go downhill, it won't matter a bit. He won't have any country to come back to."

Stark did not feel like pressing the issue. He had never liked Terhune anyway. The man had been forced on him and ever since had proved to be an irascible adjutant, diametrically opposed to most of his programs. The decision had been made early to muzzle him, send him away on good-will trips and hope that Stark stayed healthy.

249

Stark dropped the subject.

Randall interrupted. "The UN adjourned without a final vote on censure."

Stark waved his fist. "Screw the UN! It's a goddamn disgrace! Let's get back to reality."

The President now spoke with evident distaste: "We might as well discuss the possibility of surrender. I've been avoiding it for the past week, but it's time I faced it and analyzed just what it means to this country."

Sam Riordan sipped his bourbon and branch water and watched Morris Farber scribbling furiously in the corner. Impeccably attired in a lightweight chocolate-brown suit, Robert Randall just sat quietly as the President began his purgative exercise.

"It would be so simple. Just haul down the flag, send a hot line, and wait for their representatives. I can't believe they would physically occupy this country. The logistics of it are too staggering. Is it possible once we gave in, the Russians would become more benign and leave us alone?"

He looked for an answer from his advisors. Randall jumped in.

"Did Hitler become more benign in victory? Did the Czechs get any great deal from the Russians when they decided on a new form of government? Unless I'm dead wrong about the American people, they won't knuckle under to foreign domination any more than they did in 1775. Freedom is inbred now. That's what makes us so different from the rest of the world. That's why we're more flexible, more creative, and bigger pains in the ass to our own establishment. The Russians will send occupation troops. I can't see anything but hostages being killed every day, whole towns eventually being wiped out like Lidice, and all officers in the military being eliminated like the Poles were in the Katyn forest.

"Stalin may be gone from Moscow, but those birds there now

250

are obviously every bit as ruthless as he was. Only this time they've got the capacity to make the whole world a slave state. Even Hitler didn't make it that big. It would be nice to believe that if we surrender, the Russians would merely defuse our capacity to make war and then leave us alone. But let's face it, it wouldn't work that way at all. The commissars would move in, the KGB would fan out, and we'd be in for a reign of terror worse than the Gestapo. We all know there's very little difference between the old SS and the Soviet form of intimidation. The only people who don't realize it are those in this country who have been radicalizing the campuses and the streets for the past ten years. Somehow they think Mao and Che and Ho were really wonderful men, all Don Quixotes fighting the entrenched horrors of capitalism. I even heard some professor on TV the other night saying that China was a utopia, where human dignity was pre-eminent and the future a paradise for the workers. He forgot to mention the bodies that have floated down the river into Canton over the years, bodies of those who disagreed with the Party's plans for the peasants. Mr. President, giving up this country to a totalitarian system would be signing the death warrants of those millions you'll hope to spare by not going to war. You're not solving anything. In the long run, the American people would be as good as dead. As slaves, they'd be living the life Solzhenitsyn wrote about and suffered for afterward. The Russians would not be generous with those who disagreed with their system. And except for some radicals and ultra-leftists in this country, no one would survive the transformation as a whole man or woman. We'd have sold out our country."

Randall stopped suddenly and reached for his own drink.

Stark looked at him searchingly. "Bob, you're saying I'd be committing a peculiar kind of murder by giving in. I'd be kidding myself I was saving the world while at the same time consigning everyone outside the Curtain to living in a giant concentration camp for the rest of his life."

Morris Farber wrote it all down and wished he had been able to call his wife one last time.

"What about you, Sam? What do you think I should do?"

The CIA director had no desire to make a speech. The others knew he would be loathe to surrender and that he felt the nuclear strike from Turkey, if properly carried out, could annihilate the Soviet installation. But because the President had asked him, Riordan gave his opinion:

"In an occupation we'd have the usual complement of collaborators with the enemy. Every nation has them, and, God knows, we'd be no exception. There are more would-be communists running around railing against the Establishment than I care to imagine. They'd welcome the deliverers with open arms until they realized the utopia they figured on was only the product of their fragile link with the real world. They would be shattered and destroyed by the very people to whom they pledged allegiance. But for me the major worry has to be the extreme right, the overzealous flag-wavers who would go into the hills and snipe at the occupiers. These elements would not give in peacefully, and they'd bring down the full wrath. These men would never forgive you for selling their birthright. They'd fight. And the Russians would crush them like mosquitoes. In the process, America could become a giant Auschwitz, a camp of dead and soon-to-die. The ones in the middle would suffer the same fate as the extremists, and every state would be a battleground. Even nuclear weapons might be used to snuff out the rebellion. So the question is, do we risk a holocaust now when we have the means to win, or at least bluff, or do we hand over the weapons and wait for the purge?"

William Stark drained his Scotch and sat down.

"Call a cabinet meeting right away." He checked his watch. It was 10:24, fifty-four minutes to zero hour. "We'll have a brief final discussion and go from there. I've got to have a few minutes to myself in the meantime."

Morris Farber had run out of paper. He went out into the map room, asked a colonel for a notebook and saw General Stephen Austin Roarke enter the chamber. Roarke strode purposefully toward the television screen and said in a loud voice: "So that's where the bastard lies." He pointed to the laser complex, caught in the giant eye of the Samos satellite, hovering eighty-seven miles above it. The general watched the picture carefully, noting the movement of trucks and the blatant display of SAM missiles around the perimeter. Shaking his head he murmured: "And we expected a man to blow that? Jesus, we must have been crazy. He was a dead man the minute we picked him." The general nodded to his fellow members of the Joint Chiefs and walked into the Cabinet Room, where Martin Manson was detailing plans that could initiate World War III.

In Moscow, the time was 6:30 A.M. The deadline would occur at 7:18. Marshal Moskanko, who had gone to the defense command northwest of the city, was calling Dr. Serkin's office to make sure that the order to set the laser on Los Angeles had been carried out.

The professor was not immediately available. His assistant Glasov told the defense minister that Serkin had not been in his office for five or ten minutes. The marshal roared: "Find him and tell him to call me."

Five hundred yards across the compound, Anatoly Serkin was in the laboratory talking to a bearded technician, who was standing in front of a display case containing samples of chemical solvents and by-products of research experiments. Serkin nodded absently as the man asked if the laser was ready for firing. He was searching the rows of bottles and vials, looking for a special

253

object. As the technician watched curiously, Serkin opened the glass door and picked out a sample of a colorless liquid.

"What can you possibly want that tritium for, Professor?"

Serkin pocketed the bottle, started to walk away, then stopped.

"What did you say? I'm sorry, I'm so preoccupied with everything I didn't hear you."

"I said, what on earth do you want with that tritium?"

"Oh." Serkin thought an instant. "I plan to do some experiments with it when things settle down around here. Just a silly idea I've been playing with."

Serkin waved hesitantly to the man and rushed out of the room. The technician shook his head and returned to his own work.

In his office, Colonel Lavrenti Kapitsa of the Soviet secret police had taken off his boots to rest his feet. On duty since word had come to him of the capture of the American intruders, Kapitsa had been dividing his time between interrogating the remarkable Green Beret officer and supervising the search for the remaining plastique charges Safcek insisted he had carried with him. The imminent laser firing was less a cause for anxiety to the KGB officer than the presence of Bakunin. Though immensely pleased that his security staff had foiled the destruction of the laser, Kapitsa could not rest easy while the explosives were still at large.

More important, Bakunin's prodding and Kapitsa's own instincts warned him that Safcek was keeping something from him, that the American was hiding an important detail of his mission.

His feet propped up on his sofa, Kapitsa hefted the prized Colt .45 that Safcek had surrendered and was surprised at its weight in the butt. Noticing the black button on the side, the colonel suddenly got up and went to a wall bookcase. He brought down a thin red volume, the *International Handgun Register,* and leafed quickly to a picture of the Colt .45. It had no button on the butt.

Kapitsa pushed his thumb against the lever on the bottom of the butt to move the clip out, but it did not budge. He tried again but it failed to give.

The colonel balanced the gun once more in his hand and then slowly, carefully, laid it on the table and picked up the phone.

"Get me Bruk."

Kapitsa's hand shook as he lit a cigarette.

"Bruk, come to my office quickly and bring a scanner with you."

The colonel hung up and blew a huge cloud of smoke across the desk. He sat down heavily on the sofa and stared hypnotically at his trophy lying on his desk.

When Bruk arrived breathless, Kapitsa jumped up and motioned at the pistol. "Run your gadget over this."

The scientist took a pocket-sized implement from his smock, pressed a switch on it and slowly passed it over the gun. Kapitsa sucked in his breath as the small screen on top of the scanner suddenly lit up, revealing the outlines of a small sphere connected by wires to a tiny cylindrical object. The scientist was subdued. "It is some form of explosive device; that much is certain. Where did you get it?"

"Never mind that. What kind of bomb is it? How powerful?"

Bruk asked Kapitsa to wait a moment while he got another instrument. When the scientist returned, he had a Geiger counter, which he held over the pistol. The needle jumped to the limit of the radioactivity-detection gauge. Bruk backed away swiftly, colliding with the startled Kapitsa.

"What the hell's the matter with you, Bruk?"

"Colonel, you are standing in front of an atomic bomb."

Twelve hundred feet beneath the crest of the Maryland mountain, the President of the United States had heard about Marshal Moskanko's cable to Serkin. The giant radar installation on the northern coast of Turkey had picked the sentences out of the air and translated the code in one minute and twenty-five seconds. By phone, Stark had absorbed the dreadful news that the Soviet Union was evidently determined to incinerate Los Angeles. Utterly defenseless, it would substitute for Washington, and Stark had no time left to evacuate the new target. Eight million people would die in the next half hour, and he could prevent it only by surrender. Even in surrender the President wondered whether Los Angeles might be annihilated for effect.

He was in a final meeting with his cabinet, most of whom were still trying to cope with the shocking story the Secretary of State, Martin Manson, had just revealed to them. Each had retreated into his own world, thinking of families supposedly evacuation from the capital. Some had already recovered enough to grapple with the awesome decision to fight or surrender, and, spending the night in Virginia or Maryland as part of the general when Stark asked for their views, the room erupted into a babel of divergent opinions. Stark tried to sort out voices but finally threw his hands up and shouted:

"Gentlemen, hold it down. I don't have any time left to seek all your opinions and frankly I want to apologize for not letting you in on this earlier. But I had my reason, and it was simple. The fewer that knew about this, the better. Newspapermen would have been after you. If they saw cabinet sessions late at night, the word would have gotten out quickly, and I'd have had more trouble answering them than trying to figure out this horrible situation.

"At any rate, I'm glad you're with me now for the final decision, and I want you to participate in it. Secretary Manson has fully explained my choices. Now with this latest word on Los Angeles, I have precious few minutes to act. We must either send in the SR-71 and notify the Russians as to our intention, or we must surrender. I will not send in hundreds of missiles. Given this insane situation, the single plane General Roarke suggested is a reasonable alternative at this moment. There is little doubt it will get over the target. The only question left then will be the Soviet response. And, as I said, I will tell them by hot line the plane is all we will send against them. If they still choose to fight and launch their missiles against us, the decision is theirs and not mine. But their response could bring death to our civilization."

Propelled by the emergency before him, Stark was speaking hurriedly. His face was calm, his voice deep and confident. He had come out of his bedroom determined to move firmly toward a resolution of the crisis. He was satisfied he had done all he could to defuse the situation in the past days. Now his options were running out.

"I am going to ask you to vote with me on this issue. Please mark the white slips of paper before you with the word *yes* or *no*. You need not sign your name. A *yes* will signify your willingness to use the atomic bomber. A *no* would express your decision to capitulate and avoid nuclear war. I have no other reasonable alternatives to offer you."

Like schoolboys, they glanced furtively at one another and cupped a hand over the word they wrote down. Each folded his paper in two, sometimes three sections before handing it to General Roarke, who walked back and forth collecting the votes. Roarke brought them to Stark, who sat expressionless at the head of the table. He read the first one: "Yes," then on to another "Yes"; "Yes"; the fourth one was called out: "No," and General Roarke stared wildly down the ranks of civilians, who ignored him.

Stark now had two piles in front of him. The sixth and seventh both called upon him to surrender, and the atmosphere in the room was heavy with unconcealed tension. Robert Randall knew what he wanted to do. Sam Riordan knew too, but the President had surprised them by asking for this vote, and they were not sure what he had decided. The eleventh vote was for attack, and Stark, betraying no emotion, placed it on the pile to his right. He read the last three aloud, and Randall who had counted them silently figured it as eleven for fighting and three for quitting. He glanced nervously at the President, who checked the clock on the wall—it read 10:32 P.M. Stark pushed all the papers together, and rose briskly from his seat.

"Thanks very much for your opinions. To those of you who voted against using a nuclear weapon on the enemy, I appreciate your profound concern for the lives of millions. But we will go with General Roarke's plan and pray to God that the Soviets stop this insane game."

Nodding to Randall and Riordan, Stark hurried out to the Situation Room. There he picked up a red phone, spoke curtly to General Ellington at Incirclik Airbase, and hung up.

On the runway at Incirclik, the three-man crew of the SR-71 listened to Ellington on the intercom. Quickly the pilot cut in power to the jet engines, and the plane moved off down the field. In two minutes it was airborne.

In the control tower, General Ellington held the red phone in one hand and watched the atomic bomber disappear into a cloud bank. He was momentarily distracted by an aide who noted: "Thirty-seven minutes to drop." Ellington nodded and held onto the phone in case Stark had any further word.

The clock in the Maryland Situation Room pointed to 10:48 P.M. Stark had just handed the text of a message for the hot line to Sergeant Arly Cooper, who had received the ultimatum message at 11:18 P.M., just seventy-one hours and thirty minutes before. Cooper had spent the last days in a terrible state of anxiety, for he among very few knew the entire truth behind the strange happenings in and around the capital. Cooper had not been able to confide anything to his wife. He had become irritable with his family and hated himself for behaving so badly. When the summons came to accompany the President into the mountain, Cooper was almost relieved to be able to take the awful secret with him into the cave. He told his wife he would be back in several days, and she had smiled tightly and bid him a curt farewell. Now Cooper sat before the machine, preparing to relay Stark's answer to the Soviet High Command.

The President's mind was whirling as he considered last-minute details before the irrevocable commitment to his policy. He called the Samos and Midas tracking unit and heard the same report: No sign of detonation or damage to the laser. In addition, Samos had just begun to record the emergence of the laser from its lair.

Stark ran to the wall, and the television screen jumped to life. His heart pounded as he watched the silvery weapon protruding from the building eighty-seven miles below the stationary satellite. Stark felt he could almost glimpse figures moving about in the shadowy cavern beneath it. He called for Randall and Riordan to join him at the wall. General Steve Roarke moved up behind them and stared at the apparition:

"They're getting ready. Just twenty-eight minutes."

The entire cabinet now gathered around the giant wall screen. Secretary of Labor Bruce Hinton was weeping openly as he waited for the imminent deaths of millions in Los Angeles.

Robert Randall looked at him without comment. General Roarke snarled: "Stop sniveling, Hinton. For Christ's sake, this is the time to be a man, not a mouse."

Roarke made a mental note that Hinton had probably voted to surrender. He reminded himself to find the other two "peaceniks" in the coming days, if there were any days to come.

"OK, let them know about the SR-71."
Cooper began typing.

ONE PLANE ENTERING YOUR AIRSPACE NOW TO
VICINITY OF TASHKENT. IT WILL DESTROY LASER GUN
AND RETURN TO BASE. NO OTHER WEAPONS WILL BE
EMPLOYED AGAINST YOUR COUNTRY.

STARK

Stark kept his eyes fastened on the television screen.

In the scientists' briefing room, a concrete blockhouse with one glass wall, Marshal Bakunin sat before a closed-circuit television screen linking him with Moskanko in the defense command headquarters northwest of Moscow.

Bruk was with Bakunin, giving both marshals an explanation of the inner workings of the atomic bomb, now laid bare on the table. Bruk had carefully pried loose the butt cover and snipped out the vial of acid with a pair of fingernail scissors. On the television monitor, Moskanko had listened in amazement as the white-smocked scientist extolled the sophistication of the device. He explained that when the two wires linking the battery to the nuclear mass were disconnected, the plastique cover would immediately implode onto the fissionable material. He estimated that it was capable of pulverizing a six-square-mile area.

Beside him, Marshall Bakunin listened impatiently to the recital and finally exploded.

"Viktor Semyonovich, you have seen this damned bomb, and how it works. But more important, I have just seen a copy of the order you sent to Serkin changing the target to Los Angeles.

260

You very neatly bypassed me until I went to the signal center and found this transmission from you."

On the wall, the face of Moskanko seemed to expand into a cherry-red bulge.

"I do not know what prompted you to do this," Bakunin went on, "but you must rescind the order right now. I went along with the Israeli strike because I could justify it as a legitimate military requirement, but this, killing several million human beings . . . it's not war, Viktor Semyonovich. It's an abomination."

Moskanko's mouth moved on the screen, and his words thundered out from the wall.

"You are talking foolishness, Pavel Andreievich. You learned years ago that a civilian population in modern warfare is on the front lines as much as the foot soldier. The missiles you developed for a strike against an enemy will kill millions of people when you launch them. You have always known that."

Bakunin cut him short. "But that was only in defense of the motherland. I never doubted I could send them out against someone who attacked us first, but what you propose to do is wanton murder of the innocent. For effect, you say." Bakunin got up, strode to the glass wall, looked through it into the laser chamber, then returned to look at the television.

In the Moscow defense center, Marshall Moskanko studied his agitated brother-in-law on the wall screen. Patiently, he tried to reason with him. "Pavel Andreievich, please do not interfere any more with me. I am not a fool. I know who the enemy is and always has been, and I am taking the proper steps to eliminate them as a menace to us."

"That is nonsense, Viktor Semyonovich. You are just trying to justify—"

An aide appeared at Moskanko's elbow and handed him Stark's hot-line message. The marshal read it and jumped up. "Nonsense, Pavel Andreievich? Well, they have just sent a bomber against us. And it is heading right for you. Wait there until I settle this." As Moskanko rushed away to the hot-line machine to answer Stark's challenge, the television screen went dead.

Marshal Bakunin sat in the briefing room in Tashkent and waited anxiously for the monitor to come to life again. It was his only link with the unfolding tragedy he had predicted.

In the Soviet defense command center north of Saratov, monitors locked in on the SR-71 as it approached the Soviet border at a speed of 1,980 miles an hour.

"Altitude?" asked a colonel at the control board.

"It's at a hundred and two thousand feet, heading due east. Just crossing the Caspian Sea south of Baku."

The colonel was at the phone talking to Marshal Moskanko.

"Sir, a bomber has just penetrated our airspace."

"Shoot it down, goddamnit."

"Yes, sir."

The colonel hung up and called: "Intercept with surface-to-air immediately."

In the complex twelve miles north of Tashkent, the laser had stopped its climb into the sky. It hung there on its hydraulic lift, while below technicians scanned instruments. With the roof opened, the morning sunlight poured onto the floor of the building. The gun was cocked, ready to perform. Only a word from Moscow was needed.

Glasov was at his station beside the laser, monitoring the telemetry that recorded the weapon's vital functions. At 9:56

A.M., twenty-two minutes to zero hour, Anatoly Serkin appeared at his elbow, and Glasov said: "Where have you been? Moskanko is in a rage, and I have been looking all over for you."

Serkin did not answer the question.

"Feed in the power, Glasov."

"But we do not have to do that until Moskanko gives word to fire."

"Feed it now. I want to make sure everything is perfect."

"Yes, sir." Glasov punched a button, and his gauges immediately recorded a huge surge in energy intake.

When Glasov turned back from his board, Serkin was no longer beside him. He had gone down the steps of the catwalk that spiraled around the barrel of the weapon and was approaching the safety door at its base. The astounded Glasov followed him down and saw the professor working swiftly at the pressure valve that kept the door sealed tight. Serkin had it opened in seconds.

Glasov screamed: "Professor, have you gone crazy? You will be burned to death."

Over the wasteland of the Kara Kum Desert, the electronics countermeasures officer on board the SR-71 spoke rapidly: "Six SAMs on way up." He pressed a switch to initiate jamming of the missiles' electronic-guidance systems.

The pilot nodded and looked out his left window. Far below, he saw flaming trails and just above them what looked like supersonic telephone poles that were reaching up to touch and kill him.

The commotion at the base of the laser had brought scientists and technicians away from their posts to the railings of the catwalks to peer below.

Serkin faintly heard Glasov screaming at him. From his left pocket he pulled the bottle of tritium and held it high. He reached into his right pocket and felt the cool disk of the shaving mirror. Serkin knew death was seconds away. When he focused the mirror in front of the escaping rays of the laser, it would reflect the rays back onto the bottle of tritium and ignite the isotope. Before Serkin's hand was melted by the rays coming out of the bottom end of the barrel, the entire building would be demolished.

He pulled the mirror out, and Glasov saw the glint of light.

The assistant leaped down the intervening ten steps and threw himself at the professor. His hands clawed at Serkin and dragged him back from the opening. The mirror flew in one direction and splintered against a railing. The bottle of tritium fell through the grating on the catwalk and crashed harmlessly into the blackness around the hydraulic lift. Serkin was whimpering as his assistant held him down. His glasses had broken, and he could not see Glasov very well.

"Why did you stop me? It was the only way." He cried in frustration as a voice from above said: "Take him outside."

Glasov helped Serkin to his feet and led him up the stairs. Someone punched a button, and the microwaves of energy from the nuclear generator ceased to flood into the laser barrel. It was unharmed, still ready to fire at 10:18 A.M., Tashkent time, now just seventeen minutes away. Anatoly Serkin was marched outside.

Still jamming the electronic-guidance system of the surface-to-air missiles, the SR-71 pilot veered the plane sharply to the right. The cluster of missiles faded suddenly and fell back toward the earth. The bomber resumed course, boring across the parched and serrated crust of Central Asia while the pilot spoke briefly to Incirclik:

"First SAMs detected and evaded. ECM officer now monitoring dozen MIGs trying to catch up."

In the Situation Room at the underground White House, General Roarke listened in on the call and relayed information to his audience: "SAMs licked so far. Incirclik says ten minutes to drop." On the wall clock the second hand had just swept past 11:02 P.M.

In the infirmary, Colonel Lavrenti Kapitsa had just entered Joe Safcek's room. The colonel was carrying a copy of the *International Register of Handguns*. Safcek acknowledged his greeting groggily just as the walkie-talkie at the colonel's hip crackled.

"Kapitsa here."

"Colonel," the voice came metallically from the walkie-talkie, "we have trouble here at the laser. Dr. Serkin has just attempted to destroy the weapon, but the attempt was blocked. He is being taken out to the quadrangle now."

"Is everything back to normal inside the building?"

"Yes, sir."

"Good." Colonel Kapitsa broke the connection and went to the window.

Outside, on the grassy quadrangle, the professor's shirt, pants, and underwear had been removed, and his captors were looking him over for any further evidence of sabotage equipment. A guard put grease on his middle finger as Serkin was forced to bend over.

Across the compound, the colonel turned back from the window with a satisfied grunt and said: "Colonel Safcek, this place is crawling with fellows like you."

Joe Safcek's close-cropped head struggled up to look at the

friendly colonel, who added: "But fortunately we have been able to catch all of you. Even our best Scientists have turned against us." The officer shook his head in disbelief.

Safcek's face fell, and the colonel approached the bed.

"I thought I would leave something here for you to read. I was fortunate enough to learn a great deal from it this morning."

Kapitsa opened the book to a certain page and laid it on Safcek's lap.

"If you look closely at the picture of the Colt .45, Colonel, you will see that it has no black button on the butt."

Safcek's eyes betrayed him. They darted up at the smiling police officer, who shook his head in awe. "You almost fooled me, Colonel. I must admit I never thought that weapon you carried could be so deadly. My compliments to you and your scientists."

Joe Safcek did not answer. As the realization of his ultimate failure engulfed him, his head slumped back onto the pillow.

The *International Register* fell to the floor, and the walkie-talkie crackled sharply:

"Colonel, you are wanted in the scientists' briefing room right away. Marshal Moskanko's orders."

Kapitsa hurried out of the room. Without saying goodbye to Joe Safcek. Safcek stared straight ahead as Kapitsa's broad back disappeared.

It was 10:06 A.M., Tashkent time. Out of breath from running, Colonel Kapitsa entered the briefing room, where Bakunin sat alone, toying idly with the fingernail scissors left by Bruk. The Colt .45 still lay on the table, its workings exposed. Beyond the marshal, Kapitsa could see on the other side of the glass wall the floor of the laser chamber. There the huge gun, under the care of a team of scientists now headed by Glasov, was

266

poised to fire. On another wall of the briefing room, the television screen had just filled with the shape of Marshal Moskanko, talking from the command platform in the defense center control room.

"Pavel Andreievich," the defense minister shouted, "the American plane is about three hundred fifty miles out. We have a mass salvo due in three minutes from the missile batteries. Even a near miss from their atomic warheads will crack the plane like an egg. Now I want you to get right down there and make sure that laser is fired in two minutes' time. Two minutes, do you understand? Stark has forced us into this."

As he stood in the midst of his frantic staff, monitoring the approach of the SR-71, Moskanko watched in dismay as the blurred television image of Bakunin shook its head sadly.

"Do you understand?" Moskanko repeated.

"Viktor Semyonovich, you have gone mad," Bakunin said softly, gesturing at Moskanko with the scissors. "Once you had my loyalty, but now I can no longer believe in you." Bakunin's face was oddly untroubled despite his words.

The defense minister roared: "Kapitsa, arrest that man!"

The stunned secret police officer was reaching to pull his gun from his belt as Marshal Bakunin leaned out of television view and using Bruk's fingernail scissors deliberately snipped the wires that connected the transistorized battery to the marble of Einstinium 119. In the Moscow defense center, the television screen went blank before Moskanko's eyes.

Gazing at the morning sunlight streaming in through his window, Joe Safcek was imagining Martha waving to him as he came up the driveway. She was reaching for him at the moment when the plastique imploded onto the marble of dark gray particles. In the next millisecond, Colonel Joe Safcek was incinerated in his bed.

At the moment of detonation, an intense bluish white light lit the sky. In seconds a brilliant orange fireball formed over several hundred yards and vaporized the laser and all buildings in the complex. It lapped at the surrounding slopes and roared through the gullies toward the highway a mile and a half away.

In the Maryland mountains, the time was precisely 11:08 P.M.—zero hour minus ten minutes.

On the road leading north from the laser complex, a terrified driver crawled from the wreckage of his vehicle and watched a herd of sheep bleating mournfully as they trudged, blind and helpless, along the roadway. Their blistered flanks were turning into blackened running sores, and the sheep stumbled and retched onto the grass as radiation invaded their bloodstreams and raced to consume them. The long line of animals trampled unseeing over the blackened corpse of their shepherd.

In a field two miles south, a farmer was driven head first through a tree trunk.

Two teen-age girls hiking through the desert flowers two and a half miles east of Ground Zero were blinded by the glare and felt a scorching wave of heat pass over them.

At a Soviet Army training camp three miles away, men standing in line for a meal felt the hot blast and saw their uniforms erupt in tiny puffs of fire that caught and fed on them. All military vehicles in the motor pool fused into grotesque lumps of steel.

Marshal Moskanko had sat staring a moment at the dark screen. Then he lunged to the phone and tried to raise Tashkent. The line was dead. Moskanko cursed loudly. "Have we got a satellite anywhere near Tashkent?"

The duty officer at the control board ripped a piece of paper from a computer and handed it to the defense minister. The numbed Moskanko read it with a growing feeling of doom.

Friday, September 13

NUCLEAR DETONATION NORTH OF TASHKENT IN FOUR-
TEEN KILOTON RANGE . . .

In the depths of the Maryland mountain, William Stark stood ashen-faced as he watched the television. In his hand, the knuckles white, he clenched a cable, Moskanko's reply to his hot-line warning that the SR-71 was coming in:

RECALL BOMBER IMMEDIATELY FROM SOVIET
TERRITORY. DESTRUCTION OF LASER WILL BE
REGARDED AS AN ACT OF WAR AND WILL BRING
INSTANT RETALIATION AGAINST YOUR COUNTRY
BY ALL SOVIET DEFENSIVE SYSTEMS.

V. KRYLOV

On the screen, the mushroom cloud had changed colors in seconds from pink to salmon to azure and ugly black. The laser works had just disappeared in the enormous pillar of energy beneath the lurking Samos. General Stephen Austin Roarke could not believe it.

"The strike plane isn't due over the target for four minutes, but it's gone anyway," he screamed into the President's ear. "It's gone! It's gone!"

Stark grabbed at the red phone. To Ellington on the other end he shouted: "Call it back! Call it back! Right now!" Ellington screamed into the ratio: "Abort, abort" as he punched the recall alarm. Two hundred and twenty miles west of Tashkent, the SR-71 crew had no need to be told. From their perch in the sky, the men could see the twisting column of flame ahead of them and feel the spreading shock waves.

The strike plane turned quickly to the right. The pilot spoke to Incirclik: "Roger on abort, roger on abort. The target is no longer functional."

At Incirclik, General Ellington repeated the words over the telephone to William Stark, who sank into a chair and watched the mushroom in horrified fascination. The spectators in the underground White House held their breaths as they witnessed the fury unleashed by the tiny marble of nuclear material. No one spoke. Only the impersonal chatter of radios and teletypes intruded.

On the third floor of the main hospital in Tashkent, Luba Spitkovsky was blissfully unaware of the violence swirling around her. Still unconscious after surgery for massive gunshot wounds in the stomach, she lay motionless as the ceiling cracked and plaster showered down on her. The KGB man guarding her ran into the hall in panic. Luba did not stir.

At the Navoi Opera House the roof ripped, and beams cracked. Inside, three glistening chandeliers whirled wildly, then crashed sickeningly into the rows of seats beneath.

On Komsomol Lake, amateur sailors with their girl friends were swamped by the suddenly thrashing waters, which soon smothered them and stifled their screams.

In the Soviet defense command center, Marshal Moskanko stared at the men around him. His shaking hands betrayed his turmoil. Omskuschin and Fedoseyev looked at each other in silence while someone switched on the cameras in a Cosmos orbiting two hundred miles northeast of Tashkent on a course leading it over the Chinese Communist nuclear-test facilities in the Sinkiang Desert.

The marshals of the Soviet Union looked at the wall screen and saw clearly the mushroom that Joe Safcek had planted.

Because the bomb was set off at ground level and in a sparsely populated region, its destructiveness did not match the horrors of Nagasaki and Hiroshima. The fireball was blocked by the hills and valleys from spreading wildly down toward Tashkent. Even the full effects of the blast were muzzled somewhat as it reached the northern outskirts of the metropolis. But the inhabitants would never be the same after that day.

They saw the malevolent mushroom rising over them and then felt the concussion reach out to touch them.

Slivers of glass, carried like rain through the air, slashed thousands of pedestrians. On every street, houses buckled and crumbled under the impact of the shock wave. They swayed and fell, spewing out their collection of human flotsam and furniture. Streetcars and busses overturned, and automobiles were rammed into buildings with the velocity of artillery shells. The cries of the trapped and dying were joined by the clamor of ambulances and fire trucks, rushing to extricate them from the debris.

In the town of Chirchiz, eleven miles to the east, Olga Spitkovsky heard the rumble, then was thrown to the floor by the shock wave, which broke every window in the house. As Mrs. Spitovsky rose, she stepped on a picture of her daughter, Luba, gone for so long from her country and her family. Luba's mother wiped the blood off her face and ran outside to see what had happened to her town that day.

It had taken the bomb less than five minutes to spend its terrible fury.

Stark roused himself from the hypnotic vision on the screen to ask for Midas readings. Sam Riordan spoke to California. The monitor said Soviet missile sites were not on alert yet. Stark listened.

"The next hour will give us their reaction. Prepare to issue Red Alert to all strategic weapons systems just in case we get word they're revving up." He continued to watch the screen while the Midas satellite conversed with its master:

NUCLEAR EXPLOSION IN FOURTEEN KILOTON RANGE
AREA TEN MILES NORTH OF TASHKENT. HEAT AT
CENTER IN EXCESS OF FIVE MILLION DEGREES.
BLAST EFFECTS IN RANGE TEN MILES TO FIFTEEN ON
ALL SIDES . . .

Marshal Moskanko had retreated to his office, where he drank from a mug of vodka. What had gone wrong? He had just learned that the plane Stark warned him about on the hot line had turned back two hundred miles from the target. Yet his laser was gone. Could Bakunin have done that? Did the American bomb have a secret timing mechanism on it? Could there be some other explanation? Moskanko's eyes had been fixed unseeingly on a piece of paper lying on his desk. The defense minister picked it up now and found himself reading a copy of his last hot-line message to Stark.

Inside the mountain, William Stark was in the bedroom with Pamela. She held his hand tightly while he told her what had just happened. Stark was waiting for Randall or Riordan to

272

summon him momentarily with word from the spy satellites whose electronic eyes and ears were fastened on nuclear missile and bomber installations inside the Soviet Union. While he waited for news, Pamela listened to him describe the awesome cloud over Tashkent.

Marshal Moskanko had been reading the hot-line copy again and again, brooding angrily over the phrases "act of war" and "instant retaliation."

As an orderly entered to tell the defense minister that his deputies wanted to see him immediately. Moskanko lunged to his feet and ran out to the central command post. He glanced at the wall screen and saw the laser works still shrouded in smoke and dust. Small fires continued to lick at the edges of the blanket of destruction. Moskanko grabbed a phone and spoke to SMAG, the Soviet Strategic Missile Armaments Group in Chelyabinsk. The marshal was crisp.

"Priority Alert. Attack will be based on Operation Neptune, using multiple warheads against silos and Polaris systems only on first strike. City strike will follow later based on Operation Cygnus A. Execute order on receipt of computer voice code *Suvorov*."

The voice on the other end repeated Moskanko's words, and the defense minister slammed down the receiver and went along the corridor to a conference room. As he entered, he found Marshals Fedoseyev and Omskuschin waiting somberly. Moskanko walked to the head of the table, tossed the hot-line copy on the table and said: "Comrades, we are in a state of war."

273

William Mellon Stark heard the knock and Randall's voice saying urgently: "Mr. President, we need you out here immediately." Stark pressed Pamela's hand once more and left her sitting trembling on the edge of the bed.

One look at Randall's eyes confirmed Stark's fears. He went to the wall screen, where Riordan and Roarke were staring at a closeup split image of Soviet missile silos. The President asked: "Is this it?"

The shaken director of the CIA turned. "It was all quiet until just two minutes ago. Then we intercepted attack orders to all Soviet subs in the Atlantic and Pacific. At the same time the Samos began picking up these silos getting ready. The ones on the wall are at Novosibirsk. Notice that the big doors have been opened. Our radio monitors report that countdown is at T minus thirty seconds and holding. They're just waiting for a final Go."

"Are all the missiles like these?"

"They're all going operational from Novaya Zemlya to Khabarovsk. What's the true count, Steve?"

Roarke snapped: "Six hundred five and rising toward a thousand."

President Stark shook his head in despair. "They leave me no choice, the fools. Put everything up to Red Alert."

Roarke was talking on the phone immediately to NORAD in Cheyenne Mountain.

Stark rattled off further instructions. "As soon as the radar picks them up at the horizon line and verifies their trajectories, give me the word, and we'll let go."

Randall said: "God, what about the people in this country?"

"They're already dead." Stark answered tonelessly. "And so

is everyone in Russia." He tore off his suit jacket and fell into a chair. "But what else can I do?" Nobody spoke for a moment, and Stark broke the quite: "Tell the television and radio networks to get ready for a switch to CONELRAD. That will help some of the survivors anyway."

While the President sat watching the screen for the emergence of the Soviet multiple warhead missiles, the Bagman came up beside him and unlocked the black satchel containing the coded orders to initiate nuclear war. He held it open for William Stark's next move.

Marshal Moskanko was in the midst of an unforeseen argument with his deputies.

"The laser is gone," the stocky peasant Omskuschin said in his ponderous manner. "When I came in here there were no further signs of aggressive activity on the enemy's part."

"How can you be so shortsighted?" Moskanko railed. "We are in an impossible position. Stark can move anywhere in the world now and expect us to do nothing about it *unless* we show him otherwise."

The door opened, and a Soviet air force major came up to Moskanko: "The Americans have just gone to their Red Alert. All port-bound Polaris systems are getting under way for the open sea."

The defense minister interrupted the man: "So, comrades, we *must* attack. I have ordered SMAG to fire when I give the computer password."

There was a stunned silence in the room. Finally, Marshall Fedoseyev, commander of Soviet land forces, cleared his throat.

"I want no part of a nuclear exchange," he intoned. "It would be suicide." With a look of impatience, Fedoseyev, whose normally taciturn manner was a Soviet army legend, now stood up.

"Viktor Semyonovich," he said forcefully, "you have misjudged once too often. First, you should never have sent the message threatening instant retaliation. If the laser went, as it did, you would be left with your mouth open and your options nil. Now, without consulting anyone, you have ordered the missiles to priority alert. It is no surprise that the Americans have suddenly done the same thing. But your most serious misjudgment concerns the President of the United States. You thought he would avoid the ultimate decision to go into a hydrogen bomb war. You were absolutely wrong, comrade. Absolutely."

Moskanko's face was beet red.

"We cannot afford more such misjudgments," Marshal Fedoseyev continued. "And when you talk of still proving we are strong, we say you are ignoring the facts. Viktor Semyonovich, we will not allow it to happen again. We cannot let you go out of here and give the code word to attack."

Fedoseyev pressed a button on the table, and the door opened to admit two plainclothes KGB officers from the Center. They took up positions on either side of the door. As Moskanko watched in disbelief, former Premier Valerian Smirnov walked into the room and stared silently down at him.

After a lengthy silence, Marshal Omskuschin addressed the defense minister. "Your biggest mistake, Viktor Semyonovich, was losing. Losers must pay. We must survive you and be the wiser for it. But *you* cannot continue. You are too reckless, too dangerous for the Soviet people. We have brought Smirnov to defuse the situation and try to salvage something with the Americans. They can take a very hard line with us now, and we think Smirnov may be able to return relations to a reasonable status without losing too much. And that we want, much more than we want you to continue."

Marshal Moskanko glared at Smirnov, who returned his look calmly. The two KBG officers watched the defense minister.

"We have arranged a comfortable dacha for you at Sochi on the Black Sea," Omskuschin went on. "You will not need for anything, and you will not have to fear any retribution from—"

"You sniveling bastards!" Moskanko roared. "You have been with me in this from the very first moment, but I am the one chosen to fall." Spittle forming at his lips, Moskanko lunged toward them. "You cannot—"

The two KGB officers moved simultaneously and forced the defense minister back into his chair. He pulled against them, but they pinned his arms. On a signal from Fedoseyev, they forced Moskanko to his feet and led him to the door. Smirnov stepped aside, smiling mockingly. "I will give President Stark your regards, Marshal." The police pulled the raging Moskanko away from the premier, who turned his back and walked over to the hot line. He handed a sheet of paper to the operator. "Send this immediately."

Behind him the two marshals of the Soviet Union watched Moskanko struggling down the hallway into oblivion.

At the television screen in the Maryland mountain, no one stirred. The President's shirt was soaked with sweat, and his cigar had gone out several times as he alternately puffed on it and laid it down. Eight hundred and sixteen Soviet missiles were now poised along the arc of the Soviet heartland, but Stark

277

saw only four on the screen. They hypnotized him as he waited for them to vault toward the orbiting Samos camera.

At precisely 11:42 P.M., the hot line chattered, and William Stark stiffened in his chair. Randall ran to the machine, and someone said, "This is it." The President leaned over Randall's shoulder to read the print as the Bagman jostled his elbow with the opened satchel.

TO THE PRESIDENT OF THE UNITED STATES OF AMERICA FROM THE PRESIDIUM OF THE UNION OF SOVIET SOCIALIST REPUBLICS:

THE SOVIET UNION DEPLORES THE SENSELESS ACTS OF CERTAIN DISSIDENT ELEMENTS WITHIN ITS OWN GOVERNMENT IN THE PAST WEEKS. THE NUCLEAR DETONATION NEAR TASHKENT SHOULD NOT BE CAUSE FOR FURTHER BREAKDOWN OF RELATIONS BETWEEN OUR TWO NATIONS. ABSOLUTELY NO COUNTER-MEASURES WILL BE INITIATED BY OUR ARMED FORCES. PLEASE ACKNOWLEDGE AND STATE YOUR INTENTIONS.

SMIRNOV

As he read the final lines aloud, William Stark had tears in his eyes. The room erupted in cheers and whistles as men pounded one another on the back and hugged their neighbors. General Stephen Austin Roarke, his face a mixture of awe and triumph, offered his hand to the President.

"Mr. President, you're one helluva man. If I didn't know otherwise, I'd swear you were from Texas."

Stark shook his hand and mumbled, "Thanks, Steve," as Sam Riordan forced a Scotch into his left hand. "And Steve," Stark added, "tell NORAD to kill the alert." Sam put his arm around the President and whispered: "Bill, you and you alone saved us." He raised his glass to the President, and Stark started to accept the toast until he remembered the ugly mushroom in the Central Asian desert. He quickly put the drink down and reached for a chair. As the revelry in the room swirled around him, the President of the United States put his head in his hands to blot out the joyous scene.

At the wall screen Sam Riordan watched the concrete doors of the Soviet missile silos at Novosibirsk slowly close back over the warheads. He switched off the screen and went to refill his drink.